D1005843

BAD BLOOD

BAD BLOOD

A Henry Christie thriller

Nick Oldham

This first world edition published 2016
in Great Britain and 2017 in the USA by
SEVERN HOUSE PUBLISHERS LTD of
19 Cedar Road, Sutton, Surrey, England, SM2 5DA.
Trade paperback edition first published
in Great Britain and the USA 2017 by
SEVERN HOUSE PUBLISHERS LTD

British Library Cataloguing in Publication Data
A CIP catalogue record for this title is available from the British Library.

ISBN-13: 978-0-7278-8680-4 (cased)
ISBN-13: 978-1-84751-783-8 (trade paper)
ISBN-13: 978-1-78010-852-0 (e-book)

All Severn House titles are printed on acid-free paper.

Severn House Publishers support the Forest Stewardship Council™ [FSC™],
the leading international forest certification organisation.
All our titles that are printed on FSC certified paper carry the FSC logo.

MIX
Paper from
responsible sources
FSC® C013056

Typeset by Palimpsest Book Production Ltd.,
Falkirk, Stirlingshire, Scotland.
Printed and bound in Great Britain by
TJ International, Padstow, Cornwall.

For Belinda

ONE

It was an idyllic day for a killing.

Although the shadows had grown long as the sun began to set, visibility and all other attendant conditions – such as hardly a wisp of a breeze, a superb line of sight (albeit from 1,000 metres) plus an unsuspecting target who was just literally standing there, half-drunk, waiting to have his head blown apart – were excellent.

And blown apart it would be.

The man holding the Accuracy International sniper rifle, peering through the Carl Zeiss telescopic sights, knew the damage the hollow-point .338 Lapua Magnum shell would cause. He had seen such damage, had indeed inflicted such damage to the human head many times. He knew the resultant injury to the target's head – based on the fact that the bullet would enter the man's forehead one inch above the bridge of his nose, then exit through the back of his skull – would be catastrophic and that death would be instantaneous and the man, the target, would know nothing about it.

He would be alive one minute.

One second later – or less – he would be dead.

There wouldn't even be any pain, just instant blackness.

He would not know what had hit him, or even that he had been hit. He would not know that a massive round had been fired and entered his skull at a velocity of almost 2,000 metres per second (so, in parallel calculations, the sniper knew that from discharge to impact would take less than half a second) and would exit at a slightly lower speed having destroyed his brain on the way through (and in another concurrent thought, the sniper visualized a man armed with a panga slicing his way through thick jungle because that was how he saw a slowed down version of the path of the bullet ploughing through the brain) and completely shut down all bodily functions.

He would crumple, be dead, and there would be a lot of blood and brain and spray and bone matter on the door of the pub behind him.

The man aiming the rifle was settled in a warm, comfortable hollow beside an oak tree. He had been there for two days, applying all his long-acquired skills and knowledge to the task in hand, particularly the skill of being ready and willing to pull the trigger at exactly the right time.

The right time being now.

His breathing was controlled.

His heartbeat was also under control because he had learned how to do this, to consciously slow it down to the exact pace required in the moments before squeezing the trigger. It was a skill few assassins could master.

He blinked once more, then refitted his eye to the telescopic lens, perfectly adjusted to his exacting standards.

Then, for the last time, he took his right forefinger off the trigger, then carefully slid the tip back into position and began to exert the tiny amount of pressure required to fire the deadly weapon.

The target was still standing there for the taking.

The crosshairs of the sights were on the exact killing spot.

2,000 metres per second. Half a second away from death.

'Shit,' he breathed, and removed his finger from the trigger but continued to look through the sights whilst grinding his teeth and feeling his heart start to beat faster.

Someone had stepped into his line of fire.

The name of the man standing one kilometre away from the sniper, whose forehead was in the centre of the telescopic sights, was Henry Christie.

He was standing on the front steps of a country pub/hotel called the Tawny Owl situated in the centre of the tiny village of Kendleton in the wilds of the far north-east of Lancashire, essentially the middle of nowhere.

He was exhibiting all the stereotypical outward signs of a drunken man.

In police parlance – words Henry Christie had used often in the early part of his career when he had been a keen uniformed cop dutifully chasing drunks around town centres – he was unsteady on his feet, his eyes were glazed, his breath smelled strongly of intoxicants and his speech was slurred. Add to that the almost empty bottle of Jack Daniel's hanging loosely in the grip of his left hand, the square whisky glass in his right, his tie askew and a stupid expression on his face, he was the epitome of the happy inebriate.

'Well?'

Henry's eyes dropped and looked at the woman suddenly standing in front of him.

A moment before he had been staring across the car park at the front of the Tawny Owl towards the thickly wooded area on the far side of the village green, just beyond the stream, and although he had been enjoying the view, he was also revelling in the last few minutes of direct warmth caressing his face before the sun sank below the horizon.

He was standing there in a lazy, relaxed posture, left shoulder lower than the other, in the hand of which was the aforementioned bottle of JD he had secretly liberated from the stock room unbeknownst to the lady who had taken up the challenging position in front of him. At least he thought he had snaffled it without her knowledge, but she clearly knew – and could see it, of course – because as his watery eyes levelled with hers he saw her glance at the bottle, which he tried to hide behind his back.

'Stealing from your employer again?' she teased.

'Caught red-handed,' he admitted. 'Fingers in the till, so to speak.'

The woman reached across and peeled a piece of pink confetti from Henry's shirt collar with her fingernails. She rolled it into a tiny ball and flicked it away.

'You could get sacked for that,' she smiled.

'I won't make a habit of it,' he promised.

'No you won't,' she said, but not in a serious way. Henry now half-owned the business and the woman standing in front of him, who had unknowingly saved his life, owned the other half. A flicker of a half-smile played on her lips, a sexy look Henry had come to love, along with the rest of this lady.

'Anyway,' he said, attempting to marshal his disconnected thoughts. 'Well what?'

She shrugged her slim shoulders. 'Good day?'

'The best, I would say,' he replied, although the word 'say' was pronounced with a noticeable 'sh'.

It had been the first wedding at the newly refurbished and extended licensed premises and it had gone extremely well, hopefully a portent of things to come as another four were booked over the next few weeks, plus a big twenty-first party, and this was pretty much a dry run. It was also another milestone in the resurgence of the Tawny Owl following an inauspicious beginning when it had been taken over several years before as a run-down business on its last legs. The woman in front of Henry had transformed its fortunes.

'Maybe we should book *our* wedding now?' she suggested primly.

Her name was Alison Marsh, she was Henry's fiancée and just to prove it she held up her left hand and displayed the shiny ring on her finger for him to try and focus on.

'Only if we get it at cost price,' Henry said, still slurring his words.

'I think that can be arranged . . . boss says yes,' she laughed brightly, her eyes sparkling, although she had yet to drink any alcohol that day.

She went onto tiptoes and kissed Henry.

'Next Monday let's book in to see the registrar in Lancaster and pick a date,' he said, amazing himself.

She stood back slightly, unsure whether or not to believe him.

'Honestly?'

'Honestly,' he said.

'Not just the drink talking, making you brave? I know what you're like when you've had a few, all lovey-dovey and full o' bull.'

'I mean it,' he said earnestly.

And he did. He was now completely ready to move on with Alison. His wife, Kate, had been dead for over four years now and whilst her memory was still very much alive inside him, he knew it was time to seal her in his heart and surge forward with Alison and a new life, retired from the cops and with the excitement of a new business venture with the woman he loved and who loved him back. He wasn't desperate but he did have the feeling that Alison was his last chance for a wonderful shared life and he wasn't about to lose her.

She kissed him again and he felt tears welling in his eyes as she stood back and regarded him.

'God, I'm a soft-arse,' he said.

'What's going on here?'

Henry and Alison spun at the voice to see Alison's stepdaughter Ginny emerging from the pub door. She was in her early twenties, the daughter of Alison's deceased husband, and with whom she had moved to the Tawny Owl to rebuild their lives. She was a willowy, beautiful young lady who worked and lived in the pub with Henry and Alison.

'Hi, babe,' Alison greeted her. 'Just fixing up a date for a marriage.'

Ginny's face broke into a wide grin. 'Hurray!' she said. She came up to Henry and Alison and they embraced as a trio. 'About time.' She gave Henry a peck on the cheek, then hugged Alison. 'Can I be your chief bridesmaid?'

'There is no one else in the world,' Alison told her genuinely. The two had stayed together since Alison became a widow and she an orphan and were very close.

'Thank you.' Beaming, she looked at Henry. 'Does this mean you'll be my stepdad?'

'I have no idea what it means other than I'll always be here for you and Alison.' He swayed slightly, as if in a breeze.

Once more, assisted by alcohol, Henry found himself on the verge of blubbing and his bottom lip actually started to tremble.

Ginny saw it and hugged him tightly until he needed to breathe.

'Love you both, need to get back in.'

She detached herself and went back inside the pub, leaving Henry and Alison alone, again. Henry placed the bottle and glass down on the low wall by the front steps and held open his arms to Alison: more huggy time.

The sniper, 1,000 metres away in a direct line of sight through the trees, observed the touchy-feely performance through the telescopic lens.

As he watched, his jawline hardened, tensing as his back teeth grated together with a rising inner fury. He found he could no longer control his heart rate, which rose and pulsed against his ribcage; his breathing became ragged and his whole being lost the required physical and mental state to accurately fire a killing round into Henry Christie's head.

First he had seen the woman step into the line of fire.

Then the girl had appeared, followed by the group hug.

'Happy families,' he had spat at that point.

Then the young women had gone back into the pub, leaving Christie and the woman.

The sniper tried to make himself calm again, refitted his eye to the scope, placed his finger on the trigger and focused, this time on the back of the woman's head as she kissed Christie once more.

The sniper's rage turned ice-cold.

'Move,' he urged her, 'move away.'

She did, once more revealing Christie's head.

Ripe for a bullet, ripe for splitting like a melon.

He settled quickly: heart rate, breathing, psyche.

Killing time.

He watched through the scope as the woman – he knew her name, Alison Marsh – placed the palm of her hand tenderly on the man's cheek, then the ever so touching scene as she walked away from him, slid her hand all the way down his arm until their hands were palm to palm and then just their fingertips touched and they shared a sickly, loving look as she walked back into the pub and Christie watched her all the way to the door where she turned coyly, blew him a tender kiss which he pretended to catch on his lips, then she was gone back inside and he was alone with a stupid, crooked smirk of superiority across his self-satisfied, drunken face.

The sniper forced his heart rate to slow even further.

Henry Christie staggered back a few drunken paces, then regained his balance.

The sniper swore contemptuously under his breath as he realigned and sharpened his aim through the crosshairs, seeing Christie take a swig from the last dregs of the bottle he had picked up again.

'Piss-head,' the sniper mumbled.

His finger curled on the trigger.

The target was now standing relatively still.

'Got you now,' the sniper whispered, imagining the furrow the soft-tipped bullet would plough through Christie's alcohol-filled brain cells.

It was almost a pity he would die instantaneously with no knowledge of his own death.

To make him suffer would have been much more satisfying. To peel his skin from him, to make him die very slowly.

But this would have to do.

His body had now stabilized again.

Christie's head was in the sights. The pad of the finger lay across the trigger.

The trigger began to move backwards.

And suddenly the view down the scope went black as a huge shape traversed his line of sight and completely obscured the target.

'Fuck.'

The sniper raised his head angrily to see that a magnificent red-deer stag had stepped right in front of him, maybe twenty metres beyond the treeline. He was a beautiful specimen, ripping muscles and not black as he had first thought but a stunning golden brown, the colour of a lion's mane.

The stag was looking directly at the sniper who believed their eyes met and locked for an instant.

Then, with a haughty shake of his head, the stag plunged down a steep hill and disappeared into the woods.

Quickly the sniper refitted his eye to the scope but all he saw was the pub door closing as Henry Christie walked back inside to safety.

The sniper began to cry.

TWO

The newlyweds that day were Rik Dean and Henry Christie's sister, Lisa. They were the first ever couple to get married at the Tawny Owl, which now had a licence to hold ceremonies.

The day had gone extremely well for a first attempt.

Rik was now a detective superintendent in joint charge of Lancashire Constabulary's Force Major Investigation Team, otherwise known as FMIT. He had taken over, stepped into Henry's shoes on his retirement some months previously. Although Rik was a protégé of Henry's to some degree – Henry had backed him many years before to get him on to CID – and a friend and now his brother-in-law, Henry was secretly pleased he wasn't finding the job quite as easy as he had anticipated especially following Henry's own muted departure from the force which wasn't accompanied by a fanfare.

That said, Henry was happy for them because he thought they were well suited to each other – 'Mad as hatters,' he called them – and because they were the guinea pigs by being the first couple to get hitched at the Tawny Owl, although Henry's family connections did not mean they got a reduced price.

In fact, Henry had gleefully enjoyed taking several thousand pounds from Rik for the 'Summer Glade' wedding package.

As Henry wandered unsteadily back into the pub from the front steps and the setting sun, he had just glimpsed a red-deer stag in the distance, just in front of the woodland on the opposite side of the village, but the magnificent beast he had christened 'Horace' was there and gone in a flash – as usual (he had seen him many times) – and he entered the premises with that daft smile on his face, realizing how lucky he was all over again.

Yes, it was a deep sadness that his wife, Kate, had died so tragically from cancer, but also a source of great joy that Alison had come into his life and they were now moving forward together and he was determined to grasp that life ahead with both hands and make a success of it and the Tawny Owl.

What could be better, he often asked himself. Getting married to a gorgeous woman who was also a landlady and living in a beautiful country pub in the bargain with the big plus that he loved her to bits. He knew life as a landlord was no easy option – and the addition of the wedding business made it all the more tough – but certainly at the moment he was revelling in it and not even remotely hankering for his past life in the cops or with Kate.

There were around ninety guests at the wedding and the DJ

in the function room was doing a sterling job of getting everyone up to dance. Henry came in just as the newlyweds were about to begin their first dance together, twirling gently to an Ed Sheeran song all about getting old and staying in love.

Henry watched from the back of the room.

Soon it would be him and Alison. He was actually looking forward to the day.

The entertainment licence allowed the bar to stay open until one am by which time there was no sign of Rik and Lisa anyway. They had sneaked off to the bridal suite an hour before where champagne and strawberries awaited them (all part of the package) and by one fifteen a.m. the guests who were not staying had left and the ones with rooms in the new annexe were drifting off contentedly, if unsteadily.

Henry was leaning on the bar, having collected many empty glasses which would be washed in the morning.

He had not had a drink for about four hours and whilst he would never have claimed to be sober, a lot of the alcohol in him had dispersed in the usual ways.

The security shutter clattered down, pulled and locked by Ginny. The DJ finished packing and hauling his gear and shouted a farewell before heading out to his van and away.

Finally, all that remained were Henry, Alison and Ginny.

'Well done, guys,' Alison said. She hugged Ginny, who plodded weakly away towards the private quarters at the rear of the pub where her bedroom was located.

'Nice one,' Henry said thickly, suddenly very tired.

'It went well – thanks,' Alison said. 'I think we've got the makings of something special here.'

'Us or the business?' Henry asked.

'Both.'

'Night cap, security check, bed?' Henry suggested. 'In that order.'

'OK, sounds good.'

They walked down to the main bar at the front of the building. Alison unlocked the bar and poured them each a tot of Talisker Skye single-malt whisky and they went to sit on the bench in the front bay window.

Henry was glad it was only a sip. He'd drunk enough that night and anything more could have reignited his inebriation.

They clinked glasses, said, 'To us.'

Out of the corner of his eye, Henry caught sight of a movement on the car park, a dark shape crouched between the cars belonging to the guests who were staying over. At first he wasn't certain if he'd actually seen anything or that maybe it was a fox, but when his head quickly cricked around he was sure. It was a man who knew he'd been seen and who darted behind the bulk of a Jeep Renegade.

Henry placed his glass on the copper-topped table.

'Someone out there.'

Alison peered out, could not see anything. 'You sure?'

'Yeah – could be nicking from the cars.'

Henry stood up and twisted around to the front door, stepping out into the night.

The security light came on, activated by his movement, but only illuminating the very front of the pub and steps, not beyond. Henry had to shade his eyes to see into the car park, where about twenty cars remained, including his, Alison's and Ginny's.

He trotted down the steps, beyond the light.

Alison watched from the door and called, 'Be careful.'

Henry made his way directly towards the Jeep, which he knew belonged to his American friend Karl Donaldson who, with his wife Karen, was up from near London to attend the wedding.

Henry was positive he had seen a man between the cars.

'I've seen you,' he called to that effect. 'Cops are on their way,' he added, lying. The nearest cop was the village bobby, Jake Niven, who had been at the wedding and would be tucked up in bed asleep in his home, which was the police house on the other side of the village. The nearest serviceable cops would therefore be in Lancaster, almost a dozen miles distant.

So, with Alison bringing up the rear, Henry was alone.

In his short tenure at the Tawny Owl there had never once been a theft of or from a vehicle on the car park. He did wonder if the wedding had attracted thieves into the village. There had been a lot of cars parked up earlier and were relatively easy targets for crims coming in from Lancaster, and in a parallel line of thought, Henry was already considering the need for better security than just a pretty weak light around the doorway.

He paused, listened.

There was a scuffling noise, then he saw a shape flit from behind the Jeep, keeping low, taking cover behind another car.

Henry sprinted between the two cars, shouting, 'Oi!' as he ran and having to gag himself from shouting, 'Police, stop,' which was on the tip of his tongue.

He skidded to a stop on the thinly gravelled surface just as the figure rose in front of him in a blur of speed and the next thing he recalled was that he was sitting on his backside, having been punched hard in the face by the man who, as Alison ran down the front steps screaming, vaulted over the low wall and ran across the village green and disappeared without a sound.

Henry swilled his face delicately in the warm water, raised his face and winced at his reflection in the mirror above the sink. His cheekbone was red and swollen, but fortunately he had been punched on the side that had not been previously broken and had taken so long to heal properly. He was fairly sure that other than a bruise under the eye there would be no permanent damage – other than to his pride.

But it did hurt, in a dull throbbing sort of way. He scoffed two paracetamol caplets and washed them down with a couple of handfuls of water from the cold tap.

He was naked now.

Alison came into the bathroom and stood behind him. She had a worried look on her face.

She was in her nightie – quite a short one that displayed her shapely legs – but unlike Henry, who threw off his clothes at any opportunity when he and Alison were alone together, she was shy and conservative around the bedroom, except of course when they made love, when all the barriers came down with abandon.

'How is it?' she asked, looking over his shoulder at his reflection.

'OK, I think.' He touched his face carefully.

'What did the police say?'

Henry had taken the trouble to phone them and eventually

connected with the newly opened Contact Centre at police head-quarters in Hutton, near Preston, which now dealt with all incoming calls and subsequent deployments for all of the force. With his eyes rolling, he had spoken to a comms operator who had no idea where Kendleton was, let alone the Tawny Owl. Henry's boast of being an ex-detective superintendent was met by a belittling moment of contemptuous silence, which immediately let Henry know that an 'ex' anything meant nothing to a twenty-year-old comms operator who probably only knew how to follow a satnav and had no idea what an actual map looked like.

After admitting the offender had legged it and that, no, he did not need an ambulance, it was clear the young lad had no interest and Henry was informed that all Lancaster patrols were too busy to drive out to the sticks and that a message would be left on the local bobby's scratch pad for attention when he next came on duty.

'Forget it,' Henry had said at that point and hung up with a heavy heart. 'I'll tell him myself,' he muttered.

In response to Alison's question, he said, 'They were as much use as a chocolate fireguard.' He turned slowly and displayed his injury to her.

'That's going to be a shiner,' she commented.

'Well, what's a wedding do without at least one black eye?' he said, then added, 'It could be loved better.'

She sighed sternly at him and simply and firmly said, 'No,' a decision he accepted gracefully.

The sniper gained control of his breathing once more as he settled in the deep grass on the far side of the village green, watching the ridiculous prancing about of Henry Christie as he called the police on his mobile phone, following the altercation on the car park.

The sniper cursed himself for being spotted, but the plus side of it was the feel of the impact of his knuckles on Christie's face, though it was tempered by the regret it wasn't the best punch he had ever delivered. That said, it had tasted sweet and just confirmed one thing – it would be a great pleasure to kill the man.

Finally Christie finished poncing around and he and Alison Marsh retreated into the pub, locking the big double front doors behind them.

The sniper eased himself into a sitting position.

In his mind he could not erase the view down the telescopic sights of Christie and the two women, the vomit-inducing family hug.

There was also another urge inside him, almost as strong as the one to kill the ex-cop and which might give him the possibility of killing two birds with one stone and achieving his overall ambition in a more convincing manner.

After they had gone back into the pub, the sniper returned to the location in which he had lain prone for almost two days and settled down for another hour, keeping watch on the Tawny Owl in the company of a snuffling badger and then a fox that walked by unconcerned. He inhaled the close-up reek of both beasts, each distinctive and pungent. In fact he could probably, blind-folded, have identified the scent of fifty different large animals, from a camel to a lion, from all the different places he had lain in wait to kill all over the world. He had even once been eyeball to eyeball with a curious leopard whilst waiting for the appear-ance of a murderous West African warlord he had dispatched with a single bullet to the skull as the man drove home from his boyfriend's house in an open-topped Land Rover. The man had been singing away as if he had no cares in the world, a man who had butchered thousands, raped, tortured and mutilated hundreds of young girls and boys, all in the name of his religion. The world had become – for a short while – a much better place for that man's death. Something the sniper had been proud of.

And the leopard had padded away, unharmed.

This was a whole different thing, though, much more to it than just a killing.

It was an obsession.

The Tawny Owl became black and silent, all lights extin-guished, all movement ceased.

The sniper rose and edged through the shadows to the front of the pub, then around to the side, where, on a previous visit, he had arranged an easy way into the premises.

THREE

Henry had never believed alcohol delivered a good night's sleep. That night he was proved right as he lay alongside Alison with a dry mouth from the night's intake and his face pulsing from his encounter with the masked man in the car park, though he was pretty sure that a combination of paracetamol and alcohol was helping with the pain.

Alison had gone to sleep quickly. She always did, but she was particularly exhausted that night after the weeks of build-up, prep and finally running the wedding day to perfection. She deserved a long sleep and a long lie-in, but Henry knew that would not happen.

The working day at the Tawny Owl always began around six a.m. and Alison would be up, fresh as a daisy, pushing things along from breakfast onwards. Henry would be around, too, though his first hour or two was usually spent in a haze, or at least until he'd had sufficient coffee to kick-start a bit of life into him.

He usually managed a half-decent night's sleep, five or six hours, but he knew that was not going to happen tonight.

So far, he'd had none.

Alongside him, Alison made a little buzzing sound.

Henry folded his arms across his chest, annoyed with himself, unable to get properly comfortable, but he closed his eyes and tried to sleep by listening to the building.

He had grown accustomed to the noises the old pub made. It wasn't a silent building by any means, especially this part, the original bit, as opposed to the newly built annexe connected to the back of the pub by a beautiful glass-roofed conservatory in which morning coffee and afternoon tea were served.

Henry listened.

Everything creaked. The old hardwood windows, the doors, the central-heating pipes, the timber floorboards, all contracting and expanding. It was like living inside the wheezing chest of an old man.

He had grown to love the sounds. Even those emanating from Alison who, although Henry never mentioned it, had a very wide repertoire of snores.

Finally he was beginning to fall asleep. He recognized he was in that strange, twilight zone, the moments between wakefulness and proper sleep, when dreams and ridiculous thoughts unconnected with anything, began to mingle and tumble around in his brain.

Until his eyes shot open – and he knew.

He lay there, straining to hear, because he had heard something different, the sound of a footfall. Unless Ginny was up and about for some reason, no one should be walking around this part of the pub, the private, owners' accommodation, only accessible through doors Henry knew he had locked. Only he, Alison and Ginny were resident that night.

He held his breath as a strange feeling of dread zipped through him.

He knew Ginny's habits. They very much reflected her stepmother's. She was a deep sleeper, who went out like a light as soon as her head hit the pillow, and she rarely woke until her alarm came alive next to her ear. She had an en-suite shower room and toilet, but Henry had never heard her use it during the night and he had never known her go walkabout, so unless things were different that night, he knew someone else had entered the private area.

He swallowed dryly, then sat up slowly on the edge of the bed, swung out his legs. He always slept naked but with a pair of shorts and a T-shirt within reaching distance just in case one of the residents needed something or there was a fire alarm or other emergency.

He slid the shorts on as he stood up, still trying to listen above the thump of his heart and the rise and fall of his lungs. He pushed his feet into his slippers and walked to the bedroom door. In the corridor outside he knew that if he turned right then went through the first door on the right he would end up in the expansive lounge, dining room and kitchen area.

Directly opposite was the door to the rarely used main bathroom, then further along to the left was Ginny's bedroom.

He opened the door and stood quietly on the threshold, allowing his eyes to adjust to the lack of light in the corridor, and looked along it both ways. To his left, at the far end, was a set of alarmed fire doors which were closed and locked as they should be. They led out to the yard at the back which was surrounded by a high wall. The door at the opposite end of the corridor was the one leading back into the pub just by the side of the main bar.

All looked OK from his position at the bedroom door, with one exception.

The corridor lights were off completely, but Henry knew he had dimmed them low, the last thing he always did before entering his bedroom.

'Henry?' Alison called sleepily from the bed, sitting up and squinting at him. He did not turn, simply held up his left hand in a gesture for her to remain quiet. 'What is it?' she hissed.

This time he turned and placed a finger on his lips: 'Shhh.'

She frowned. Henry turned away, every nerve now on full alert.

He stepped into the corridor, then took one stride to the bathroom door, which he opened slowly and looked inside. The light was off, the room empty. He closed the door, reversed back into the corridor by which time Alison had scrambled out of bed and was at the bedroom door tightening a dressing gown around her.

'What is it?' she whispered.

'Thought I heard footsteps,' he whispered back.

'You sure? Not a guest upstairs?' she asked. On the floor above were the original bedrooms, old, but beautifully refurbished, including the bridal suite.

Henry knew the difference between the footsteps of the guests up there and someone at ground level. He shook his head and pointed to the floor. Alison nodded.

Their heads swivelled to Ginny's door.

Henry shrugged and walked towards it, Alison a step behind him, now wide awake.

Henry rarely entered Ginny's room. It was her secret lair and she often spent the night in there with her boyfriend, but she had recently split up with him, so Henry knew she would be alone. The door did not lock from either side, none of the private rooms did. Henry curled his fingers around the door knob and placed his ear to the door itself, his face strained as his eyes narrowed and he concentrated hard, but heard nothing.

Alison clamped her hand around his bicep, dug her nails in, making him jump, sensing his trepidation and also believing his senses. Then she released him.

He turned the knob very slowly and stealthily, then finally believing the tension was going to give him heart failure, he shoved the door open.

Ginny was in bed, her long hair splayed out across her pillow, asleep.

And the man in her bedroom had one knee on the bed and the corner of the quilt in the grasp of his fingertips, about to draw it back from her.

He turned: froze.

In the light – and there was enough of it – Henry instantly identified him as the man he had encountered in the car park, same dark clothing, same balaclava, same build.

'Stop right there, you bastard,' Henry shouted and lurched across the room towards him, flinging the door fully open.

The man threw down the cover and came head-on to meet Henry halfway across the carpet.

This time Henry was slightly more prepared for a clash, and swung a fist at him.

The man jerked his head sideways and Henry's punch sailed past, missing him by an inch, which was a long way in a fight.

Alison screamed a warning, but the man forced Henry to the floor as the ex-detective pummelled him about the back of the head and shoulders, hitting him as hard as he possibly could with his fists, connecting with the bone of his cranium and the muscle of his neck.

They rolled back in a clawing, punching lump, but suddenly the intruder had the better of Henry, straddling him, pounding his face mercilessly, blow after blow, hard and accurate as Henry tried to deflect them with his forearms and by twisting his head.

Alison burst across from the door and launched herself into the man, dislodging him and sending him sprawling across the carpet.

Henry tried to move but he was suddenly groggy and in a whirling world of disorientation.

The man backhanded Alison, knocking her spinning away from him, but as she rolled she grabbed his ankles, trying to bring him down. He stepped out of her grasp like he was stepping out of a tyre in an obstacle course, then stamped hard into her face and said, 'Bitch.'

Henry's senses flooded back. He threw himself at the man who was too fast, too lithe, and he jigged sideways out of Henry's grip, sprinted to the door, was gone.

'How is she?'

'Still very groggy.'

'Definitely been drugged, sedated?' Henry asked the paramedic.

'I'd say so,' she said. She was perched on the bed beside Ginny, re-checking her vital signs. All seemed good in respect of heartbeat and breathing but she still had not resurfaced from whatever drug had been administered to her.

The lights were all on now. Henry was holding a cold compress, made from a folded tea towel packed with ice, to the side of his newly swelling face. Alison dabbed a handkerchief at her nose, which dribbled blood. She stood next to Henry and his free arm was wrapped around her shoulders. Both of them were now dressed and he was trying to comfort and reassure her, but she continued to shake like a leaf.

And who could blame her? Henry thought.

He was feeling it too as he looked at Ginny but he was also covering it with rage at the violent intrusion into their lives. He was actually strangely taken aback about how much he was feeling for Ginny, who was not a blood relative. He had two 'real' daughters from his marriage to Kate, both now grown and living away, and he would not have said that Ginny was any sort of replacement for them or that he was a 'dad substitute' for her. The fact was, she came with Alison and he and Ginny liked each other immensely, maybe even loved each other a little, too. To see her as a victim of a crime in a place where she should have been totally safe had affected him deeply and demonstrated just how deep his feelings were for her. She was part of his family now, he supposed, and anyone violating her also violated him.

After the intruder had gone, after assaulting him and Alison, he had called the cops and ambulance again on the treble-nine system whilst Alison cared for Ginny, who was completely out of it.

This time he got a promise from the operator he'd spoken to earlier that a patrol car would be dispatched, but gave no estimated time of arrival. When he was transferred to the ambulance people, they sent one immediately. It had to come from Lancaster but was there within fifteen minutes.

In that intervening time Henry called the local bobby's mobile number. He had been at the wedding, so Henry knew him well enough. In fact, Henry had been instrumental in getting PC Jake Niven the job of the rural cop for the area, which was about the last thing Henry ever did as a detective superintendent prior to retirement.

The phone clicked to voicemail three times before Jake picked up in person, answering thickly, probably with his tongue glued to the roof of his mouth.

'Henry . . . what the fuck?'

'Get showered, get dressed, sink a pint of water and get yourself out here if you're fit enough . . . Someone's broken in and tried to abduct Ginny and assaulted me and Alison along the way.'

'Eh?'

Henry could visualize Jake's screwed-up face as he tried to make sense of the information, probably thinking he was listening to a hoax call.

'You heard,' Henry said bluntly.

'OK, OK, ten minutes,' he promised. Henry knew it would take him a little longer than that but at least he was on his way.

By this time the ambulance had arrived and pulled up silently in front of the Owl, no blue lights or sirens, neither being necessary, and few minutes later the nice lady paramedic had delivered her confirmation of Henry's thoughts, which were not rocket science.

The man, the intruder, had obviously injected something into Ginny, probably via her neck, and this was evidenced by the syringe on the floor by the bedside drawers. He had drugged her to subdue her and had also stuck a strip of gaffer tape across her mouth, though he had probably done this before injecting her. As Henry took this in, the sequence of events was slightly unclear, but the facts were Ginny had been drugged and her mouth taped over.

He had not got as far as trussing her up by tying her wrists and ankles, but this was probably on his to-do list as evidenced by the roll of tape, and it seemed that once this had been done he had intended to roll her into the sleeping bag he had brought along just for that purpose, zip her in tight and carry her out over his shoulder like an old carpet.

Henry and Alison, it seemed, had entered the bedroom just before the trussing-up section of the proceedings.

Going into cop mode, Henry warned the paramedics not to touch anything other than was necessary as this was a serious crime scene and it was vital to protect and secure any evidence. He took responsibility for removing the tape from Ginny's mouth before the paramedics arrived, easing it carefully away and ensuring he only touched one tiny corner of it between thumb and forefinger. There was a good chance of fingerprints or DNA on the tape and the same applied to the roll of tape and the syringe and maybe the sleeping bag left behind. He put the strip of tape that had been over her mouth into a plastic sandwich bag.

'Will she be all right?' Alison asked fearfully.

The paramedics were easing Ginny into a wheelchair. One was holding up a saline drip that had been inserted into her arm just for good measure.

'We need to get her in to be on the safe side,' the lady paramedic explained. 'A doctor needs to examine her and we need to get her blood tested to find out what drug has been used on her. The police will want to know. Can one of you come with us?'

Alison looked at Henry uncertainly, trying to think things through.

The male paramedic who was holding up the drip and who had treated Henry and Alison for their injuries, which were superficial, said, 'She'll need someone when she comes round.'

Henry knew what Alison's conundrum was: there were guests staying and it would be another couple of hours before the chef arrived to begin breakfast preparations.

'What should I do?'

'Go with her,' he told her. 'It's you she'll want to see, not me. I'll sort things out here, not least because I want to go and rouse Rik and Karl from their slumbers.'

'No, don't, don't bother them,' she pleaded.

'Trust me, neither will thank me if I don't wake them and tell them what's happened. They'll want to know and help if they can . . . but I'll leave it a while . . . maybe.'

'OK.'

'When everything's sorted, I'll come out to the hospital, OK?'

'Right, right, OK,' she said.

They stood aside as the paramedics manoeuvred the wheelchair through the narrow door, Ginny strapped into it to stop her slipping out, barely conscious, her eyes just watery slits.

'Why?' Henry whispered.

'Do you think it's connected to the guy on the car park? You think it was him?' Alison asked.

'I'd put a hundred quid on it . . . but that doesn't answer why. Is something happening in her life we don't know about?'

'I don't know,' Alison answered, then frowned fleetingly, an expression that was gone almost instantly, but one that Henry noticed.

They all trailed out to the ambulance on the front car park. Ginny was hoisted into the rear. Alison put a foot onto the back step of the vehicle, stopped suddenly and turned to Henry. Her eyes were filled with tears.

'She'll be all right,' he assured her again.

'What if she isn't?'

Henry blinked at her. 'Not going to happen, got that?' He gave her another embrace and a kiss and tried hard to project a strong front. He wasn't sure how convincing he was, but he did his best, trying to give his impression of a rock face.

She stepped back up again, but then stopped dead again and said, 'Damn!'

'What?'

'Lord Chalmers,' she said.

'What about Lord Chalmers?' he said, but even as he spoke the words, he knew.

'I said I'd go and see him at ten this morning – about that twenty-first-birthday party for his granddaughter.'

'I'll go and see the old git,' Henry said.

'B-but . . .'

'I'll be all nice and professional, honest, and we'll get the gig. You go and take care of Ginny, just concentrate on that.' Henry saw the shadow of doubt scud across her face. 'I *will* take care of everything and then I'll come over to the hospital and pick you up, because everything's going to be OK. Now go.'

This time she stepped into the ambulance. The paramedic shut the doors and the vehicle drew away en route to the A&E department at Royal Lancaster Infirmary. Henry watched until it disappeared out of sight, then exhaled, checked his watch and wondered where the fuck the cops had got to.

He went back inside the Tawny Owl to the private accommodation and to Ginny's room, where he stood on the threshold. He slid his hands into his jogging pants.

It seemed such a long time since he had been to a crime scene but not everything he'd had ingrained into him in over thirty years as a cop had left him, some eight months into retirement. He knew he was blunted, not as sharp as he had been, and was aware that his knowledge of police procedure was not as up to date as it had been, but the basics of crime-scene management – securing and preserving evidence – were not difficult and he had done the thing that he had first learned at the Police Training Centre when attending a crime scene. As the instructor had screamed at him, 'Put your fucking hands in your fucking pockets and use your fucking eyes first. Look, but don't touch.'

That little gem, strangely, had stayed with him all his service.

Not that there was an awful lot to see in this particular crime scene, and things had already been moved, but he still took a few moments of reflection which had not been possible earlier because of the circumstances.

The strip of tape from Ginny's mouth was already in a plastic bag, but neither the syringe nor the full roll of gaffer tape or the sleeping bag had been touched.

Henry knew those items could hold a forensic treasure chest. Or not.

It depended on how forensically aware the offender was, how prepared he'd been, and, also, perhaps, what this was all about.

Henry closed his eyes tight and tried to re-visualize the scene he had encountered on opening Ginny's bedroom door.

It did not help that he had alcohol in his system and it annoyed him he could not recall if the intruder had been wearing gloves or otherwise. If he had been, and had prepared everything with them on, then the forensic side could be more problematical.

'C'mon, brain, work,' he chided himself.

But he knew this wasn't the only crime scene. The man had entered the Tawny Owl somewhere else and Henry knew it was vital to identify the point of entry. The whole of the old part of the premises was therefore a crime scene.

With that depressing thought, Henry decided he needed a coffee to give him some stability and brain power. He walked back down the corridor and out into the public reception area just as the local cop, PC Jake Niven, arrived. He was in uniform, smart, but his face betrayed a night of boozing and it looked as though Henry's instructions about water intake and a shower hadn't worked well.

'What's going on, Henry? I've had comms bleating at me, but I've cancelled any other patrols for the moment – even though this is my day off,' he stressed.

'Oh yeah,' Henry said sarcastically. 'My heart bleeds for you. Coffee?'

It was at that moment Jake saw Henry's injured face properly for the first time and his jaw went slack.

'What the—' he began.

Henry silenced him with a wave of the hand. 'I'll tell you in a minute.'

Henry switched on his amazing coffee-making machine behind the bar, ground some Kenyan beans and began the brewing process for which he had even become a trained barista. He was a great coffee-maker now.

Then he took a half-pint glass from a shelf and filled it with cold tap water and guzzled it in one, tipping it down his throat, feeling his Adam's apple rise and fall as the cold liquid spread downwards.

He looked at Jake who had watched the little ritual with patience.

'Yeah, I'll have a coffee,' he said.

Henry made two Americanos with hot milk and explained the night's events to him. Jake listened, increasingly perturbed.

'Shit,' he said as Henry concluded. 'Is she OK?'

'We don't know yet . . . she's in medical hands.'

Henry looked expectantly at Jake as the incident had now been officially reported to the police – something that filled Henry with dread. No disrespect was intended towards Jake or to other individual officers or staff, but Henry thought that police forces had completely forgotten how to give the public what the public wanted – a response.

He did not want to tell Jake what to do, but knew that if it had been him in this situation, having just been told of such a serious crime, he would have been calling for backup. He would be on the blower for CID and Scenes of Crime and also maybe thinking about putting together a search team come daylight to start combing the area for an offender still at large. He would also have an officer at the hospital to check up on and possibly guard Ginny, the victim.

Henry watched the cogs rotating through Jake's skull for a moment. The PC then took his coffee outside and began to make some radio calls to mobilize what Henry called 'the Circus'.

Henry sipped his coffee, watching Jake, fairly certain he was at least trying to put some of Henry's thoughts into action. Jake was a good cop and knew his business well, one of the reasons Henry had supported him in getting the job in the village. He and his family had had a baptism of fire but as he came out of that, Henry knew he had been taken to the heart of the locals . . . but as an example of the way Henry's mind had just been working in the respect of the police losing focus, Jake was already feeling the tug of being pulled away from the village to cover staff shortages in Lancaster. So far he had managed to resist, but it would not be long before the bosses ordered him because policing the city was more important to them and they thought rural beat officers were a luxury these days. In fact Jake was one of only a handful of such officers left in the county, those who lived and worked in the communities they policed.

Anyway, Henry thought with a heavy heart, he was here at the moment – and on his day off, as he had so bluntly reminded Henry.

The water rehydrated Henry and the coffee gave him the kick he needed to start the day which, he knew, would be long, wearying and emotional.

And he still had a peer of the realm to see.

Jake came back in. 'Right,' he declared, 'crime scene investigators turned out, a detective's on the way and we're looking at the possibility of getting a support unit serial over later and there's a PCSO on the way to the hospital to meet up with Alison and Ginny.'

Henry nodded. Good enough for the moment.

'He's out there somewhere,' he said.

'But if he has a vehicle, he could be miles away.'

'Mm.' Henry mulled that over. 'I've been trying to think what he smelled of.' He searched his olfactory memory because it seemed important. Then he had it. 'He stunk of grass, that's what it was.'

'Weed, you mean? Marijuana?'

'No. Actual grass, the stuff cows eat . . . like maybe he'd been lying low in it.'

'Watching and waiting?'

'Maybe, maybe.'

They regarded each other.

'You're certain it's one and the same guy who assaulted you in the car park?' Jake probed.

'Yeah.' Henry scratched his rather ragged left ear, the one he had nearly lost when someone fired a shotgun at him some time ago. It resembled a half-made gear cog, but at least it didn't hurt any more, though it remained intriguing to play with. 'I'm sure.'

They chatted some more then when they had finished their coffees, Henry refilled the mugs.

Outside, the late-summer dawn was not very far away. Henry suggested it could be worthwhile checking the exterior of the pub to see if the intruder's point of access could be found.

Essentially, the Tawny Owl consisted of two main sections. The old part contained the public bars, dining room, kitchen, the living accommodation with guest bedrooms upstairs, plus the refurbished function room where weddings were held; this old section was connected to the newly built annexe by way of a nice conservatory. The annexe consisted of a dozen bedrooms, six either side, all on the ground floor, all en suite and all with terraces looking out towards the village at the front or the woods at the back.

Henry and Jake found where he had entered fairly quickly – by way of the ground-floor gents' toilets, the open window being a bit of a giveaway.

Without spoiling any evidence, they inspected the window and as they did, Henry's chest tightened as he became increasingly angry because the closer they looked, the more it became apparent this was a planned break-in.

He was furious with himself because he hadn't physically checked that the window was secure on his rounds. The offender had clearly been into the pub, either posing as a customer or a hiker (as he and Alison happily allowed hikers to use the facilities even if they didn't buy anything). The man had unscrewed the screws that fixed the stays and hack-sawed them down almost to the screw head and replaced them so it appeared that the window was secure. All he had needed to do was prise the end of a jemmy or screwdriver under the window frame and pull and he was in.

Henry felt like a fool. He remembered checking these windows from the inside only the day before and they had looked all right to look at, except they weren't.

Jake was picking up on his bitterness. And also a couple of sawn-off screw shafts from the grass under the window.

Henry swore.

'The window would have looked locked,' Jake said, stating the obvious. He was trying to make Henry feel better, but was not succeeding. At least they had found how he had got inside the building.

After sliding through this window into the gents', it was an easy enough journey to the main bar but then he would have somehow had to force his way through the secure door dividing the public area from the living area – or enter the four-digit code on the keypad by the door.

Henry did not recall seeing any signs of forced entry on that door.

He growled internally, thinking, 'If someone wants to break into your property, they will.'

'Bastard.'

'Planned,' Jake said.

Henry tried to recall when he had last opened and closed that toilet window, just to try and put together some sort of time frame for this. It wasn't something he did regularly, usually just when he was cleaning the window frame. He guessed it could have been two weeks before, which didn't really narrow things down too much, and fourteen days gave a bad man plenty of opportunity to do bad things.

The pub opened its doors at seven a.m., offering breakfasts for the guests and a small but steady stream of locals who started their day with a hearty meal and, of course, great coffee before work. The business then often stayed open until after midnight, when the boozy locals were ejected. That also gave a lot of hours each day for someone to come in unnoticed and prepare a break-in.

'What about CCTV?' Jake asked.

Henry's mouth twisted. There were a few cameras dotted around, one in the bar which covered the bar itself and one scanning the front doors. The images were recorded on a computer in the office in the kitchen. Henry conceded it was a poor set-up. The new annexe was much better protected with cameras everywhere and new, tamper-proof windows throughout. The old section of the pub had been neglected and was definitely vulnerable but Henry had not realized until now, just how much.

He gulped and decided the alarm company would be in that afternoon.

'I'll have a skim through some of the disks,' he told Jake, 'but I don't hold out much hope . . . there is something I need to check, though.'

He spun and both men went back around the pub, inside, and to the door leading to the private accommodation with the security keypad next to it.

Four digits needed to be pressed in the right order to gain access.

'You got a UV torch?' Henry asked Jake.

'Out in the Land Rover.'

'Will you get it?'

It did not surprise Henry that Jake had such a piece of kit. They were useful for inspecting crime scenes and highlighted such things as sperm stains on bedding, that sort of pleasant stuff.

Henry took the torch from Jake as he came back in with it, then shaded the keypad with one hand, switched on the torch and shone it over the numbers. It was totally obvious which of the four numbers from zero to nine made up the entry code because those keys were the only ones with greasy fingerprints on them.

Four, eight, nine, zero.

Henry knew it would be relatively easy to guess the correct combination with patience and some luck and the application of the statistic that most people when deciding on number combinations were intrinsically lazy and usually just went in ascending order to keep it simple for themselves and, unfortunately, others. The combination had not changed since Henry had moved in, which did not make him feel any better.

Once more he kicked himself mentally very hard.

As a cop he would have given himself totally different advice – you can't be too careful, you never know when something bad might happen, blah-de-blah-de-blah.

He had become complacent and paid the price.

After that, all they could do was wait for the circus to arrive.

In that time the chef arrived and began to prepare breakfast. With the wedding there was a full house of guests overnight and the chef would be extra busy that morning with two staff down – Alison and Ginny – and only Henry in their place.

As much as he wanted to just think about the break-in and Ginny, there was still a business to run and Henry tried to concentrate on the practicalities of that, preparing the dining room, laying out the Continental breakfast choices and setting up the heated trays for the self-service full English 'eat all you can' as well as firing up the coffee machines so that as guests eventually began to filter down from their rooms, everything would be ready.

Henry also made a call to a local girl who waited-on part-time and asked her if she would be willing to come in early to help out. She was happy to do so and that eased the burden.

Even without the events of the night, Henry's life was so incredibly different now.

Not all that long ago, as a detective superintendent, he would have sauntered into his office at headquarters, got a coffee, plonked himself at his desk and got others to do his bidding with a flick of the fingers like a modern Caligula.

That life had gone, but he didn't miss it, and usually his day now began with a coffee and a piece of toast out on the front steps of the pub, watching dawn arrive before getting stuck into the complexities of running a business, learning as he went.

He loved what he had now, a life with Alison, and whilst it was physically and mentally taxing and the remuneration was nowhere near what he had earned as a cop, it was fantastic and his stomach crawled when he thought that someone had entered it with such evil intentions.

He knew he would not rest until he found that man.

And punished him.

FOUR

Although the mobile phone signal in the area of Kendleton was at best unreliable, Henry managed to call Alison for an update on Ginny's condition. She told him they had arrived safely at the hospital and she was being treated but it all looked good. She was coming around slowly from whatever sedative had been injected into her system but was still disorientated and confused about what had happened. Alison sounded very stressed but there was little Henry could do other than re-assure her everything would be all right and that he had a grip on the Tawny Owl.

Because of the early start at the pub, in addition to the steady stream of early-rising locals who came in for breakfasts, one or two gamekeepers occasionally showed up, one of whom was chatting to Jake on the front doorstep as Henry ended his call to Alison.

To be truthful he was actually a trainee gamekeeper by the name of Tod Rawstron, who was attending the local agricultural college and working as a gamekeeper in his spare time. He was just nineteen years old and Henry knew he had been a bit of a rogue, but college and work had kept him on the straight and narrow for a while now and if he did manage to get a full-time job after college, he would have a bright, if not well-paid future.

Jake had developed a good relationship with all the local keepers. There were quite a few of them, several who worked on the vast expanse of land around Kendleton owned by the Duke of Westminster and other landed gentry such as Lord Chalmers, who also owned a big chunk, but nowhere near as much as Westminster.

One of the by-products of Jake's job as a rural beat officer was that he was also a wildlife and conservation officer and he knew that gamekeepers weren't averse to blasting the daylights out of protected birds of prey in order to protect their own home-reared birds, so he had already made inroads into getting to know as many keepers as possible whilst recuperating from his injuries.

Henry walked out into the middle of their conversation and nodded at Tod, who was kitted up for a day in the outdoors. His short-wheelbase Land Rover was on the car park and his loyal canine companion, a black Labrador called Nursey, leaned out of the open window, tongue hanging out.

'Morning, Tod,' Henry greeted him.

'Mornin', Henry.' Tod almost doffed his tweed cloth cap at Henry, which, Henry thought, was only right.

'You in for breakfast?'

'I am.'

'Be ready in a few minutes.'

'Great, thanks.'

Jake interrupted. 'We've just been having an interesting chat,' he said to Henry, then glanced at Tod and urged him, 'Go on, tell him.'

Henry knew Tod wasn't the most garrulous of people, but he tried anyway. 'Not much to tell, really, but I've seen a guy in the woods a couple of times recently, just, fleetin' like. But he moves quick an' I never actually caught up wi' 'im . . . did have a rifle of some sort in his hands. Spotted t'cunt twice in two days nah.'

'Whereabouts?'

Tod pointed across to the woodland on the other side of the village, the trees Henry had been looking at the night before when he had seen the stag. The land belonged to Lord Chalmers, Henry knew.

'An' it weren't a shotgun.'

'What d'you mean?' Henry asked.

'It were a proper rifle, so he weren't out rough shooting.'

Rough shooting was putting up game, such as rabbits, hares and birds, often using a dog, working hedgerows, and blasting the poor animals with a shotgun when they broke cover, ran or flew for their lives.

'It had sights on it an' a tripod.'

'But you didn't catch up with the guy?'

'Nah, but I know me guns, even from a distance.'

Henry took it in. 'OK, thanks Tod . . . go get your breakfast – and it's on the house today,' he said generously then regretted the words instantly because he knew what Alison would think. He had become a businessman but he still liked giving things away. It was hard not to. He knew he needed to develop a more ruthless edge in respect of taking money out of people's hands.

When Jake gave Henry his puppy-dog eyes he relented with him also, so all three then went inside to eat.

Because Jake and Tod were in deep conversation about pheasants, partridges and grouse as Jake was also a keen shooter, Henry blanked over, made himself a sausage butty on a barm cake, grabbed another coffee and went back out to the front of the pub to sit, eat and cogitate.

He was exhausted. The previous day, being the first wedding the Tawny Owl had ever hosted, had been long and arduous, topped by him drinking too much, then sort of sobering up followed by the incident on the car park and then in Ginny's room. However, the coffee hit the spot and the sausage barm injected some energy into him.

Henry was sipping yet another coffee around about nine a.m. when Karl Donaldson emerged from the hotel annexe, dressed in his running gear, stretching his muscular frame, rolling his neck muscles and making Henry feel like a couch potato.

The two men had known each other for a good twenty years, having met initially when Donaldson was an FBI field agent investigating American organized crime links to gangsters in the north-west of England. They had become good friends and had worked together on and off over the years after Donaldson had got a job at the American embassy in London as a legal attaché. He had also married a lady who used to be a police woman in Lancashire, though she had subsequently been transferred to the Metropolitan Police and had now retired. They had a strong marriage and a couple of kids who were growing too fast.

'Jeez, Henry,' Donaldson uttered mid-stretch on seeing his bashed-up face. Henry squinted back through swollen eyelids. 'What the hell . . .?' He stopped stretching. 'The wedding wasn't that bad, was it?'

Trying not to wilt under his sympathy, Henry gave him a succinct account of the night's events and the probability of a link between the man on the car park and the man in Ginny's living room.

Donaldson listened seriously, then said what Henry knew he would have said.

'Why in hell didn't you get me up, man?'

'Decided I didn't want to disturb you, spoil the day.'

'Asshole,' he blurted. 'What about Rik? Did you get him up? This is a serious crime.'

Henry shook his head. 'He would have been no use and I'm certainly not going to involve him. He's due to go home and get ready for his honeymoon tomorrow with his lovely bride.'

Donaldson reluctantly accepted Henry's point of view. Although he had a senior investigating officer on tap in the form of his new brother-in-law, Rik would have been too drunk to operate. In fact, Henry wasn't sure he could have raised Rik from his alcoholic slumber based on his recollections of trying to revive him when they had been in Budapest for a three-day stag party. Henry did not expect to see him until at least midday and even then knew he would be like a zombie.

Donaldson was insistent that he should cancel his run and somehow help. He was as keen as a terrier but Henry steadfastly refused the offer. Everything was under control and Donaldson and his wife were travelling home later all the way down to Hartley Wintney in Hampshire and he did not want to mess up their travel plans.

In fact Henry wanted all the guests to get up, eat their breakfasts and go, but he knew the morning would be long and tedious dealing with a whole bunch of folk with hangovers, himself included, although Donaldson was as fresh as the dew because he never drank too much as he did not hold his liquor well. About two pints was his usual limit.

'No, you go, have your run,' Henry told him. 'This is all covered, honestly.'

He frowned, unconvinced, but then sank a large glass of water from the dispenser in the dining room, nodded at Henry and set off at a trot giving Henry a view of his tight backside in his tight shorts. He was a bit younger than Henry and kept his body – and his all-American college-boy good looks – in much better shape.

'Good-looking bastard,' Henry whispered.

'I heard that,' Donaldson responded and without turning, jerked a middle finger in Henry's direction.

He left a trail in the damp dew on the village green that had still not evaporated away.

Coming in the opposite direction were two cop cars. At last, the circus front-runners had arrived, possibly the monkeys, Henry thought.

He spun plates metaphorically and in reality that morning. The really important bit was to ensure the police dealt with the crime scene properly and also to speak to the detective constable who had turned up, a young man Henry did not know, but who seemed quiet but efficient.

They did a good job, up to Henry's exacting standards.

He also gave a brief written statement in between meeting and greeting the rising guests who, without exception, were feeling rough. Many paracetamols were dispensed.

The detective left after a short while, telling Henry he was going over to the hospital to check on Ginny and Alison. He promised that a dog patrol was on the way, just to sniff out the route the man had taken when fleeing from the pub. Henry shrugged, not believing there would be much to find.

It was after ten a.m. before Henry's brain-Rolodex flipped around and opened up on the name Lord Chalmers, and he cursed himself.

He should have been on his way to see him and he knew that in spite of everything going on, Alison would not be best pleased if this business opportunity was missed.

Henry found Chalmers' number on the pub phone and dialled from the office, expecting no response or for the butler to answer, but it was actually Lord Chalmers himself who picked up and said brightly, 'Chalmers.'

'Lord Chalmers' – Henry tugged his forelock – 'this is Henry Christie. I co-own the Tawny Owl with Alison Marsh. We had an appointment to see you this morning and I apologize but I'm just running a bit late. I wonder if I could come to see you now.' Henry was using his best telephone manner.

'Fine, come over,' he said and hung up leaving Henry holding a dead phone to his ear, but only for a moment for as soon as he hung up, it rang. Alison was on the other end.

'Hi, darling,' he said, doing a quick check of the wall clock and hoping she would not put two and two together and ask why he was answering when he should have been doing a deal with the gentry.

Her adding up, as ever, was spot-on.

'Why are you there, Henry?'

His 'Err . . .' response told its own story.

'You forgot, didn't you?'

'W-well, yeah, but on the plus side I've just remembered and been on the phone grovelling to his lordship. He'll see me if I go now.'

'I'll let you off, then,' she relented.

'How are things?'

'Ginny's OK. She's awake and fine now. They've taken blood samples to see if they can identify whatever it was that was injected into her, although that could take for ever . . . but she's OK, which is the main thing. They want to keep her for an hour or two just for observation and then she can come home, so could you drive over after you've seen Lord Chalmers and pick us up?'

'Yeah, will do.'

'I gave a bit of a statement to the police; they spoke to Ginny but haven't taken a written statement from her. They say someone'll come and see her.'

'They might even ask Jake Niven to do it, once she's back home.'

'That'd be better.'

'Have you spoken to her about it?' he asked cautiously.

'I have. She doesn't remember anything as yet. Maybe she will in time.'

'Hopefully.' He told her the police had arrived at the Tawny Owl and that he had given a statement too. He also reassured her about the running of the pub and how efficient he had been. She seemed underwhelmed by that and Henry got the impression she thought he might be blagging her.

They ended the call after a couple of 'I love you's,' and then after checking everything was running OK in the pub – the chef was hard at it on the lunch menu, the barman had landed, the ladies who did all the bedrooms had started work as they became vacant – he set off to see Lord Chalmers in his new car.

Except that he ended up having to use Alison's huge four-wheel-drive monstrosity, a massive Nissan Navara, because all four tyres on his almost new Ford Mondeo Estate had been slashed.

FIVE

Lord Chalmers was one of the richest men in the country. His wealth was nowhere near the vast riches of his close neighbour, the Duke of Westminster, but the figures published in the *Sunday Times* Rich List had made Henry Christie's eyes almost pop out.

Eight hundred million pounds at the last count. Some inherited, but the majority self-generated over the last fifty years from property in London, the north-west of England, New York and Paris and also some very successful dabbling in the steel industry in India and the Far East, or so Henry had read in the little blurb. However he read it, Chalmers was worth more than he could possibly dream about, having been a salaried employee all his life and thinking he didn't have it too bad.

Chalmers had homes all over the place, but tried to spend as much time as possible in his country mansion on his north Lancashire estate, set under Mallowdale Fell with the tiny River Roeburn trickling through its grounds. There were rumours of politicians and celebrities staying at Brown Syke (named after a small lake up the fells), but Henry had never seen anyone famous passing through, though it was possible they could have landed on the helipad or on the airstrip at the mansion, or via dark-windowed Hummers zipping through Kendleton on the way to the house.

Chalmers was known to keep a low profile. He rarely made the media, though Henry had once read some tittle-tattle about him meddling in high-level politics, a claim that neither interested nor surprised him. People like Chalmers knew people like Chalmers.

With a cloud of uneasiness hovering over his brain as he tried to juggle getting ready to see Chalmers and the discovery of the damage to his car – and trying to get his head around that new development (was he a target too, he wondered, and if so, why?) he drove out of Kendleton and out towards Mallowdale Fell, quickly onto tight roads, some not much wider than farm tracks, some clinging precariously to steep hillsides with sheer drops, hoping he wouldn't meet anything coming in the opposite direction because he really wasn't in any mood to give way to any bastard that morning.

Eventually he arrived at the entrance to Brown Syke, a huge double-fronted intricately wrought iron gate with an intercom set into one of the pillars.

It irked him he had to climb down from Alison's beast and call. He guessed this was usually the job of the chauffeur.

He pressed the buzzer, waited for a response.

'Identify yourself,' came a tinny male voice.

'Henry Christie for Lord Chalmers, from the Tawny Owl.' As he spoke he glanced up to see a security camera peering down at him from the branches of a tree on the other side of the high wall.

'Drive up.' The intercom clicked dead and the big gates began slowly to open. He jumped back into the car, selected drive and released the brake.

Henry half-wondered what he was doing here, but Chalmers' granddaughter, some flaky London socialite with more money than sense, had once popped into the Tawny Owl on a day he wasn't there – he had been at the cash-and-carry warehouse, a whole new experience for him, buying sackfuls of peanuts and dozens of tins of food – and the girl had got into a conversation with Alison which included the plans to turn the Owl into a wedding and function venue and the purchase of a huge marquee out the back which would be semi-permanent. The young lady had been so impressed by the quaintness of the place she immediately booked it for her upcoming twenty-first-birthday party on the proviso that the marquee was up and running.

It was due for delivery and erection next week and the said birthday party was pencilled into the diary in a month's time.

Henry and Alison expected to separate Chalmers from about five thousand of his pound coins, hence his visit today to finalize details and also to take the second stage of the deposit. The granddaughter had already paid £1,000 on her first visit to the Owl, producing the cash out of her handbag.

The big wheels of the Navara crunched on the fine gravel as he headed up towards the house with the River Roeburn on his left-hand side and the well-tended grounds on the right, up to the point where the drive turned sharply away from the river, through a wooded area and then the mansion was revealed for the first time in all its shabby glory.

It looked as though it had seen better days, but that could have been a ploy because as Henry drove closer he saw the outside, clad in creeping holly and other such climbing plants he could not identify, was much nicer close up.

Two cars were parked in the turning area, a grey Range Rover and a red Aston Martin. Beyond a copse of trees he glimpsed a helipad, beyond which was a finely trimmed grass runway.

Henry swerved deliberately to throw up some gravel from his tyres and climbed out, bringing his file on Chalmers with him. He set off towards the front doors – double-fronted and constructed of heavy wood, painted a deep, rich blood red – but he stopped in his tracks when he spotted the pair of Dobermann pinschers sitting side by side on the top step, ears erect, like guardians of an Egyptian pharaoh. He realized they were not actually intricate bronze statues, but real, living, breathing beasts.

Their eyes twinkled with bad thoughts as they surveyed him along their snouts.

'Shit,' he said. He didn't mind dogs he could kick skywards, but not monsters like these, both, he now saw, slavering snot-like dribble from the corners of their mouths.

Fortunately the door opened at that moment and a man Henry recognized as Lord Chalmers, fit-looking but mid-seventies, stepped out, laughed and said, 'Stand down, lads.'

The dogs came to life and ran towards Chalmers.

He rubbed their heads and called them, lovingly, 'My boys,' walking towards Henry as he did, one dog either side of him, eventually getting close enough to reach out a dog-saliva covered hand to shake Henry's.

'Mr Christie, I'm Chalmers . . . that's what you can call me, just Chalmers,' he said magnanimously and in a friendly uncondescending manner with no edge to it.

'You can call me Henry,' he responded, extending his hand. The men shook and Henry was pleased the dogs did not chew his off.

'These two fellers will be OK with you now,' Chalmers promised, giving the dogs another big rub of their heads, then gestured – a flick of the fingers – and they hurtled away down the front steps towards a man Henry had not noticed before, a guy dressed in sporty black joggers and a black hoodie with the hood pulled off, exposing his closely shaved head. He looked very former-soldier-ish to Henry.

'Security,' Chalmers said off Henry's glance. 'One of two guys I have roaming the place just in case.'

Henry held back from asking, 'In case of what?' He assumed rich men were often targets.

'Anyway, come in,' Chalmers beckoned. 'We'll have a chat about my granddaughter's party.'

He led Henry through those big front doors, across a vast tiled entrance foyer, along a wide hallway and out to what he called the orangery, basically a huge conservatory, at the back of the house with sweeping views of manicured lawns leading down to the river and beyond, the breathtaking views of the Bowland Fells.

'My favourite place,' he said smiling. 'Puts everything into perspective.'

'It's lovely,' Henry agreed, coming quite late in life to be a big fan of hills now that he lived nestled in amongst them.

He gestured for Henry to take a seat next to an ornate occasional table on which a large pot of filter coffee and a pot of tea on hot rings awaited with appropriate crockery, heavy mugs or delicate china cups.

He sat across from Henry. 'What's your poison? Redbush tea from Kenya or Kenyan coffee?'

'The coffee would be great.' Henry was still in need of its reviving qualities.

As he poured he looked at Henry's face and commented, 'You've been in the wars.'

Henry shrugged. 'Trouble with a burglar in the pub, but he managed to get away.'

SIX

Tod Rawstron's parents made him attend college to ensure that if all else failed he would have at least some recognized qualifications to fall back on. He attended dutifully if not enthusiastically three days a week but the remainder of his time he spent as a trainee gamekeeper on the Westminster estate in north Lancashire.

He had been born for the outdoors. As far back as he could remember he had always visualized himself as a gamekeeper, but he knew his parents were correct. Not many gamekeepers existed these days and the few who did make a career of it were very lucky and very hard workers with great skills and commitment.

Tod had decided it was his vocation and he would do everything he could to make it happen for him. He had become skilled with a shotgun, worked many hours without pay, did his best to learn the actual job, continually increased his countryside knowledge and tried to become indispensable to the head keeper of the estate. He had been volunteering since the age of twelve – in between stealing cars and other stupid behaviour which landed him in youth custody for some short spells. The head keeper had taken him on with no promises other than he 'would see what he could do' provided Tod managed to keep his nose clean, and got professional with it.

The result of these years of graft had been a poorly paid part-time job as a trainee, although he did make huge amounts in tips through the grouse- and pheasant-shooting season from rich people who came north to gun down the birds Tod had helped rear.

That was until yesterday when the head keeper called Tod into his office and, true to his word, offered him full-time work plus free board in one of the tiny en-suite rooms over the stables if he wanted. The other proviso was that Tod had to finish college and pass his courses.

Tod accepted immediately and he was an ecstatic young man with a gun and a dog and a job.

His dreams had come true, his commitment paid off, but he was canny enough to know it was still a job that could disappear at any moment.

He went home after his meeting with the head keeper, broke the news to his parents and thanked them for insisting he went to college and although he still had some time to go before he finished the courses, he had already picked up some low-level engineering qualifications which he'd used to set up a small vehicle-repair business he ran from his parents' garage specializing in all-terrain vehicles (ATVs) – quad bikes in other words – a business that ticked over nicely because such vehicles were always going wrong.

He had enjoyed a lazy breakfast at the Tawny Owl, probably spending too much time over it, but he was feeling in a celebratory mood. The local cop, Jake, who he'd come to know quite well, had told him about the masked intruder in the pub, but had not gone into great detail. Jake, though, and Henry Christie, had shown interest in the man Tod had seen skulking through the woods with a rifle. Jake wondered if it could have been the same man who had tried to abduct Ginny, so Tod thought he would keep an extra eye out on his travels that morning. He liked and fancied Ginny.

Probably the guy was just another local poacher, but even so he needed to be collared. Tod relished the thought of a bit of a manhunt that morning.

He waved goodbye to Jake, who was still busy at the pub, thanked the chef for a great breakfast, then jumped into his tired old Land Rover and set off for a look around.

Tod knew the whole area intimately. He drove out of Kendleton, west towards Brookhouse, then looped off the road on to a forest track that followed Rushbed Gutter, one of a series of small streams in the area which ultimately fed, via other streams and rivers, into the River Lune, which flowed out through Lancaster into the amazing expanse that was Morecambe Bay.

The track he followed became narrow, rough and eventually petered out to nothing until Tod was surrounded by high, dense trees, their rich summer canopies cutting out much of the morning sunlight. To his right was the bulk of Abbeystead Fell and in the distance in a break in the trees he could glimpse Jubilee Tower, the high viewing point that gave a stunning view across Morecambe Bay, Blackpool and the Lake District.

Tod had actually stopped on the edge of Tarnbrook Fell, very much a part of his beat. Through the woods away to his left, although quite a distance away now and a hard walk, lay Kendleton.

'Well, Nursey, you up for a stroll?' Tod asked his loyal wide-eyed Labrador who seemed to smile and almost say yes, she was raring to go.

Tod climbed out, followed by the dog, went to the back of the Land Rover and removed one of his shotguns from the locked metal case. He broke the weapon for safety, made sure it was not loaded, balanced it over the crook of his arm, chucked a handful of cartridges into his jacket pocket and set off into the woods, the dog obediently at his heels.

Henry was surprised that Chalmers was dealing with the matter of his granddaughter's party by himself, but as they chatted Henry saw how much he doted on the girl who, it seemed to Henry, was a bit of an airhead, but clearly Chalmers loved her to bits.

'She was absolutely entranced by your little hostelry,' he was telling Henry, 'and I said I'd happily fund the twenty-first . . . not, of course, that it will be her only celebration. She'll be down in Mayfair, then Ibiza, no doubt, but she wanted to give some of her friends a taste of rural Britain. How many bedrooms do you have?'

Henry told him.

Chalmers did some mental arithmetic. 'We'll put all her friends up there for a couple of nights, including her. The older contingent can stay here with the fogies, like me. Would that be in order?'

Henry nodded with alacrity, seeing pound signs leap up before his eyes like an old-fashioned till in a haberdashery. No room bookings had been taken for that weekend just on the off-chance of this business, so the Chalmers clan could have the run of the place. Henry did his own mental arithmetic, not something he was terribly brilliant at, but he liked the look of this ballpark figure.

'I'm not into the detail of costs,' Chalmers told him. 'If we say ten grand for the weekend, would that cover it?'

Henry's ballpark just got bigger. He tried not to grin as he said, 'Yes, fine, but it won't come to that.'

'That's what I'm paying . . . don't forget, you'll need to order the best champagne and caviar . . . the best food, et cetera.'

'Good point,' Henry conceded.

Chalmers' eyes narrowed. 'I believe you were a police officer once over.'

'Happily retired, pulling pints now.'

'A detective superintendent?'

'I reached those dizzy heights against all the odds.'

'Not what I've heard. I'm told you were good, very good.'

'By whom?'

'That doesn't really matter.' Chalmers dismissed the question. 'But if you ever tire of the licensing trade, I'm always on the lookout for good people.' He raised his bushy eyebrows, asking the question.

'I'm good, thanks.' Henry could not have imagined anything worse. 'Look, what I'll do is price up the weekend accurately, champers and all, send you a quote and take it from there, if that's OK?'

It was cool in the trees, dark and not a little mysterious. Tod picked his way quietly through the underbrush with Nursey at his heels, moving with him, not straying. Tod liked this environment, a place he felt he could have been the first human being to set foot and up to a point that was true, for very few people did venture into these woods.

It was almost as if he was the only person alive in the world.

But Tod had also developed a sixth sense as a tracker and suddenly, as a wisp of cool breeze flitted around his neck, he felt he was not alone at all. A strange, unsettling sensation underneath the canopy.

He stopped moving, gave a sharp hand signal for Nursey to stop also.

Then he backed up against a tree, sank slowly to his haunches, laid a hand on Nursey's head and listened hard, inhaled slowly, as his eyes roved between the foliage.

Just something.

He sniffed in deeply.

Something.

Then, rather like focusing on one of those paintings that, if stared at long enough, if the mind is allowed to relax, the picture reveals something else, and a hidden image appears as if by magic, he saw a hide of sorts. Branches, leaves, scrub, all resting against and covering something between two trees.

A vehicle.

He did not move, just allowed his eyes and brain to fully comprehend what he was seeing. A green-bodied, white-roofed Volkswagen camper van had been driven into the woods and then someone had taken the time to very effectively hide it. Someone skilled and very careful had gone to a great deal of effort.

Tod's nostrils flared as he sniffed the air again and he found himself to be slightly afraid.

Slowly he rose off his haunches and walked towards the vehicle until he was alongside it. He moved a twig and peered in through a side window, saw cooking utensils and a camping stove on the tiny kitchen work surface, a kettle on the hob with a wisp of steam coiling out of the spout, a mug alongside it.

He held his right hand over his eyes to shade them.

He saw the rifle laid out across the sofa and recognized it for what it was – the weapon of a sniper. Maybe the one he had seen in the hands of the mystery man in the woods.

Ten metres behind him, standing alongside another tree, the owner of the VW and of the rifle watched Tod's actions, knowing he had to act now to avoid detection and exposure.

The handgun dangling in his right hand by his outer thigh was a Browning 9mm automatic, a Carswell noise suppressor screwed on to the muzzle.

He raised it slowly as Nursey growled a warning and Tod spun around.

Henry rose to his feet, collected his paperwork and extended his hand to shake Chalmers'.

'I'm certain we'll put on a great weekend for your grand-daughter,' Henry assured his client. 'Other than the public areas, the whole of the Tawny Owl will be exclusively for her and her party.'

'Sounds excellent. I'll show you back out and keep the dogs from eating you,' he said with a grin.

The Dobermanns had retaken their positions side by side as if they were the guardians of Hades, but they paid Henry no attention, which pleased him as did the fact they were chained to the pillars on either side of the door.

From the top of the front steps there was a view along the close-cropped runway, which looked flatter and better maintained than a premiership football pitch, just as wide and many times longer.

'You could land a Jumbo on that,' Henry quipped.

Chalmers laughed. 'Just long enough for a small plane . . . in fact,' he checked his wristwatch which Henry noticed was slim Patek Philippe (Henry had a thing about nice watches and actually owned a Rolex, though wore it rarely), 'my wife's due to arrive in her plane fairly shortly.'

'Not that I know anything about it, but don't you have to use proper runways and all that?'

'No, not at all,' Chalmers said. 'We file flight plans, keep the local commercial airports updated, keep out of the way of passenger jets and the military . . . we have council permission to have a private runway and we don't really use it often enough to annoy the neighbours, not that we have any to annoy . . . just think what parachute clubs do.'

Henry nodded. 'Very nice,' he said, although the prospect of being in a tiny plane with just one engine and propellers made him queasy. 'Anyway, I'll take my leave and send you that quote.'

They shook hands again.

In the distance, but getting closer quickly, Henry heard the sound of two car engines approaching.

He looked back along the gravel driveway just as two black Range Rovers with blacked-out windows burst through the treeline.

The reality is that a silencer – or more accurately, a noise suppressor – does not completely deaden the sound of a bullet being fired from a firearm. There was no whispering, 'Phtt', but more a sound like a china cup being dropped onto a tiled floor.

Within the context of the woodland, though, the sound of the bullets leaving the muzzle of the Browning automatic was quite loud.

Tod had seen the pistol rise in the man's hand and tried desperately to dig into his pocket, find two shotgun cartridges and load his weapon but he had no time or chance and the 9mm rounds spat out and slammed into his chest, both entering his heart and shredding the muscle. It was an almost perfect double-tap, the shooting technique where two shots are fired in rapid succession at the same target.

Tod dropped the shotgun, slumped down onto his knees, then fell face first into the ground, dead.

The sniper approached slowly.

Nursey stood over Tod's unmoving body and growled menacingly at the man who, without compunction, also shot her.

The Range Rovers were new and looked impressive, speeding along the gravel drive, the lead one throwing up grit and a cloud of dust that almost shrouded the one behind.

They circled into the turning area at the front of the house and crunched to a halt.

Henry glanced to his left and saw that Chalmers' two security guards were racing towards them on quad bikes from the direction of the airstrip, bouncing across the grass, the men on them standing astride in a very macho way.

Henry looked back at the Range Rovers, the dust starting to settle around them. No one got out. Henry could see a male driver in each car, biggish individuals.

'Friends of yours?' Henry asked Chalmers.

There was no response.

He looked at the millionaire, who had frozen.

'No,' he replied then.

The security guards skidded to a halt on their ATVs by the Range Rovers, kicking up their own gravel and dust storm. They dismounted quickly as the drivers' doors of the four-wheel-drives opened and two men climbed out.

The guards strutted to the interlopers, their body language clearly stating their tough-guy credentials, men who meant business. The lead man had his palm out towards the new arrivals in a 'stop right there' gesture.

Henry watched the scenario unfold, already feeling uneasy about the whole thing. He was too far away to hear anything that was being said, but the lead security guy seemed to be questioning or lecturing the men from the cars, who Henry would have liked to think had wandered innocently into Chalmers' grounds and were being given a dressing down before being sent on their way. 'This is private property, get the hell off it,' sort of thing.

Except Henry knew the Range Rovers were there with a purpose.

There was nothing accidental about this incursion.

The two drivers stood with their arms folded, feet shoulder-width apart, looking cool and unperturbed at the security guard who was lambasting them.

They were late twenties, Henry guessed, both in short-sleeved shirts, three-quarter-length cargo pants and trainers. They had close-cropped hair and had sunglasses pushed up on to their foreheads.

Intuitively, what Henry was seeing gave him a bad vibe, sensing this was bad news but not knowing why.

He knew the type of men, could tell they were trained, versed in the art of violence. He had come across many such people in his life as a cop, come face-to-face with some of them – but always with backup on its way.

Henry's eyes jumped from the two interlopers to the two

guards, trying to get a handle on what was happening when something else clicked with him that confirmed his suspicions: the Range Rovers must have been allowed in through the electronic gates as entry was controlled by someone inside the grounds, one or both of the security men. The guys in the Range Rovers had been let in and unless there was someone else on site today that he had not seen or heard, Henry concluded it must have been one of the security guards.

'Sure you don't know them?' Henry asked quickly.

'Positive.'

The security guard who had taken the lead in confronting the men was beginning to remonstrate with hand gestures and a threatening stance when one of the interlopers began to laugh at him.

Henry frowned, did not get it for a moment.

Then he did.

The second guard, standing behind his colleague, slid his right hand around to the small of his back, to his waistband underneath his T-shirt. It reappeared quickly with a small handgun in it and in a single, flowing motion, with coolness and without hesitation, he brought up the gun. Before Henry could cry out – his voice croaked in his throat – the guard fired two shots into the side of his colleague's head, a cold-blooded execution, one that the two men from the Range Rovers totally expected.

The guard crumpled as blood fountained from the terrible, fatal wounds, then became a dribble.

Henry said, 'Christ!'

The Dobermanns suddenly came to life, flinging themselves towards the incident, but dragged roughly back by the chains. They began to bark madly.

'What the fuck's happening?' Chalmers demanded. He made to go towards the men who all looked at him, then moved as a team towards him.

Henry grabbed Chalmers' upper arm and swung him back into the entrance hall, slamming the big double doors closed. In the microsecond before the doors closed Henry saw that guns were in the hands of all three of them. As the doors came together, Henry jerked away as at least four bullets – he wasn't counting – crashed into the thick, solid wood, but did not pass through.

'Run,' Henry said.

He grabbed the confused-looking Chalmers, who appeared reluctant to move, completely dumbfounded by what he had just witnessed.

Henry ducked instinctively as more bullets thudded into the other side of the doors.

Without any finesse, Henry yanked the older man across the hallway towards the rear of the house.

'Just move,' he demanded of him.

Chalmers tore himself free of Henry's grasp. 'I need to tell her not to land,' he insisted.

'Tell who?'

'My wife, for God's sake. She can't land, she mustn't.'

Henry jerked his head towards the front doors as what now sounded like a machine gun was being fired into the thick wood, and this time the doors began to splinter, particularly around the lock.

These men were coming in and very soon.

He shared a desperate glance with Chalmers.

'I must warn her, I must,' Chalmers said firmly.

'How?'

'There's a brick-built shed on the airstrip.' Henry recalled seeing it, a small building with a very tall aerial on its roof. 'The radio's in there.'

Chalmers looked pleadingly at Henry, then jumped as another series of rounds thudded into the door, causing more splintering and more weakening.

'This way.' Chalmers turned and began to move, although not as quickly as Henry would have liked.

They raced through to the rear of the house, back into the orangery, past the table with their mugs on it, and out of the double doors onto a series of Indian stone steps leading down to the lawn. Chalmers veered right onto a paved garden path that plunged behind a high trestle fence beyond which was an ornate walled rose garden that Henry had not realized was there. He assumed there were many surprises to behold in this rich man's domain, not least of which was a brutal murder and three men coming after him armed to the teeth.

There was more gunfire from the front of the house.

Henry thought they must be through the door now and if they were it gave him and his Lordship about a thirty-second lead which would reduce dramatically once the men started to run through the house. They were young, fit and healthy looking. He and Chalmers were not as well equipped as that.

Henry did keep himself as fit as he could. He knew the temptations of running a pub were rife so he tried to control his diet, with the exception of his morning bacon bap, and he did jog two to three miles every other day in a very sedate manner and he was only about half a stone overweight, and his slight paunch and man-boobs were camouflaged by his height.

He couldn't speak for Chalmers, who he tried to shoo along.

Neither was he sure why he was doing this, a question he asked himself as Chalmers stumbled ahead, but was effectively answered by the shouts of the men chasing them who emerged from the orangery obviously having got through the front door. They didn't seem like the kind of guys he could have waved past. He knew he was fleeing for his life because he realized that if such a thing as a hit squad existed, these men were it and to approach them with placating body language would simply result in him being riddled by bullets.

They were getting close.

The odds were very much against him and Chalmers but Henry knew he would rather die trying to help this man than not, although Chalmers was obviously the target in this scenario, not himself, but he knew he would be seen as collateral damage.

There were other reasons he did not want to die on that day, not least of which was his desire to know why the men had turned up to assassinate Chalmers, who the hell they were and what this man could possibly be embroiled in.

Hit squads don't just turn up for fun.

Henry managed to grab Chalmers as he tripped and they ran on through the rose garden to a door set in the wall on the far side. They reached it without any of the armed men coming into the rose garden, making Henry wonder if they had split up to search the house as well.

It was an old, rotting door, but that did not mean it opened easily. In fact it was stuck fast. Henry had to barge his shoulder against it to force his way through. It opened with a loud crash and immediately after there were more shouts from the men, who had clearly heard it.

'Shit,' Henry said, bundling through the opening, dragging Chalmers with him and closing the door, forcing it back into its tight frame.

Chalmers ran ahead to a gap in a high hedge, Henry on his heels. They ducked through the opening and came to a small tarmacked area on the north side of the house. Directly ahead was the helipad, beyond that the airstrip with the radio shack to one side.

Chalmers' arms pumped. His face was cherry red and he was panting heavily, beginning to slow right down, but still determined to reach his goal.

Henry thought a heart attack seemed more likely than a bullet at that stage.

He came alongside, twisting back as he ran, keeping an eye over his shoulder on what was happening behind.

No sign of the men. Just yet.

He glimpsed the tableau at the front of the house. The two Range Rovers, Chalmers' two cars, the quad bikes, Alison's Navara and the dead body of the security guard splayed out on the gravel.

So it had been real.

He and Chalmers reached the shed and dipped their heads to get in. It was sparse. Just a metallic table on which stood a very ancient-looking radio set, headphones and a microphone on a stand. A small table to one side had a kettle, two mugs and brewing tackle on it.

Chalmers, gasping hoarsely for breath, thudded onto the plastic chair in front of the radio table and with dithering hands, fitted the headphones over his ears and flicked on the power switch. Henry could have sworn he heard the unit start to hum.

He took it all in but remained by the door, keeping it open a crack and peering through with one eye.

No sign of the shooters.

'Base to Ella, base to Ella,' Chalmers said urgently into the mike. 'Base to Ella, come in please . . . urgent.'

Henry continued to look back towards the house and gardens; still the pursuers did not appear.

'C'mon, c'mon,' he intoned to himself, working out what the best escape route would be if he and Chalmers managed to make it out of the shed. It would have to be straight across the width of the airstrip and then plunge into the woodland opposite, then put as much distance between them and the gun-guys.

'Ella, come in, please,' Chalmers begged.

'Edward, Edward? What's going on, dear?' came, Henry assumed, the voice of his wife piloting the plane. The signal was weak, her voice distorted by static.

If it was actually possible, Henry tensed up even more at that moment because he was sure that in the distance he heard the drone of an approaching plane. Ella, it seemed, was not far away.

'I'm almost there,' she said.

'Ella – do not land, repeat, do not land,' Chalmers shouted. 'Pull away, land at the parachute club near Pilling and contact Brooks. Do you copy?'

The sound of the plane grew.

He took a chance, bobbed his head out of the door and narrowed his eyes down the airstrip and there she was, just a tiny black dot in the distance, but definitely getting larger and noisier, and intending to land within the next ninety seconds, Henry calculated.

Chalmers screamed into the mike, 'Do not land, do not land!'

There was no response from the plane.

'Fuck,' Chalmers cursed.

Henry pulled his head back into the hut. 'We need to move. They'll find us here.'

Chalmers hurled down the mike. It came to pieces on the table top.

'Can you keep running?' Henry asked. 'If we get into the trees we might have a chance.'

The older man looked at Henry, his watery eyes weighing up the options.

The sound of the plane grew louder.

'I cannot allow her to touch down,' he said – at which point Henry had had enough. His own survival instinct kicked in strong and was assisted by Chalmers who said, 'You go.'

'We can both make it if we go now,' Henry said, giving the old man one last chance.

'No, go.' Chalmers flicked his fingers at Henry, shooing him away.

Henry cocked his head, nodded and glanced out of the door.

The sound of the plane was much louder but there was still no sign of the gunmen. He gave Chalmers one last glance, then went for it. He contorted out of the shed door and sprinted across the airstrip, his pumping arms impelling every last bit of energy and speed out of him. It was perhaps sixty metres at most but felt like a half-marathon and his legs felt weak and heavy as he tunnel-visioned his goal – a split in the longer grass on the far edge of the strip, a parting into which he could dive, then roll into the trees.

As he ran his head jerked one way, then the other.

To his left, still high in the sky but now more definable, was the single-engine plane approaching down the valley formed by the River Roeburn, with Salter Fell to the right and Mallowdale Fell to the left. In that glance Henry could not even begin to estimate how far away the plane was, he just knew it was closer.

Then, with a head jerk to the right Henry saw the gunmen emerge from the garden, reminding him of a team of mercenaries, killing machines, and in that glance he saw each man was now brandishing a machine pistol as opposed to a handgun, much deadlier and requiring less skill.

They must have seen him, he knew that, but he powered on, knowing that to hesitate would get him killed.

Then he was there, launching himself into the dense grass and rolling until he stopped with a jar against the roots of a tree, an impact that winded him, but he kept on moving, doing a snake crawl further into the trees where he came up onto one knee and hid behind several low-hanging branches.

With horror he saw that Chalmers had run into the middle of the airstrip and was standing, facing the oncoming aircraft which was on its final descent. He was making a gesture that resembled repeatedly opening an up-and-over garage door.

Henry got the meaning. He was telling the pilot to stay up, do not land.

But the plane was getting closer.

Henry stretched his neck to see without actually sticking his head out of cover.

To the right, the plane was virtually on the airstrip, the wheels only feet above the cut grass.

Dead ahead of him stood the desperately gesticulating Chalmers.

Away to the left were the gunmen, each now holding their machine pistols in firing positions. They had fanned out into a line and were jogging inexorably towards Chalmers, who continued to throw his arms upwards.

The plane touched the ground.

Chalmers ran towards it, waving, signalling, but he had run only a few yards when the men opened up and fired a short burst from each weapon, cutting him down face first into the grass as a criss-cross of bullets slammed into his back.

It was the second horror Henry had witnessed in the last few minutes, another brutal, seemingly senseless killing, and Henry was as certain as he could be that Chalmers was as dead as his security guard.

Henry ducked down.

He heard the sound of the plane's engine growl as the pilot pushed the throttle forwards, sending more power to the pistons. The wheels had touched the grass but now as the wing flaps were turned down, it rose easily and flew over the heads of the gunmen who followed its trajectory with their upturned faces and also their weapons as they opened fire as it skimmed overhead.

Henry heard the bursts of fire above the roaring sound of the engine.

He also heard the metallic slap as at least eight bullets punched into the fuselage.

Henry saw the plane wobble uncertainly, but then lift and continue to rise, banking, rise again and then it was gone.

He ducked flat down on his belly, rubbed his hands in wet soil and scrubbed his face with it, primitive camouflage, and attempted to control his breathing and his fear. He watched through the grass as the three men approached Chalmers' splayed-out body. One of them flipped his machine pistol on its strap over his shoulder and took a handgun from his waistband. He stood over Chalmers and put two further bullets into the back of the man's skull.

Literally overkill, Henry thought: professional overkill.

Terror swept through him like a tidal bore when all three men turned as one towards the spot where he had disappeared into the trees. In a line they walked towards him. One of them extracted a paper folder from his waistband.

SEVEN

That morning's flight from a private airfield to the north-west of London had been uneventful. The German-built Ramos GX, a high-wing single-engine light aircraft, had been piloted by Lady Chalmers, the wife of Lord Chalmers, flying having been one of her passions since her teens. She loved the sensation, the sense of freedom it gave her, but although she was a skilled and highly competent amateur pilot, as she aged she became a fair-weather flyer and fortunately the conditions that day were excellent.

She had owned a variety of planes throughout her life, all financed by her husband's business dealings, of which she knew little and, mostly, wanted to know less. The Ramos GX was the latest in a long line of light aircraft and although not new – some nine years old – it was her favourite and was always kept in superb condition.

However, she approached that morning's flight with some trepidation.

Usually she was keen to get up to the house, away from London. It was a lovely, secluded, chill-out place.

The package made that all different.

She had been told to wait for it before flying. Her husband had given her those instructions and she had wanted to say no, but there was little choice. She had become aware that Chalmers had become involved in some very ugly financial and property shenanigans involving unsavoury characters, including so-called 'clean' politicians (who weren't so clean), businessmen and gangsters. She had learned by accidentally overhearing a conversation that the 'package', whatever it contained, would be the 'deal-maker'.

Her wait at the airfield had been nervous and edgy with the Ramos ready, waiting and raring to go.

Finally a man in an old silver-grey Aston Martin DB9 pulled onto the car park, climbed out and approached Ella. He had an attaché case in his hand.

He was in his fifties, smartly dressed, but was overweight and sleazy in Ella's estimation. She had seen him skulking about in her husband's company a couple of times. Once he had even been round to their house in Eaton Square and she had not liked what she saw. He made her tremble with repulsion.

'Lady Chalmers,' he said. 'Good morning, very nice to see you.'

'OK,' she said dubiously.

He held up the case. 'Your husband asked me to give you this.'

'Thank you,' she said, seeing his eyes flit over her slim body with lust in them. She was in her mid-fifties, quite a bit younger than her husband, and good dieting and exercise had kept her fit and healthy and she was still proud of her boobs, which so far had no need for any supportive surgery. Normally she enjoyed an appreciative glance from a man, but not this slimy individual. For a horrible instant, she had a creepy image in her mind of the man's tongue licking her between her legs.

He handed over the case, allowing his fingertips to touch the back of her wrist as she grabbed the handle. She almost dropped it as she mentally recoiled.

'Tell him it's all there,' he said, his eyes lingering on her breasts, then rising to look meaningfully into hers.

'What's all there?'

'Don't you know?'

She shook her head, wishing she hadn't asked the question because he took a conspiratorial step towards her, invading her space, and whispered, 'You might want to share it with hubby . . . wank each other off as you do.' Then he stepped back, laughing dirtily. 'On the other hand . . . well . . . you know what you could be doing with the other hand.'

'You revolt me,' she said simply. She spun and walked towards the waiting plane, totally aware that the man's eyes were watching her behind and slender legs which were clad in tight-fitting three-quarter-length leggings.

Five minutes later, after redoing the pre-flight checks, she was in the air, flying north-west from the airfield, tilting the thirty and a half feet wingspan and steadily reaching a cruise speed of 120 mph, which would bring her to the private airstrip at Brown Syke about two hours later.

She settled in for the flight, picked up the radio, called ahead and spoke to one of the security guards who worked for Lord Chalmers, telling him she should be on time.

It did, however, take a few more minutes to get her bottom comfortable in the seat and purge the gruesome thought of that man's tongue.

The man – his name was Brooks – watched the plane rise from the airstrip, but he wasn't trying to clear his mind of the fantasy he was visualizing with Lady Chalmers. As the plane became a speck, he turned back to his car and walked uncomfortably to it, grasping his erection via his trouser pocket.

The airstrip was just a few miles from the M40, reached by a series of narrow and winding country lanes on which Brook met two black Range Rovers coming in the opposite direction, hogging the lane, making no attempt to move over.

Irritably, Brooks slowed down his Aston Martin and pulled into the side of the road, flashing his headlights at the approaching cars which stopped, one behind the other, completely blocking passage and offering no chance of squeezing past at all.

For a few moments the three cars were involved in a stand-off.

Brooks opened his driver's door window and poked his head out.

'Get out of the fucking way,' he bawled.

There was no movement or concession.

'Shit.'

Brooks selected reverse, realizing he wasn't going to win this one, recalling a passing place maybe a hundred metres back into which he might be able to pull. He began to edge backwards in a car with a limited view at best and certainly not designed to be reversed, other than into a double garage.

He continued to swear.

The Range Rovers moved with him, as though herding him. The front grille of the leading one was almost eyeball to eyeball with the front of the Aston, harrying him like a sheepdog.

'Get fucking lost,' he shouted, but began to get a bad feeling about the situation.

Finally, after having avoided putting the rear wheels of the meaty sports car into the ditch, he manoeuvred into the widened passing place and scowled at the driver of the lead Range Rover as the guy drew alongside and stopped. The second Range Rover swerved slightly in front of Brooks' car, blocking it in.

'Bastard,' he roared.

The driver's door window of the lead Range Rover slid down. The man at the wheel was young-ish, close cropped hair, wearing a baseball cap.

'Have you delivered the package?' the man asked Brooks.

'Eh? What the hell are you talking about? What package? Can you just get out of the way, please?' Brooks' voice faltered, his instinct about the Range Rovers right on the nail. 'Got the wrong guy,' he blustered.

He looked at the other Range Rover, which was angled across the front of his car, boxing him in.

He swore internally now and panic began to creep with a horrible taste into his mouth.

The driver of the first Range Rover opened his door and slid down to the road, just a few feet away from Brooks. Then he took one stride and there he was at the window, suddenly with a gun in his hand pointed at Brooks' head.

'Christ, what's going on?' Brooks demanded, his voice faltering.

The man leaned in. 'The package . . . where is it? Please do not mess me around or I'll kill you here, now.' His voice was cold, calm, hardly above a whisper. Menacing. 'Your blood will never clean off your car,' he added.

If anything, Brooks was a realist. He pointed to the sky. 'It's up there, on its way to Lancashire.' He saw the man's expression flicker as he took in this information. 'May get there in two hours. You seem to have missed it, sorry.'

Brooks could see the man knew exactly what he was talking about.

'That's a shame,' he said.

'Hey, I've told you, now can I get going?'

'Nah.' The man shook his head and a moment later, as predicted, the blood and brain matter from Brooks' head had decorated the inside of the pristine Aston Martin, never to be cleaned away. The man was then on his mobile phone, having a hurried conversation before dashing to the second Range Rover and shouting orders to the occupants. 'We've got two hours to get to Lancashire,' he said grimly. 'And we've got to beat a plane there.'

Fortunately for the men in the black Range Rovers, Lady Chalmers was in no hurry. In a direct flight she could have made her destination in two hours at top cruising speed, but because the day was gorgeous and because she simply could, she dawdled through the skies and treated herself to some sightseeing along the way, enjoying twenty minutes swooping over and across the Peak District almost in a delightful dream, taking in Bakewell, Buxton and the high moorland at Howden, before adjusting course to skim the southern edge of Manchester and use the motorway system to guide her across to the M6 which she then followed directly north over Preston and Lancaster, before bearing north-east and loping across to line up on the private airfield at Brown Syke.

She was only minutes away from landing when she received the urgent-sounding radio call from her husband, which she could not really make sense of and she needed to land just as urgently because she needed to pee. It was almost painful.

On the final approach with the beautiful house visible at the head of the airstrip, the beautiful fells of Lancashire on either side, she saw the figure of her husband gesticulating madly, clearly signalling for her not to land, and the three figures behind him.

The wheels of the Ramos had just touched grass, and her husband was running towards her, still gesticulating, when suddenly he pitched forwards and Ella made out the guns in the hands of the men.

She slammed on the power and heaved back on the joystick, willing the little plane to respond and lift its nose skywards.

Miraculously, it did.

She flew over the body of Lord Chalmers, saw the raised faces of the three men and also the guns in their hands coming up as the plane rose and banked towards the hills, then jumped as she felt bullet holes being punched into the underside of the plane, then the near miss as one skimmed her left leg, but then the pain as another entered the sole of her shoe into her foot and another smack as yet another one came up through her seat and entered her lower abdomen.

She lurched on the impact, tried to fight the quickly spreading agony in her lower belly, but hissed when she glanced down and saw blood already pooling on her seat. She had been wounded very seriously and knew it. She swooned for a moment, then tried to get a grip of herself, tried to convince herself that it could not be as bad as it seemed.

The plane rocked.

She corrected it, but then all her limbs and joints started to tingle weakly. She forced herself to keep a grip on the control column, concentrate, find somewhere safe to put the plane down.

She blinked repeatedly as her vision swirled sickeningly.

The pain in her belly became a flame.

In the seconds before she passed out, she was aware of the Ramos flipping sideways, flying at ninety degrees to the ground and plunging towards a tight gulley sliced into the moorland, though when the plane crashed she was unconscious and was killed instantly.

The man held up the file, waved it in the air.

'I know your name,' he called into the trees. 'I know where you live.'

Henry heard the words and slated himself for, somewhere along the line, dropping the paperwork he had completed for the quote on Chalmers' granddaughter's party, which he assumed would not now be happening. In his rush to outrun the gunmen he hadn't even realized it had gone. It had been unimportant in the grand scheme of things. Now it was the most important thing in the world.

'Henry Christie. Tawny Owl,' the man shouted.

It sounded like a roll call for a transgender scout in a Girl Guide group.

Henry remained still. He watched one of the men – the Judas of a security guard – whisper something then run back across to the radio shack and disappear into it.

'Henry,' the other man continued, 'come out. You're going nowhere because we hunt down people for a living. That's what we do. That's what we're paid to do. That's what we're good at. Save yourself some agony at least because if we have to come in there and find you, it will be much worse. Promise. Henry Christie, Tawny Owl,' he concluded.

Henry's nostrils flared. He was not going anywhere in their direction.

The two remaining men stood shoulder to shoulder, their machine pistols at hip height, facing Henry.

He knew what was about to happen.

This was a firing squad. They were going to strafe the trees.

The man who had called to Henry said something to the other guy. They made a show of cocking their weapons, as if they weren't ready to fire, then on another word out of the corner of the man's mouth, they sprayed whatever bullets remained in the magazines into the treeline.

By this time Henry had rolled sideways and tucked himself half-underneath an all too slim fallen log, rather like a dog who hides his head and thinks no one can see the rest of his body.

There was a short burst of fire, not a long 'drrr', and both guns clicked on empty chambers because they had already fired many rounds into Lord Chalmers and the light aircraft.

Even so, Henry had braced himself for the worst and cringed as bullets flew just inches above him or smacked and splintered his protective log or sent spits of soil or rotting foliage from the ground around him.

Then it was over and he had not been hit.

Henry knew they would have to reload. This would entail a change of magazine. He wasn't naive enough to think they would fumble about. They would be well-practised and fast and would probably do the swap quicker than a Formula One pit-stop.

However, it gave him a quick window of opportunity which he took advantage of because he knew he had to put serious distance between himself and these cold-blooded killers. It would only be a few seconds, but he could not afford to dally.

He rolled, came up onto his feet and keeping low and trying to make as little noise as possible he ran, zig-zagging between low branches and deciding to go left because he had a vague plan in his head which he hoped would fool them if only for a little while. They would perhaps expect him to simply run away from them, not parallel to the runway back in the direction of the house, because that is where the cars were parked and he knew that his best chance of escape would be to make it back to the Navara and drive away.

He didn't feel remotely confident in trying to out-manoeuvre them in the woods.

He was almost surprised when he made it in one piece to the edge of the lawn surrounding the gravel turning circle at the front of the house where all the cars and ATVs were still parked and on which the body of the security guard was still laid out, his blood soaking into the chippings.

Keeping low, he looked back down the airstrip to see the men had not made any progress. They were in a tactical huddle, making plans. He then looked at the cars, weighing up distance and time. Could he get into the Navara, fire it up and then get away before the men surrounded him?

Looking at them he saw all three of them slowly walking towards the treeline like a line of beaters on a pheasant shoot. They were going to put him up and shoot him down.

Henry waited until they had all entered the woods and were out of sight, then he dashed across the gravel and jumped into the Navara, fumbling for the keys in his pocket. He started it and looked up. One of the men had reappeared from the trees and seen him and was shouting and beckoning to the others.

Henry revved the engine.

'Keep your cool,' he told himself.

He selected reverse and swung the big car backwards in an arc so it faced down the drive, managed to get it into drive and gunned the beast, hoping the front gates would be open. The thought of having to crash out through them was not appealing.

He almost stood on the accelerator but as he came around the last curve in the drive before the gates he saw with horror that, though they were open, they were starting to close.

He tried to get more from the engine, but it was a sluggish chunk of machinery.

'Come on,' he urged it.

There was perhaps half an inch either side as he shot through the gates and swerved on to the road back to Kendleton, tight, twisting, precarious, clinging to contours of the hills with a steep, craggy drop into the River Roeburn to his right as he drove in a north-westerly direction along the road he had earlier travelled.

He gripped the wheel, ground his teeth, and felt a little flush of victory. He had out-run some seriously bad guys, but now he needed to make it to the safety net of civilization and that meant reaching Kendleton, the Tawny Owl and, hopefully, the cops who should still be there.

Looking in the side mirror, he gave a tight gasp of despair when he caught sight of two menacing-looking black Range Rovers maybe a hundred metres behind.

EIGHT

FBI employee Karl Donaldson was enjoying his morning run through the countryside around Kendleton as much as he could in spite of the worrying news from Henry about the attempted abduction of Ginny during the early hours. Otherwise, Donaldson was enjoying the break in north Lancashire, a couple of days' respite from his job in London.

He was mainly a gatherer and disseminator of intelligence, working with many police forces across Europe and the world, and was currently deep into a multi-agency investigation into an Albanian crime family with connections to Central American drug cartels and who, Donaldson also believed, had just murdered an undercover FBI agent. Donaldson was close on the coat tails of this particular family and he was keen to mete out some summary justice, hopefully in the near future because, as Henry

Christie suspected, but could not prove, Donaldson's remit in the FBI extended far beyond paperwork and desk-jockeying.

The break to attend Rik Dean's wedding to Henry's sister had been welcome. He had not been spending enough time with his wife recently and chilling out, having a drink and then getting very intimate with her had been fantastic for them both.

He had jogged away from the Tawny Owl with no real plan, other than to make it long, keep going for a couple of hours at least, maybe do a little off-road exploration along a few woodland tracks and paths, but generally come around in a circular route back to Kendleton using the GPS on his very fancy wristwatch for guidance.

About ninety slow minutes out, Donaldson had followed a few tracks, met dead ends or impossible terrain, spun around, followed others, but finally found himself on a forest track that narrowed and almost disappeared to nothing in a plantation.

This is where he found the Land Rover, which he knew belonged to a local gamekeeper as it had been parked outside the Tawny Owl as he'd set off for his run.

He thought nothing of it. Gamekeepers, he guessed, parked in isolated places, but even so, he slowed down and came to a standstill alongside the mud-splattered vehicle.

He caught his breath. He'd been going slow, but maybe he'd pushed himself too far. His regular running track was the rather flatter Hyde Park. Even so, he felt good and alive, inhaling the beautiful air around here.

When his breathing was normal, he stood still and listened.

Listened to nothing. The silence. Unlike running through the capital which constantly bombarded his eardrums and senses with heavy traffic and people.

That was when he heard the double 'cracking' noise, like two light coughs.

Then nothing.

Then another single crack.

All three noises were accompanied by a metallic snickering sound.

Donaldson remained completely still because he knew exactly what he had heard. Suppressed shot from an automatic pistol, in the trees, maybe sixty metres away from where he stood.

He wondered if the gamekeeper was having a bit of fun with an unapproved weapon, though he doubted it. Shotguns were the tools of that trade and to be found carrying a handgun would at the very least be dismissal from the job.

Donaldson knew exactly what he had heard, although he questioned himself momentarily because the sound in this context did not make sense. He had lived with firearms all his working life, fired them regularly at targets and sometimes at people, had even taken a bullet himself and even now, years later, could still feel the track the slug had taken up through his abdomen, almost killing him.

It wasn't so much the suppressed coughing sound. What made it odd was the bit that wasn't silenced, the metallic action of the breech, the ejection of the spent cartridge. Each gun had its own distinctive sound in that respect, so Donaldson, who had fired hundreds of different weapons in his life and become familiar with many of them, would put money on the noise he had heard as being that of a Browning 9mm, once very much a military favourite, especially with British armed forces.

So, he wondered, a Browning in the middle of a woodland glade in rural Lancashire?

He walked up to the Land Rover and peered into the cab, shading his eyes.

Empty. He wandered to the back door, which was locked, and looked in through the window where he saw a shotgun cabinet secured to the bulkhead. It was open with a shotgun visible inside it. He tried the door handle. Locked.

He hesitated, rolling his chiselled jaw.

There was something very uncomfortable about what he had just heard and because the need to investigate had been drilled into him, become part of him, in over twenty years with the FBI, he knew he had to check it out and would rather do so armed and dangerous.

He picked up a stone about the size of half a house brick and weighed it in the palm of his hand.

'You shouldn't have found me,' the sniper whispered to Tod Rawstron as he dragged his dead body through the grass by the legs. 'You idiot.'

He dropped the legs which thumped down, then went back for the damned fucking dog.

His intention was to scoop out a shallow grave and basically cover boy and dog with some soil and foliage, then get the gamekeeper's Land Rover and drive it deep into the woods and hope neither man, animal nor vehicle would be discovered for a day or two, long enough for him to complete his task.

He looked down at the young lad, angry with himself as much as anything.

It had all started to unravel and he, himself, was to blame.

His anger had made him break cover and do ridiculous things when deep inside he knew he should have controlled himself, stuck to the plan, been patient, but fury had driven him, made him vulnerable.

His brain seemed to be waging a war with itself, making him lose it.

'OK, OK,' he said under his breath, 'let's get back on track from here on in.'

His inner calm began to self-restore, the inner calm required of a sniper. A calm shattered by the noise of breaking glass.

Donaldson dropped the stone and reached inside to release the door catch. He stretched in for the shotgun, broke it and found it to be empty. It was an old weapon, but well cared for, double barrelled, twelve-bore, basic and reliable. All he needed. He shook the last three cartridges out of a box and slid two into the breech, the third into his shorts pocket. He closed the weapon and released the safety catch.

The sniper knelt on one knee behind a tree, his breathing shallow, his heartrate reduced, his concentration now total. His Browning was in his right hand, muzzle pointing at the ground, his left hand cupping the right.

He watched and waited, then saw the man approaching through the trees, creeping slowly with a shotgun in his hands.

The sniper recognized him: Karl Donaldson, one of Henry Christie's friends. He knew all about Donaldson, that he was much, much more than a pen-pushing legal attaché.

He too, the sniper knew, was also a trained killer.

He was getting on a bit now, had to work twice as hard to maintain his fitness levels and speed, but a very big part of what Donaldson was sometimes called on to do was all about attitude. The sniper knew Donaldson had all the attitude necessary and going up against him would not be anywhere near as easy as facing the dumb cop, Christie.

But Christie was the one he wanted.

He had no argument with Donaldson just like he had no argument with the gamekeeper and he hoped he would not have to kill the American here and now, but if it was necessary, he would not hesitate.

He knew it would be necessary.

Donaldson moved quietly, very, very slowly, gently edging his way through the grass that tickled his shins, placing his feet carefully. The shotgun felt good, balanced.

For a few seconds he stood just inside the treeline, allowing his eyes to adjust to the more dappled light and shade filtering through the leaves and also allow his other senses to adjust. The sound was different in here, the smells also.

Mostly it was a compost-like smell, decaying leaves and trees on the ground, but then there was also a brief, tantalizing and transient aroma that touched his sense of smell, then it was gone, but to Donaldson it was unmistakeable.

Gunpowder.

He moved slowly, crouching.

Then stopped.

To his left, lying in a bed of grass, was a freshly killed dog, blood still oozing from a head wound. Donaldson registered what he was seeing but did not react to it. The dog was a Labrador, the same breed and colour as the one belonging to the young gamekeeper, Tod. Donaldson recalled seeing it as he set out on his run, sitting in the Land Rover, resting its chin on the open window frame, big, dopey-eyed, waiting for its master to return.

Donaldson was shocked by the sight but tried not to give away that he had seen it just in case he was being watched; the creepy feeling he had told him that eyes were on him.

He also spotted flattened drag marks in the grass where it looked as if a body had been lugged away.

Again, he did not show he had seen this, nor that he had now seen the shape of a vehicle hidden between the trees.

Someone living rough, he thought, trying quickly to piece all these little things together.

Had Tod stumbled across someone? A vagrant or a criminal on the run? Or someone who might want to kidnap a young woman from her bed?

Donaldson remained still and quiet, aware he had nothing to protect himself other than the shotgun.

Someone very dangerous?

Donaldson took a few steps.

His mouth was arid as adrenaline gushed into his system. He became more tense and alert. His forefinger tightened slightly on the shotgun's trigger whilst his left hand, supporting the double barrels, gripped more firmly.

The figure moved quickly.

There was a rush, a rustle of bushes behind Donaldson who threw himself sideways into a clump of thorny gorse, twisting as he did, trying to pivot and bring the shotgun around and if necessary fire at the shadow of a man. Donaldson registered the shape of a pistol in the man's right hand and at the exact moment the American saw and heard the flash-bang of that weapon being fired, he too fired one barrel of the shotgun. It was not well aimed, a shot on the move, and the jerk of the recoil flipped the gun skywards at the same moment he felt the slipstream of a bullet zip by his right ear, barely an inch from his head.

He continued with the momentum of this move and rolled sideways across the bush, firing the shotgun a second time but only at thin air because the man had vanished as quickly as he had appeared. Donaldson broke the shotgun and picked out the spent cartridges, tossing them aside, reloading just the one barrel with the remaining ammunition. He didn't fumble, did not waste time, but knew he was vulnerable as he did this.

Unless he had hit and wounded the man, which he thought he had.

Detective Superintendent Rik Dean awoke with a monstrous headache alongside his new wife, Lisa, who was still deep asleep, having been as drunk as he had at the conclusion of the previous evening's festivities. She was snoring like a drain.

Rik squinted at her. She was on her back, mouth open. Very gently he eased her sideways and the snoring ceased.

His head felt as though he might have done Henry Christie's old party piece of smashing a metallic tray against it whilst singing the old classic, *Rawhide*, 'Get along, move 'em out,' smash, smash, smash.

He slithered out of bed onto his hands and knees, then used the bed as a climbing frame to get to his feet. When steady he headed for the bathroom where after an extended spell in front of the toilet he stepped into the shower and turned it on full blast.

Ten minutes later, with his head still beating like a bass drum, he was dried and shaved and almost back in the real world but knowing he needed a lot of water because of alcohol dehydration, followed by a lot of coffee, paracetamol and food, preferably of the greasy variety.

Today was planned as a day of recovery and to get his head around the wedding ring on his finger.

He let himself quietly out of the bridal suite into the corridor, this being on the first floor of the old part of the Tawny Owl rather than the new annexe. All the bedrooms on this level had been refurbished and were all quaint and countrified as opposed to the more clinical new ones.

The previous day had been excellent and worth the money that Lisa had forced him to spend. Alison (mainly) and Henry had done a great job of their first ever wedding and Rik was looking forward to thanking them both, his new brother-in-law and wife-to-be.

Rik walked to the end of the creaky corridor, all old floorboards and beams, and paused to glance out of the window overlooking the front of the pub and to the village green and woods beyond.

Usually a pretty sight, but Rik stopped cold when he saw the police activity outside. A crime-scene van, two marked cars, and a few others, plus Jake Niven's police Land Rover.

He raced down the steps, curious obviously, and slightly worried.

*   *   *

Donaldson remained on one knee in the prickly bushes, not moving, not breathing, willing his heart to stop making such a loud noise.

A slight breeze wafted the lower leaves of the trees but other than that, nothing moved.

He rolled his jaw as his eyes moved, adjusting themselves continually, his ears straining for any sound.

Nothing.

He re-gripped the shotgun and waited in the same position for a further ten minutes before rising slowly to his feet, feeling the blood rushing back down his legs. The gorse scraped his calf muscles, drew blood.

The attacker had moved incredibly quickly. Donaldson could not be certain if he had wounded him or not. He thought he had.

He took a step towards where the guy had appeared from, ultra-cautious, knowing he had to check it out and maybe force the issue again by putting himself in the firing line. The spot was identifiable from the broken stems of grass. Donaldson sank to his haunches, still continually looking around, and inspected the ground and grimaced with satisfaction when he saw two splashes of blood on a big, wide green dock leaf.

He had hit the guy, the question being now, how badly?

He did not want to spend too much time with his head lowered for fear of being ambushed again but from what he could see there did not seem to be a great deal of blood, no big gouts of it.

He rose again and still moving vigilantly, went to the dead dog and crouched beside it, laying a hand on its chest. Still warm.

'Stumbled into something,' he muttered, twisted around and looked at the flattened grass possibly caused by something or someone having been dragged through it. Initially Donaldson had thought body. Now he was certain of it.

Once more he stood up, went to this and followed the trail which led him to Tod Rawstron's body. He took a moment to feel for a pulse, a necessary but ultimately pointless action because he could see the young gamekeeper was dead. He had taken two bullets in the chest.

'Poor lad,' Donaldson whispered.

He stood up once more, keeping the shotgun ready to fire and made his way to the hidden vehicle, finding it to be a VW camper van, quite old but in good condition. It was unlocked. Donaldson slid open the side door and quickly peeked inside.

It was basic – camp bed, cooking stove, some food. He walked around to the rear of the vehicle and opened the engine cover to reveal the engine, which looked pristine and well cared for. He smiled grimly as he removed the distributor cap and points, which he slid into a pocket. Old engines were far easier to disable than new ones, he thought. This vehicle was going nowhere.

The early morning phone call from Henry Christie had not been welcome, but although PC Jake Niven had still been under the influence of the previous night's alcohol he had readily rolled out of bed and staggered into the shower and, as per Henry's suggestion, he'd drunk about a litre of cold tap water before turning out in response to Henry's plea for help.

Now, much later in the morning, Jake was beginning to feel it – exhausted, wiped out and still not a little disgusted by his organization's response to the incident which, in anybody's books, was a serious crime.

Jake was sitting on the wall at the front of the Tawny Owl on which, the day before, many of the wedding photos had been snapped. He had eaten the free food provided by Henry and was now having another coffee to give him more energy to carry on.

'Caught you!' came a voice from behind.

Jake turned to see Rik Dean stepping out of the pub doors with a mug of steaming coffee in his hand.

'Hi, boss,' Jake said. He took it that their working relationship had now resumed following the fun of last night. Though the men knew each other well, having been embroiled in a gruesome child abduction/murder case over the last few months, they each knew the boundaries.

That said, Rik gave Jake a dismissive wave and said, 'Call me Rik . . . What the hell's going on?' He gestured with his mug at the police vehicles.

'Henry got assaulted in the early hours and someone drugged Ginny and tried to abduct her from her bed.' Rik hoped that was succinct enough.

Rik's mug had stopped halfway to his mouth and his jaw had dropped. 'Run that by me again.'

Which Jake did but in greater detail and at the end of the mini-briefing Rik was almost apoplectic with rage.

'Why the hell didn't he get me up?'

Jake gave him a blank stare.

'Well, OK, I get it. I was too pissed.'

'And it was your wedding night, and you're not on duty, and he didn't want to bother you.'

'Bother me?' Rik blasted. 'Where is the wanker?' he asked, referring colourfully to his new brother-in-law.

'He had to go out and see a client.'

'Right – and Ginny's at the hospital in Lancaster with Alison?' Rik asked, trying to get his head around things, although like Jake this was his day off plus the first day of his honeymoon. 'Does Karl Donaldson know about all this?'

Jake nodded. 'He's gone for a jog . . . yeah, Henry said he could,' Jake added reacting to Rik's expression.

'OK, I need to speak to the detective on this. Where is he or she?'

'One been and gone,' Rik said, 'no one else landed. All busy with prisoners, apparently.'

'Which DS is on duty?'

'Jess Makin.'

'OK, and is there a support unit on the way for searching, et cetera?'

Jake shook his head. 'Got diverted.'

'The shower of shit,' Jake said. 'I'll get on to them . . .'

'No need, DS Makin's here,' Rik said as a small Toyota Hybrid pulled onto the car park and Makin climbed out. She was a detective sergeant based in Lancaster. Rik trotted down the steps to meet her and the look of horror on her face tickled Jake as he watched a low-voiced, but nonetheless ear-chewing dressing down take place. She took it reasonably well, looking contrite, and then Jake felt a bit sorry for her, but only a bit.

Since he had been posted to Kendleton he had come to realize that the public wanted to see cops on the beat and when they called for help. To Jake's simplistic mind it seemed to be an easy equation, but one which the force did not seem to comprehend.

As a consequence the cops were losing a crucial battle in a war they might never now win. He always ensured he went to see anyone who called him and consequently this community had taken him to its heart.

When the bollocking was over, the two detectives walked back up the steps, the DS looking suitably chaste and apologetic, but to be fair, it transpired she had been to see Ginny at hospital. The problem as Jake saw it, though, was that the offender was still at large and no steps had been taken to ID or capture him.

Jake nodded at Makin, who blanked him.

'Let's go and see what the crime scene has to offer us,' Rik said, leading her into the pub. 'What's your plan now, Jake?' he asked the PC as he passed.

'I know time's gone on, but a couple of things.' Jake pointed across to the woodland on the other side of the village green. 'The guy who lamped Henry ran off in that direction and one of the local gamekeepers spotted someone lurking around there with a rifle in his hand. Thought I'd just have a root around, then I'll hop into the Land Rover and have a drive around, see if I can spot any strangers and also chat to a few well-placed locals.'

'Good plan,' Rik said, stood aside for Makin, then followed her into the pub.

Jake watched them go then sauntered across to his ancient Land Rover, which was about the only resource paid for by the constabulary, an old, very past-it vehicle that had been discovered long forgotten in a garage at headquarters.

He started it up and drove across to the far side of the village green and stopped on a small car park from which various public footpaths were signposted. He slid out of the driver's seat and considered the view back to the Tawny Owl for a moment, then, without his cap on, he walked up the footpath leading to the trees.

Prior to being a rural beat officer, Jake's role was as a full time armed-response unit officer in Blackpool, before that as a PC on the beat in the resort. He recalled a time when there had been a plethora of night-time burglaries in houses on the perimeter of Stanley Park, the biggest public park in Blackpool. There had been some sightings of a man in the park who was believed to be living rough and was committing break-ins to survive, taking only food and cash, but also causing real fear amongst the community. The police ran a long operation consisting of overnight observations in the park and Jake was one of the cops involved. On one particular night he had seen a figure prowling through some trees and had tried to follow him but a foot pursuit in near pitch-black conditions had left Jake red-faced when he went flying into a flower bed and did not catch his prey.

It did show that the offender was living within the park, but despite thorough searches, including the use of dogs, the man's hideout was not found until after he was arrested whilst committing a burglary. So Jake knew that to search and find someone who might be hiding out in a wood was not easy.

As he walked into the woods at Kendleton he was fully aware of this problem and not hopeful of lucking on to a tent made of twigs and branches, things you could walk past within two feet and not realize. That is if anyone was actually there.

One thing he did think about was that if the person Tod had seen in the woods was the same one who had committed the offences at the Tawny Owl, then that smacked of planning – particularly if that person had prepared his entry into the pub and was armed with knock-out drugs.

A lot of planning and preparation, which would have included keeping observations on the Owl, which, Jake thought, would require a good, well-hidden vantage point.

These considerations suddenly made finding a hideout less of a needle in a haystack problem, unlike hunting for a burglar's secret place. This person would want to remain hidden, yes, but would also require a great view of the pub to watch comings and goings.

To Jake that meant somewhere slightly elevated and close to the edge of the treeline.

He stopped on the footpath, then spun and backtracked to the Land Rover. From there he walked to the village green, turned and surveyed the woods which rose on a wide slope. He thought, 'Now where would I go if it was me?'

After several scans, he pinpointed three good positions from which there would be a great view across to the pub.

He made his way to the first one.

The second one left him cold and not a little terrified.

He was certain this was it as he crouched down in the bushes and saw a sleeping bag open on a plastic ground sheet and by the roots of a tree there was a cushion which had a thin indentation across the middle. He looked carefully at this, his already dehydrated mouth getting even dryer.

Trying not to disturb anything, he sank to one knee and looked through an opening in the foliage from which he could clearly see the front elevation of the Tawny Owl, maybe a thousand metres distant.

A kilometre. A long way. Maybe.

His eyes followed the indentation in the cushion.

Jake knew a sniper's nest when he saw one.

'PC Niven to DS Makin receiving?' he called on his personal radio (PR).

'Go ahead, Jake.'

'Sarge – found something in the trees of great interest. Could do with a crime-scene investigator to take a look, I think, and yourself. I think it's where our offender might have been keeping obs on the pub.'

'Roger,' Makin said, 'but there's something come up here that's urgent . . . Can you come back ASAP and we'll take it from there?'

'Will do.'

Jake paused, wondering what the urgent thing could be. Even so, he took a few extra seconds to use his mobile phone to record what he had just found. Part of him wanted to seize the sleeping bag and ground sheet and cushion but he knew it might destroy vital evidence if he did.

After taking the photos he looked a little more closely at the discoloured track across the cushion.

He knew what it was. Gun oil.

He made a quick judgement call then because the last thing he wanted to do was leave this unattended for any length of time, only to return to find it gone when a CSI eventually got to it.

He seized the cushion, believing the risk would justify the reward.

* * *

Pulling up at the pub, Jake was surprised to see Tod Rawstron's Land Rover had returned.

He left the seized cushion on the passenger seat of his car because he did not want to handle it any more than necessary, and trotted up the steps into the pub where he found Rik Dean, Jess Makin and Karl Donaldson – still in his running gear – sitting around a table engaged in a very serious-looking conversation. There was no sign of Tod.

Donaldson was doing the talking, the other two listening intently. All three looked in Jake's direction.

The expressions on their faces made Jake's heart sink.

'What is it?' he asked.

'We've got a killer on the loose,' Rik said dramatically.

'I've just found that young gamekeeper's body,' Donaldson added. 'He's been murdered and whoever did it had a pop at me. I think I managed to wound him, but he still got away.'

The news hit Jake as hard as a medicine ball in the gut. He found it hard to take in because of that strange feeling of learning of the death of someone you only just saw a short time ago and had a chat with – and because Tod had been an acquaintance of sorts.

Jake sat down heavily on the spare chair at the table, dumbstruck, his eyes flickering from one to the other. He couldn't think of anything constructive to say so instead he asked Donaldson if he would retell his story, which he did, accurately and succinctly.

Then Jake asked, 'Could it be the same guy who tried to kidnap Ginny?'

They all shrugged. Jake knew everything was a possibility, but to say yes and then rush down what turned into a blind alley would be counterproductive, though the chances of two men running wild out there at the same time was unlikely.

'We need to take it one step at a time and keep our options open,' Rik Dean said, ever the detective superintendent. 'I'm now going with Karl and DS Makin to the crime scene and we'll take it from there,' he told Jake, then asked, 'Was your trip into the woods of any use?'

'Yeah,' Jake said heavily, 'it was.'

He told them what he had found. They listened with growing

concern and Rik's observation, 'That's a worry,' was an understatement.

'Gotta be the same guy,' Jake said. 'I know what you're saying, boss, I know it might not be . . .'

'I get it too,' Rik said, 'but like I say, open mind.' He marshalled his thoughts, wishing that Henry Christie was back from his foray. His input would have been, and still could be, invaluable. To Jake he said, 'You grab one of the CSIs and take him to see this sniper's nest, as you call it, and gather all the evidence you can. We'll set off to the other side of the hill.'

Jake nodded. 'As soon as I've done that, I'll come around, too, if that's OK?' To Donaldson he said, 'I knew the lad quite well and at least I'll be able to ID him in situ if you want?' He turned to Rik again. 'I'd like to be family liaison officer and break the news to his parents.'

'Yes, you can be, but I want to be there when they're informed of his death.'

Jake nodded. Even though it would not be the case, there had been occasions when a death message had been delivered to the person who had killed the victim and he knew SIOs liked to judge the reactions of anyone being told the news.

Rik then addressed Makin. 'Get on the blower, get a dog out here, a search team, an ARV, and everybody else who needs to come. No excuses, they all need to turn out. And inform control room, tell them I'm covering this.'

Donaldson himself owned a Jeep Renegade and had volunteered to drive the two detectives back to the scene in it. One of the CSIs still at work in the Tawny Owl was going to follow as far as possible in the crime-scene van whilst the other would go with Jake in his Land Rover to the woods across the village.

'We need to keep in contact, basic stuff,' Rik instructed everyone. 'There's a dangerous individual out there and no one tackles him alone.'

'Or maybe two dangerous individuals,' Jake reminded him.

'Or maybe two . . . so take care.'

'And you guys,' Jake said.

The two forensic-suited CSI officers who had been doing their jobs on Ginny's room and the rest of the Tawny Owl emerged from the pub carrying their aluminium cases of equipment. One peeled off to join Jake, the other approached Rik.

As they were all about to get into their vehicles, Jake saw a fast-moving Mercedes sports car belonging to the village doctor, an oldish man called Lott, a Tawny Owl regular, tear into the car park and slither to a gravel-spitting halt by Jake's Land Rover. Lott jumped out of the sleek motor car and trundled quickly over to Jake, looking harassed and flushed.

'Jake, boy, Jake boy, I'm glad you're here . . . you know I'm not great with mobile phones and there wasn't a good signal anyway,' he said, shaking the latest iPhone angrily at the officer.

'That's OK, Doc, what's the matter? I'm just setting off on an urgent job, can it wait?'

'No it bloody well cannot,' Lott said ferociously, causing Jake to jump. 'There's been a bad accident on the road out to Brown Skye, you know, Lord Chalmers' country pile? I was on my way to do some brown-trouting, as I call it. I've got permission to use one of the lakes on Chalmers' land, some excellent specimens in there . . . no size for eating, but lovely, nice things . . .'

'Doctor Lott,' Jake interrupted, 'you said an accident.'

'Oh yes, on one of the bad bends – you know, where the road twists through Wellbeck Gulley and there's that almost sheer drop down to the River Roeburn?'

'I do.' Jake knew the stretch of road with a perpendicular drop to one side, down a jagged scree with the river at the bottom. The last thing he needed was a road-traffic accident to deal with. He'd already decided to hand it over to what little remained of the road-policing department.

'Well, I'm driving along, all slow like . . .' Lott continued with his painful report. Jake knew that the doctor threw his sports car around country roads like he was in a rally – and often with more alcohol in his system than was healthy, or legal. 'Saw the wall at the side of the road had been knocked over and I just thought it odd because it was intact two days ago when I went past, so I was curious.'

Jake waited, his eyebrows encouraging Lott to hurry up. He would have been a nervous wreck by now if he'd been waiting for a diagnosis.

'Well, well,' the doctor said, flustered, 'I had a look over the edge – and you know it's a bloody long drop down there and any vehicle that goes over the edge is likely to get badly damaged,'

'OK, cut to the chase, Doc, please.'

'Well . . . it was, I'm sure it was, Alison's car in the river, that horrible, gross four-wheel-drive monstrosity she insists on parading around in.'

NINE

'What?'

For the second time in less than fifteen minutes, PC Jake Niven's insides turned icy cold.

'I'm sure it was Alison's car,' the doctor confirmed. 'I tried to call' – he waggled his phone again – 'but I was shaking like a leaf and there was no signal to speak of way out there . . . but I did manage to take a photo . . . bit shaky I know.' He tapped the screen of his iPhone with his gnarled finger, then showed it to Jake, who angled it to see the image more clearly in the light, then snatched it from the doctor's hand and zoomed in on what was definitely a white Navara, badly damaged and lying upside down on its roof in the river like a dead animal.

Jake caught his breath.

It was Alison's car, he was certain. The registration number was not legible because of the camera angle, but it was a very recognizable vehicle and the only white one in this area.

'What d'you think?' Lott asked.

'I think you're right. Only thing is that Alison wasn't driving it this morning. She's at the hospital with Ginny. Henry was driving it,' he said bleakly. 'Did you see him? Or anyone?' Jake asked anxiously. 'Or a body?'

Lott said no.

Rik Dean and Donaldson were aboard the American's Jeep, about to set off from the car park.

Jake dashed over and stepped in front, waving them to stop.

Rik leaned out of the window. 'C'mon, Jake, we need to get

going.' Apart from anything else he also had a new wife to attend to though for the moment she was still in recovery, as was Donaldson's wife Karen. Many of the other guests had left or were in the process of leaving, unaware of the overnight incidents.

'This is a day that keeps giving,' Jake said. 'Looks like Henry might've had an accident, presumably on his way back from his business appointment.'

'What do you mean?' Donaldson asked.

'His – Alison's – car is at the bottom of a steep ravine, according to the doctor. Badly damaged, no sign of Henry.'

Jake showed them the photo on Lott's phone.

'My God,' Donaldson said.

Stunned, but still trying to be practical, Rik said, 'We're running out of resources here. Look,' he addressed Jake, 'take the CSI with you and check out the accident. If Henry's hurt or trapped, or whatever, he's got to be your priority. Come back to the sniper's nest later,' he added, trying still to get his mind working logically. 'At least you seized that cushion.'

'What if he comes back for his gear?'

'A chance we'll have to take. Saving a life's more important at this moment in time. My call, I'll stand by it.'

'OK.'

'Excuse me.'

Jake turned to see the waitress who had come in early to work at the pub. She was trotting down the front steps holding a cord-less phone, a worried look on her face.

Jake frowned as she approached him. 'It's Alison,' she said, indicating the phone.

'Right?' Jake said guardedly.

'Can someone talk to her, please?' She looked slightly help-less. Jake held out his hand and took the phone from her.

'It's Jake Niven, Alison.'

'Jake? Is Henry there, please?' Alison's strained voice asked.

'Er, no, why?'

'It's just that I seem to have had one of those accidental calls from his mobile, you know, the sound of a phone in someone's pocket? Then it went dead. I called him back but got no reply. I just wondered where he was.'

'How long ago was this?'

'Just now, couple of minutes.'

'OK. Where are you?'

'Still at the hospital with Ginny. I'm expecting him to pick us up any time. Ginny's been discharged, so, is he there, or do you know where he is?'

Jake took a breath and said, 'Look, Alison, Henry's not here, but there's a possibility he might have been involved in some sort of accident between here and Chalmers' place, in Wellbeck Gulley. Doctor Lott's seen a similar car to yours off the road, down in the river, and I'm just going to investigate now.' He knew he was speaking bluntly but his voice was calm and he knew there wasn't time to sugar-coat anything. Henry wasn't here, there's been an accident and a vehicle like the one he had been driving was upside down in the river.

'Why was he in my car?' Alison asked.

'Er, he couldn't use his for some reason,' Jake said, looking over at Henry's new Mondeo Estate with four slashed tyres. Alison did not know about this and he did not want to complicate things or worry her any further. 'I won't know anything more for about ten or fifteen minutes, but as soon as I do, I'll call you, OK?'

There was dumbfounded silence on the phone.

'Alison?'

He heard her suppress a cry.

'Alison, I'm sorry to be so direct, but I need to get to the scene and whatever, I'll let you know immediately.'

'OK, Jake, thank you.'

He pressed the end call button and handed the phone back to the waitress who, having heard his end of the conversation, had gone very sickly looking. To Rik and Donaldson he said, 'Sounds like she got one of those phantom phone calls from Henry, no speaking, just rustling, then couldn't get through when she called him back.'

'So he could be OK,' Donaldson said.

'I'll go find out, eh?'

'Come on, let's get moving too,' Rik said, breaking the atmosphere of dread that had suddenly descended on them all.

Jake walked back to Dr Lott and gave him his phone. 'You lead, I'll follow.'

Seconds later they were all on the road, none of them knowing what they were about to get into.

Alison looked accusingly at her mobile phone, now dead in her hand, then across at her pale stepdaughter slumped on a chair opposite. They were in the A&E waiting area at Lancaster Infirmary. Ginny was tired and still quite out of it but her bloods had come back normal. Although the sedative use had not yet been analysed, the doctors were happy to discharge her and also Alison, who had been treated for her facial injury where the intruder had stomped on her. She tried Henry's mobile again but could not connect.

She sighed heavily and her mind began to race because the only thing she could now speculate about was whether there was any connection between Henry's accident and the assault. Could it have been more serious than they had thought? Supposing there was a bleed on the brain, or a clot? He should have come with her and Ginny for a check-up, she should have insisted on it, then at least they would all be here together, their little family unit with Henry the old silverback caring for them all.

Her other thoughts concerned the unknown man who had attempted to take Ginny from her bed. Was he a sexual predator, a man who hunted and preyed on young women? Had he just lucked on to Ginny, seen her as his latest victim?

Alison thought she could handle that.

As traumatic and horrifying as it was, she could accept a dangerous opportunistic criminal on the loose, taking his chances as and when.

The serious beating he had tried to inflict on Henry was an extra concern because it had been delivered by someone who knew exactly what he was doing, who knew how to put another man down at close quarters.

No! she thought.

It couldn't be.

She looked at Ginny and their eyes met. She might only have been her stepdaughter but she loved her like she was her own flesh and blood and would gladly have put her own life on the line to save her.

Ginny smiled wanly.

All Alison could now think was of that single word the intruder had spoken when he had stamped on her face.

'Bitch.'

Alison dropped her gaze, unable to look into Ginny's eyes any more as she thought, 'No, no, it cannot be.'

Jake thought if he stuck a breathalyser into Dr Lott's mouth and asked him to blow there would be a positive result; he went on to think if he did the same for himself it would also be positive as both of them still had alcohol in their systems from the previous night's revelry. Lott had actually been the wedding photographer – a sideline he was working on having just completed a photography course at a local college – but after he had done his duty in that respect following the first dance of the bride and groom, the doctor and his big friend, the local butcher, had got seriously pissed.

That was of no concern to Jake.

So long as Lott – or himself, even – did not have an accident whilst driving, he was happy. They had to get to the scene in one piece, which they did, some ten minutes later.

The road was narrow and treacherous, rising, falling and winding, and in some places only just wide enough for one vehicle. The most dangerous section, maybe a quarter of a mile in length, was where it clung to a steep hillside and on one side was a sheer drop down into the river via a rocky scree. The only safety feature was a low dry-stone wall on the road edge, which was of no great use. The rules were simple – drivers had to take great care, otherwise the result could be disaster.

The two vehicles, Lott's Mercedes and Jake's Land Rover, reached this section in one piece. Lott signalled that he was pulling in to stop.

Jake braked and rolled to a halt behind him, then he and the CSI alighted. Lott climbed out of his Merc and beckoned Jake to come to him. He led the PC to the front of his car and showed him the gap in the low wall where it was obvious a car had gone through and over and down.

With foreboding, Jake looked over the edge of the precipice, an almost vertical drop over a hundred feet to the narrow river below.

'Bloody hell,' Jake whispered in awe.

At the bottom of the scree face there was an upturned vehicle which had left the road, crashed through the wall, bounced down, maybe overturned on its way down, and was now on its roof in the river.

It was Alison's car and Henry had been driving it.

About the time Jake arrived at the scene of the accident, Rik Dean, DS Makin and Karl Donaldson got out of Donaldson's Jeep on a woodland track. At the American's suggestion they walked the last hundred or so metres to the murder scene with the CSI behind them.

Donaldson held them back short of the crime scene and pointed out where Tod's Land Rover had been parked, the tyre tracks up to that point and even some pieces of broken glass from the rear window he'd smashed to get the shotgun.

He then indicated the point at which he had entered the woods.

After this he moved on, keeping up a running commentary until they reached the edge of the trees, where they stopped again and Donaldson explained again what had happened from the moment he had entered the woods and described the location of Tod's and his dog's bodies and the VW camper van.

'Think he's still here?' Rik whispered, suddenly very uneasy as he realized how vulnerable they were and slightly regretting his insistence that Donaldson should hand over Tod's shotgun to the CSI for evidential purposes. It was the right thing to do, but having Donaldson armed with a weapon would have been reassuring. He doubted if his bosses at headquarters would have backed him up, though.

'We can only hope he's gone,' Donaldson said, 'because if he is still there, and wounded – which I think he is – then he'll be one mad mother and this will be like going after a wounded lion in the bush. Not advisable.'

'Something you have experienced?' Rik asked.

'Actually, yes.' He hadn't but it sounded good. He did, however, have familiarity with hunting down desperate murderers and terrorists and had entered many places expecting to get his head blown off.

The two men regarded each other, then the moment was interrupted by Jess Makin's PR which was in her hand.

'DS Makin receiving?' It was Jake calling her up.

'Go ahead.'

'Are Superintendent Dean and Karl Donaldson in earshot?'

'Affirmative.'

The two men gathered closer.

'Just for your information I'm at the scene of the accident with Doctor Lott.' Jake hesitated, then said, 'I can confirm it's Alison's car, the one Henry set off in this morning. It is down a ravine. I haven't managed to get down to it yet . . . it's more than just a steep climb so I might have to find another way down, but I cannot see any sign of Henry, repeat, no sign of Henry.'

Makin eyed the two men. Rik gave her a nod.

'OK, keep us informed,' she told Jake.

'Will do.'

'Shit,' Rik said. 'Right, let's get on with this.'

He turned to the trees, cupped his hands around his mouth to form a loudhailer and shouted, 'This is the police. You should now give yourself up before any more violence is committed and people are hurt.' He repeated the message, got no reply. 'In that case we are now going to enter this area and I must warn you that any violence committed towards us will be met with all the force necessary to neutralize you. You need to understand that.' Still there was no response. Rik gave Donaldson the nod to continue, which brought a cynical twist to the American's mouth, but he still went ahead into the woods.

Jake stared down the slope, although the word 'slope' very much underestimated the precipice he was looking over.

He wondered why better safety barriers hadn't been erected, though he knew this was not a frequently used route by the general public.

To descend from where he stood would require a rope and the ability to abseil. He had both. A rope in the Land Rover and the skill of abseiling acquired when he was an authorized firearms officer. However, that method was not something he was terribly keen on. Too dangerous, not something to do without skilled help and Dr Lott and the CSI were not those helpers.

His mind raced.

'Other than jumping, what's the quickest route down, Doc?' he asked Lott. 'You know the area better than me.'

'Further along, the road veers away from the river, just before you get to Lord Chalmers' place. The road drops and you can make it across to the river on foot. Take maybe twenty minutes to get to the river, then you'd have to make your way back up river, maybe another twenty minutes.'

'No,' Jake said, dismissing that instantly. If Henry was down there somewhere and needed help, that time could be crucial. Again he looked over at the upside-down car, the roof in the river. He imagined Henry half hanging inside, upside down himself, either dead or badly injured.

There was only one way to do this quickly. He would have to go down by rope.

The dog was there, dead. As was Tod Rawstron. Neither body had been moved.

The flies were already beginning to gather in numbers, their buzzing loud and sickening.

Donaldson, Rik, Makin and the CSI spent a few moments simply looking, trapped in their own thoughts about this unnecessary tragedy.

A boy and his dog murdered for no good reason, it seemed.

Rik angled to Makin. 'Circus time – and that now includes more than one dog, more than one search team, and lots of bodies.'

Rik followed Donaldson's previous path to Tod's body and crouched down alongside it, wafting his right hand to keep the bluebottles away.

'Where the fuck do these buzzing bastards come from,' he demanded angrily.

'The smell of flesh and blood,' Donaldson said.

'It was a rhetorical question but it does tell us one thing.' He looked up at Makin. 'We need to get things moving as quickly as possible because these two bodies are going to start rotting sooner rather than later.'

'I'm on it,' she said.

*   *   *

The rope was in the space underneath the passenger seat in Jake's Land Rover.

He had discovered it there soon after adopting the vehicle when he was first posted to Kendleton and had vaguely thought that one day it might come in useful. He had been thinking in terms of hauling some unlucky motorist out of a muddy field, not having to use it to shimmy down a rock face and take part in an activity well known for causing fatalities.

He pulled it out, uncoiled and inspected it for the first time, a long, thin rope that could well have been used for climbing. It was maybe a hundred feet long, just about the right length to reach the gulley floor. He did not know why it was even in the car but he wasn't too impressed by its condition. In several places it looked frayed, although when he tugged it to test its strength it seemed fine, but that could be a different story when a thirteen-stone guy was attached to it and was dangling over the edge. He winced at the thought.

Dr Lott and the CSI watched him in concerned silence as he flicked the end of the rope around the sturdy front bumper of the Land Rover and tied a decent enough knot, which he then tested for strength.

'You're not?' Lott said.

'I am.'

'Really?'

'Really.'

Jake walked to the edge and dropped the rope over. It uncoiled with a hiss and the end reached the bottom with an audible slap.

'I'm sure I used to do things like this when I was a kid,' Jake said.

'Kids bounce,' Lott said. 'Blokes just plummet.'

'Thanks for that.'

Jake looked over and felt slightly queasy, but nevertheless was determined to go for it. What bothered him most was his level of strength and fitness. Having been off work for such a long time after being assaulted he had stopped fitness training for a big chunk of that period and only as he recovered had started training again, using the bench press and weights in his garage, and running. This would be his first real test of strength.

He scanned the rock face, looking for the likely slipping points and the best places to put his feet. He turned and faced the doctor then took the tension of the rope.

'I'm going to do this quite quickly,' he said, 'because my arms will let me down first, so I don't want to give them that chance.'

Dr Lott rolled his eyes and looked on fearfully as Jake backed slowly out. He had considered running the rope around his body to act as a pulley, but visualized himself being hung halfway down.

'I can do this,' he told himself, wound the rope around his wrists, gripped it tightly.

'Gloves?' the doctor suggested.

'Good point.'

Jake found his leather gloves in the car and set himself up to go again and reversed out into space and started to lower himself inch by inch and nowhere nearly as quickly as he had envisaged.

Stones did dislodge and crumble away under his feet, but he kept hold, kept steady, concentrated, believed in himself and eventually he stepped backwards onto horizontal ground. He looked all the way back up the rope and waved at the doctor and the CSI, who waved unsurely back.

Jake flicked his hands and rubbed his fingers, getting movement back in them, then went towards the overturned car. It was a mangled, battered mess with smashed windows, crushed bonnet and side panels. Jake could tell it had somersaulted down.

He waded into the river and the chill of the water coming down from the fells made him gasp.

He sidled around the Navara and bent to look into the driver's window, saw the roof had been crushed and pounded low and the steering wheel was twisted out of shape. The remnants of the airbag hung uselessly from the centre of the wheel like some huge condom.

'Shit.' He stood upright. 'DS Makin receiving?' he called on the PR.

'Go ahead, Jake.'

'I've managed to get down to the car. No trace of Henry,' he said.

*   *   *

Makin, Rik Dean and Donaldson, huddled around the radio, looked nonplussed at each other.

'Tell him to repeat what he just said,' Rik told Makin, which he did.

Jake came back. 'Confirming, no trace of Henry – or anyone else.'

Rik snatched the PR from Makin. 'In that case you'd better get looking, Jake.'

'That's my intention.'

With one hand clutched to the flesh wound in his side, the sniper watched and listened to the scenario being enacted less than twenty metres from where he was hiding amongst a clump of large ferns.

He knew they would return. They had to. The American, Karl Donaldson, would lead them to the scene of the crime as well as to the VW secreted in the woods, which was essentially the sniper's home base when not lying out in position.

Following his confrontation with Donaldson – who had moved with stunning speed, faster than he had anticipated and at the same time returning fire with a clumsy shotgun which had ripped off a section of his skin over his ribcage – the sniper had treated the wound, which was not serious, but stung and hurt like nothing he'd felt before. Donaldson had almost killed him, and he gave him credit for that.

When the Yank had left in the dead gamekeeper's Land Rover, the sniper had returned to the VW hoping he could simply drive away and be gone before the cops returned en masse.

The vehicle did not start and a glance into the engine compartment revealed why.

'Son of a bitch.'

The sniper tried to keep a level head, something he had been able to do in some of the most dangerous situations in the past – that ability to keep calm in the midst of chaos, then fire off that one decisive round to take down his allotted target. The sniper knew this well but also that this ability had started to desert him. He could not always keep his focus on the job in hand. He had started to think about other things and also do rash things – such as killing five villagers in West Africa just because he thought they deserved to die, innocent or not.

And other thoughts began to surface, the thoughts that had brought him to this area.

He patched himself up with an antiseptic pad and plasters from a first-aid kit in the car. He then took the ammunition from the hidden compartment in the kitchen area and retired to a position from which he could watch the return of the cops.

They came in time, led by Donaldson. The sniper also knew the other male cop, Rik Dean, the man who had taken over Henry Christie's role on FMIT, but he did not know the woman cop, who he assumed was a detective, or the CSI guy in the white suit.

Blood seeped through the dressing from the wound in his side and he knew that if dogs were sent in after him, they would home straight in on the scent of blood.

But there would be more killings before that.

TEN

Jake balanced on the narrow bank of the river and looked both ways along Wellbeck Gulley, trying to work out where Henry could be – if, of course, he had been in the Navara when it sailed over the edge in the first place. He was standing close to the back of the car where the bumper wrapped around the side panel.

His eyes kept returning to two things.

Firstly to the bumper itself.

Jake knew Alison had only recently bought the car from new and it was her current pride and joy. She doted on the beast like it was her pet. She cleaned it, fed it, protected it. Jake knew she would have been devastated if it got scratched or had a bump with another car (and on that musing, he knew she would be in hysterics to see it in its present state). He was fairly certain that if it had been in a bumper-to-bumper collision with another car, he would have known about it. His eyes settled on that rear bumper again and he bent down to inspect the damage he had noticed, which was not caused by flipping over a cliff. He knew a rear-end shunt when he saw one. Someone had either crashed into the Navara, or vice versa. It could be there was no connection with the damage he was looking at and why the car was at the bottom of a cliff. He was keeping an open mind about it, though the question nagged: had Henry been forced off the road?

The second problem for him was the rear window.

All of the other windows were smashed, except for the front windscreen which, Jake saw, had come out from its frame in one piece and was lying on the river bank.

The rear window was not even broken, as such, and was still, incredibly, in place.

Problem with it was there were two holes in it.

Jake inspected them closely, and as sure as he knew what a rear-end shunt looked like, he also knew a bullet hole or two when he saw them.

Whilst his hypothesis went 'Henry's been shot at and forced off the road', his mind went, 'Eh?'

Jake's buttocks clenched tightly as he then shimmied along the side of the car and peered inside and had a good, proper look.

The roof was badly caved in, the steering wheel mangled – and there was blood splatter on the dashboard.

The next addition to his hypothesis: Henry had been shot.

He went through it all in his head, chunk by chunk, trying to see if this conclusion was just ridiculous speculation.

It wasn't.

He stepped back from the car, called Makin on the radio, made sure the others were listening, and reported his assessment of the crash scene, which was met by stony silence.

After this he kept his promise to Alison and called her via his PR using the telephone facility that was integral to all personal radios in Lancashire Constabulary.

He was upfront with her and she took the news badly, but he did not spend too much time talking to her because he knew he had urgent work to do. The first part was to radio the control room and ask them to turn out the police helicopter to the scene and also ensure the air ambulance was on standby at Blackpool airport, where it was based.

He might just need both.

He knew from experience that he would rather look stupid by

turning out the troops now rather than underplay the situation and not alert anyone, only to then find he needed urgent help. Facial egg he could handle. Dead friends he couldn't.

When he looked back up towards the road, he was relieved to see the blue lights of a traffic car. Something told him he was going to need a bit of help on this.

Rik, Donaldson, Jess Makin and the CSI stood in a loose cluster back at the American's Jeep, having back-tracked from the bodies.

Rik was doling out instructions, thinking on the hoof.

He asked Makin to set up a rendezvous point back where the tarmac road petered out, then start to deal with the arrival of the specialists and other staff as they landed. He was already trying to think ahead and prepare for what might be needed and cover all those bases. A crime scene in the woods made for its own peculiar set of problems, not least in terms of access and communication and, of course, the weather. At the moment it was good, but he knew from experience it could change rapidly in this area and therefore protecting the scene and the access to it was high on his priority list. Then he had to think about who he had to call, inform and maybe turn out beyond the usual as at the forefront of his mind was that there was still a killer on the loose and every second not trying to find him was a second wasted.

Makin took it all in as Rik ran through his requirements as all the time his mind was thinking concurrently about basic investigatory principles, such as the 5WH: Who, What, Where, When, Why, How.

Also, what was the link between location, victim, murderer?

Was the horrible, brutal killing of this seemingly innocent lad just unfortunate and tragic or was Tod Rawstron not as innocent as he appeared to be?

Rik's gut told him that Tod had stumbled across something and had paid the ultimate price, but he knew he had to keep an open mind. When he'd finished his list of requirements, Makin kept looking at him, expecting more, and he had to shoo her away.

Then he turned to Donaldson, who was not under his jurisdiction in any way but whom Rik would like to keep close, as his experience could prove invaluable.

'I don't want to spoil any evidence, Karl, but I wouldn't mind a closer look at that VW. It could give us some fast-track clues about who and what we're dealing with. If some evidence gets spoiled, but it means we get a lead on this guy, then so be it.'

'I agree,' Donaldson said. 'He didn't expect to be found so there could be something in the van . . . maybe like his name and address.'

'Stranger things have happened.' Rik looked at the CSI, a man called Ray Bower. 'Suit and boot us, Ray.'

Less than ten metres away, the sniper listened to every word.

He watched Dean and Donaldson kit themselves out in forensic suits, both looking completely ridiculous in the one-piece outfits that looked more like romper suits for adults.

He smiled dangerously, then winced at the pain in his side.

It was true what the detective superintendent had said. There would be evidence in the VW camper van that would lead them to him.

He smiled again because he knew they would never find it.

Both men, plus the CSI, walked straight past where he was secreted, laid out full length, and their elasticated shoes were at his eye level.

When they had gone past, he wriggled backwards to put some distance between himself and the event that was about to happen.

Donaldson stopped and held an arm across Rik's chest, halting the superintendent.

'What is it?' Rik said, wanting to push on.

Donaldson's face turned slowly to him, then he pulled Rik towards him so he could speak into his ear and covered his mouth with his hand.

'What do we know about this guy?' the American whispered hoarsely.

'What do you mean?'

'Exactly what I say . . . if this is the man the gamekeeper spotted flitting through the trees a couple of times, armed with a rifle not a shotgun, he could be the one in the sniper's nest with a view down to Alison and Henry's pub . . . and if he was the one who tried to abduct Ginny . . . yeah?'

Rik nodded. Both men knew it was one and the same guy really.

'He's been hiding out in the woods, so he knows survival and concealment skills. He's hidden a vehicle. He kills ruthlessly and he doesn't want to be found or caught . . . He has access to firearms and used a Browning to kill the kid . . .'

'How do you know that?' Rik interrupted.

'I just do, trust me . . . All that, plus I had to leave the scene of the crime to get you back to it . . . and I say again, he does not want to be caught, so I think he's military, or was, and military scares me.'

Though the sniper could see the whispered conversation he could not hear a word or even see Donaldson's lips moving.

'What's he saying?' he demanded of himself. 'What's he fucking saying?

In his heart he knew. Donaldson was no fool.

'What are you saying?' Rik asked.

'I'm saying that if I was him and I had the resources, I'd make shit sure there would be a little surprise present for the next person to go anywhere near my car.'

Although Jake Niven had never been a traffic cop, he had attended a good many accidents in his time, often arriving first on the scene and covering before the arrival of the road-policing unit. He had been to several where cars had left the road and although it wasn't a common occurrence, there were instances of drivers and/or passengers being thrown from their vehicles by the forces of physics as they plummeted and overturned and rolled, such as Henry's car had obviously done on this occasion.

It looked as if he had been thrown out, probably via the front windscreen.

If so, Jake expected to be able to see him somewhere close by. That was not the case here.

One way or the other Henry had left the vehicle – willingly or otherwise – survived, then somehow scrambled away from the scene, probably badly injured from the accident itself and possibly wounded from being shot.

Jake scanned the gulley.

It was very steep from the edge of the road, less so on the opposite side, which was not a stony scree but a less rocky and grassy incline.

'Jake, you receiving?' his PR interrupted his observations. 'Look up, if so . . . it's me, by the way,' the voice on the radio said, 'Jim Taylor.'

Jake shaded his eyes and looked up to the road where the traffic officer who had just arrived was waving at him. Jake acknowledged him and over his PR said, 'Hi, Jim, glad you're here, mate.'

'Yeah, looks a bad one. You found the driver yet? I heard your transmission to Jess Makin.'

'Negative, just looking now. Not in the car, must've been thrown out, but I can't see him, must have managed to get away somehow.'

'Yeah, can't see anything from up here, either,' the traffic man said. 'Just one thing, though, and I don't know if this is connected or not.' He held up something between his finger and thumb for Jake to see, though from where he was he could not actually make out what Taylor was showing him. It looked like a pencil stub.

'You'll have to be more specific,' Jake told him over the PR.

'Several spent shell casings. Looks like someone's been firing a gun or guns from up here. Nine-mill, I think.'

'Booby-trapped?' Rik Dean said.

Donaldson shrugged. 'Who knows? Just putting myself into his head.'

'Mm, you're too good at that sort of thing,' Rik commented.

'I'll take that as a compliment.'

'Better safe than sorry,' Rik said, bowing to Donaldson's extensive knowledge of dealing with terrorists of all kinds and putting together dangerous operations combining military and law-enforcement agencies, many of which entailed raiding premises occupied by suspects which were often rigged to catch out the unwary and blast them to fuck and back.

Still conversing at a whisper and with a hand over his mouth, Donaldson went on, 'OK, I know there wasn't a tripwire around it earlier,' he said of the VW, 'but he has had time to rig a basic one and there could also be something else.'

'Such as?'

'Dunno.'

Rik rolled his eyes in mock-irritation.

'Don't laugh,' Donaldson said, 'but I'm going down on my hands and knees and I'm crawling the rest of the way.'

'Be my guest.'

The American sank down and began to seriously use his eyes to see if any sort of tripwire had been strung at shin height, which would be harder to see if he had been on his feet. It would be as fine as a fishing line and maybe coloured green to match the background.

He started to move at a snail's pace towards the van, not feeling remotely stupid.

Rik and the CSI watched from a respectful distance.

Donaldson took the same route to the vehicle as he had done previously – and found a wire immediately, stretched taut between two slender trees, maybe nine inches from the ground.

He held up a hand and pointed to indicate his discovery.

'Shit,' Rik said.

Donaldson stayed down and carefully followed the line to one side and found it to be coiled around the tree trunk. Leaving that end untouched, he worked back in the opposite direction.

It might have been hastily put together, but it was dangerous nonetheless.

A hand grenade had been fixed by gaffer tape to the tree trunk and the wire had been looped through the pin in such a way that if anyone had walked into the wire, the pin would have been pulled out and the device would have exploded.

It might not have been fatal but at the very least would have caused serious injury to the lower part of the body, maybe even blowing off limbs.

Donaldson knelt upright and scrutinized the grenade. It was pretty standard military issue, nothing fancy, just effective.

'What is it?' Rik called.

Donaldson explained over his shoulder.

'Do we need bomb disposal?'

'No,' Donaldson said with certainty.

Looking closely, he saw the pin had been partially extracted so that only a tiny tug of the tripwire would jerk it out. Donaldson simply pushed the pin back into place with his thumb and the device was safe. He unthreaded the wire and stood up stiffly, sweating heavily in the forensic suit.

'We're all right here,' he announced, 'but I firmly believe in the old adage taught to me by my driving instructor about vehicles and junctions.'

'And that is?'

'Where there's one, you can bet your ass there'll be another.'

Jake Niven scrambled part-way up the less steep banking and began to move along it to look for any signs of Henry Christie, although he could not be sure which way Henry might have gone if he had got out of the Navara in one piece, which he must have done, Jake thought – unless something else had happened entirely, something Jake did not even want to speculate about. That maybe whoever had been shooting at him had taken him.

'Gotta be bollocks,' Jake grunted as he scaled a large rock, then perched on top of it and surveyed the landscape around him.

His mobile phone rang: Alison's number showed on the display.

'I thought there was no frickin' signal around here,' he said, then answered it, 'Hi.'

'Any news, Jake?' she demanded shakily.

'No, no update, sorry. Just searching the scene now.'

'OK, OK . . . what the hell? How come he drove off the road?' she said weepily.

'I don't know. I'm trying to work it all out.'

'But you haven't found him yet?'

'Not yet. Sorry. But I'm trying.'

'I know you are . . . but not finding him, that's got to be good news?' Alison said hopefully.

'Yes, gotta be.' Jake tried to sound positive.

*   *   *

Donaldson was as sure as he could be that the tripwire to the grenade was the only booby trap around the outside of the camper van. Once he had disarmed it, leaving the grenade in situ strapped to the tree, he went on to approach and circle the VW just as cautiously, still on all fours, and found nothing else before rising to his full height and turning back to Rik and the CSI.

'All clear up to this point, but I would advise we use the same route in and out all the time from now.'

Rik and the CSI joined him, all three now perspiring heavily in their forensic suits and from the tension.

'That's not to say the vehicle itself isn't booby-trapped,' Donaldson warned. 'Still need to be cautious. I think the only plus point is that he will have done this in a hurry, but that doesn't mean it won't blow your face off.'

'Maybe we should wait, get the bomb-disposal guys on to it,' Rik said.

'Your call.'

'Love it when you do that,' Rik said. 'That shifting-responsibility thing.'

'What you get paid for,' Donaldson pointed out.

'I know, I know.' Rik's dilemma was the possibility of getting quick information as opposed to the delay and the risk. To get bomb disposal to this location, he knew, would take at least two hours. 'Could we open a door, do you think?' His face was tight as he asked the question. 'Passenger side so we can lean in, check the glove box, look under seats?'

'We could try.'

'Let's do it, if you're up for it.'

Donaldson looked blandly at him. 'I love it when you do that, y'know, that shifting-responsibility thing.'

'You're good at this, mate,' Rik said.

'OK . . . let's check out the front passenger door.'

Donaldson turned to inspect it. On the face of it, it looked safe enough. There was nothing under the handle and peering through the windows it looked as if the inner skin had not been tampered with in any way, although there was a blind spot where the bottom third of the door closed against the front bench seat and it was impossible to see down that gap.

Donaldson's mouth twitched. The door might even be locked,

in which case this was all academic, but he knew it would not be a hard job to wedge another grenade down there, between seat and door which, if the pin was removed, would simply ping open and explode when the door was opened. Simple and effective, just the kind of thing a quick-thinking, practical military man might do when the enemy was bearing down on him.

'Get ready to run,' Donaldson warned. He gripped the door handle.

Rik and the CSI trembled anxiously.

The door was unlocked. Donaldson opened it just a crack but kept his body weight against it so it would not swing open. He contorted and peered into the space between the slightly open door and the seat. He could not see anything amiss, certainly no sign of anything wedged down there. He checked the hinges and felt along the bottom edge of the door with his fingers and found nothing.

Even so he continued to open the door barely a centimetre at a time until it was fully open, at which moment he realized he had been holding his breath possibly longer than the world record.

He exhaled and said, 'Ta-dah!' for the benefit of the other two who both had terror-wracked expressions. From the way they both also exhaled at the same time, they were also in contention for the world breath-holding record.

'I suggest looking with eyes only,' Donaldson said, 'and only move or open something when we're certain it isn't rigged or on a pressure pad of some sort.'

Rik patted the CSI's back. 'Careful as you go.'

Jake was on his PR to Jim Taylor, the traffic cop.

'I'm thinking we should close the road,' Jake said as he stumbled across pebbles and stones back down in the river about two hundred metres east and upstream of the accident scene where the river bed widened considerably and flattened out as well as parting company from the road which then cut away towards Lord Chalmers' house. 'Or at least until we're happy with what's going on. Is there a crash investigator on the way?'

'Yes, but an hour away,' Taylor said. 'I will close the road, though. I'm not liking what I'm seeing.'

He was walking along the road in the direction of Chalmers' house, looking for evidence.

'Why?' Jake asked, because he didn't like anything about it at all.

'There's been some shunting going on.' Taylor was taking photos with his phone. 'Looks like debris from the Nissan and also from another car, the one doing the butting, which was black coloured and there's some broken headlight glass, too.'

'Ties in with what's down here,' Jake acknowledged.

'Any joy?'

'Not so far.' Jake looked up and around. 'Hang on a sec,' he said and ended the transmission.

Donaldson squatted down on his haunches to look at the grenade strapped to the tree like a fruit of some sort. He was no great expert in explosives, but having worked regularly with Special Forces in both law enforcement and the military, he knew this was a standard anti-personnel fragmentation grenade filled with RDX explosive which, on detonation, bursts open and fragments outwards at high velocity. Had he tripped the wire he was in no doubt that at least one of his legs would have been blown off. He'd thrown a few himself in training exercises and had seen how lethal they could be.

'Standard military kit,' he said to Rik who had joined him. 'You can mess with the fuse so it detonates instantly or give a three to four second delay, say.'

'Is this guy still around, then?' Rik asked.

'Probably watching us right now.'

They had allowed their guard to slip.

The sniper watched the two men discussing the grenade whilst the CSI looked delicately in and around the VW as far as he could reach.

He realized there was far too much incriminating evidence in the van.

He wriggled backwards from his hiding position, moving as silently as a snake, until he eased himself onto his knees. The two detectives were still chatting some twenty metres to his right. The VW and the CSI were about ten metres to his left.

From inside his jacket he removed his second and last grenade, which had a three and a half second delay.

He extracted the pin, keeping his hand wrapped around the safety bar, and froze when the pin made the slightest metallic click as it came free.

Donaldson heard it.

In the same way he recognized the sound of a Browning automatic, he also knew the sound a pin made when being taken out of a grenade, especially set against the context of all the other noises in the woods.

He had last heard that noise in a hotel corridor in Istanbul when he and a team consisting of Delta Force, SAS and Turkish Special Forces were about to enter the room of a wanted, dead or alive, terrorist from Pakistan who was hiding in the city. It had been decided he would be delivered dead.

The team was silent against the background throb of Istanbul.

Way ahead of Donaldson, up the corridor, the second officer in the line removed the pin from a grenade.

Donaldson heard it.

As he had that day.

He twisted around, saw the running flash of a man emerging from the undergrowth, appearing very briefly by the VW behind the unsuspecting CSI. As he passed the CSI he lobbed a grenade into the vehicle through the passenger door, it seemed to arc in slow motion, and then he was gone.

Donaldson's warning scream was lost in the blast.

Jake Niven ran across the shallow river towards the large boulder lodged against the bank, a huge chunk of stone that probably landed there ten million years previously. He was sure he'd seen someone's feet sticking out behind the rock. He climbed over it and slithered off the other side next to the body lying face down under the overhang of the boulder.

'Found him, found him,' he transmitted excitedly over his PR in the second before turning Henry Christie on to his back.

He did not add, 'But I think he may be dead.'

ELEVEN

As far as listening went, it had been a quiet night for Basil Wentrose, twenty-four-year-old graduate in media studies. He had got a good degree from Birmingham but jobs were scarce in that industry and Basil's talent was only minimal. He had drifted more by luck than judgement and the promise of a half-decent pay packet into a role advertised as 'corporate communications' and which turned out, after a series of interviews by faceless panels, to be one of the most tedious jobs he could ever have imagined – literally listening to other people's conversations.

Basil had become what was euphemistically termed an 'eavesdropper' based at GCHQ, the government's secret communications centre at Cheltenham. It was a job he had acquired, it later transpired, because he had a smattering of Urdu and Arabic from his upbringing in the cosmos that was his home city of Birmingham. His language skills had been enhanced and much of his working day was spent listening to tapes of phone calls and also 'live' calls, delving for information and patterns which occasionally uncovered terrorist plots. He fed his findings upstairs and rarely heard anything back.

But it paid his bills. He wasn't too far from his family home and his dull job often became nothing short of James Bond when he was trying to get his hands into some lovely lady's panties. It usually worked.

His shifts therefore consisted mainly of intelligence-gathering and responding to the occasional 'red light', meaning something was happening somewhere in the here and now.

Basil worked in a small three-sided cubicle within a much larger office on the third floor and that night it was an actual red light flashing on his bank of computer monitors that made him shoot forwards and his heart beat a little quicker than normal. He placed his Big Mac down next to the Frederick Forsyth novel he'd been reading, wiped his mouth on his shirt sleeve and clicked the wireless mouse to open a little-used program linked to the light.

This was where he would find details of the reason for the alert.

He opened the message, the body of which was in code, but which also told him who he should inform immediately.

As ever Basil decoded the message in his brain and did not commit it to paper because he was not supposed to be able to read or understand the content, but he could, though would never admit it unless he was being water-boarded.

This one read simply, 'Stiletto reactivated', which meant nothing to him but there was a file attached to the message which he did not dare open because that would have meant instant dismissal and Basil wanted to keep his job at least until he found a job as a film director.

He redirected the message as instructed, erased it from his memory and picked up his paperback, which was all about tracking down terrorists.

The email Basil sent was instantly encrypted by the highest level of technology and landed a few moments later, having bashed its way through several firewalls, in two separate computers, one in London and one in Hereford.

The message in London would remain unopened until the morning, but the one in Hereford was read almost as soon as it arrived, just before midnight.

The man sitting at the cramped desk in the cramped office was called John Smith, an ideal name for a major in the Special Air Service, the SAS, a Special Forces unit of the British Army.

Smith had had a long day of physical exercise and tactical planning but found he could not sleep so he had dragged himself back over to his office at the SAS headquarters to tweak some operational orders he had been working on. Mostly they were run of the mill, but the ridiculous requirements of Health & Safety legislation that even applied to the SAS were quite complex, even for a training exercise, and he wanted to get them right before submitting them up the line for further scrutiny.

He had just finished one to his satisfaction and decided on a shot of Jura whisky from his desk-drawer stash when his email pinged.

He put up the inbox on his screen and saw the red flag on the one that had just landed from GCHQ.

It was entitled 'Birthday Party', as most of the sensitive ones were, just in case they did get into the wrong hands and the vague off-chance that some terrorist leader would not be interested in attending someone's twenty-first and might delete it before opening. It was a pretty weak last line of defence.

Smith leaned back in his comfortable chair, one purchased out of his own pocket, and considered the message before actually opening it, because once open, he was committed.

He had no idea of its possible contents.

It could be anything from an urgent deployment request, in which case two SAS units were available immediately, to something as simple as a threat update, requiring no response.

He tapped the 'enter' key, opened it.

As he read the body of the email he tipped forwards in his chair, his insides tightened up as if he had terrible wind, and the only word he could think to say was, 'Fuck.'

He downed the Jura in one.

The left side of Rik Dean's face looked as though a bucket of hot ashes had been thrown against it. And it burned and stung like hell and wept with the antiseptic cream that had been applied cool but had soon melted.

It would have been much worse if Karl Donaldson had not seen the movement in the trees and reacted instantly by screaming a warning and hurling himself at Rik just as the grenade exploded. Purely by chance, Donaldson had been shielded by Rik's body as he took him to the ground. Donaldson had received some searing burns to the backs of his hands but had avoided serious injury whilst Rik's face had taken some of the blast.

Unlike the CSI, who had not been so fortunate.

He had been facing the open door of the VW when the grenade had been tossed in over his shoulder and rolled into the footwell, then exploded.

He had taken its full force from knee level to neck. The fragments had shredded the soft portion of his abdomen from lower stomach to chest and killed him almost instantly, launching him back into the bushes. He looked as though he had been the target of a flame-thrower.

And the offender had vanished.

Somehow Donaldson had maintained his mental clarity, whereas for at least ten minutes, Rik Dean had been disorientated, his eardrums pounding from the percussive blast.

After checking Rik was OK, Donaldson had risen slowly to see rising smoke and flame from the explosion and had approached to find the body of the CSI lying in a clump of bushes. His forensic suit and clothing underneath had effectively been blown off, revealing him naked and terribly injured.

Rik and Donaldson had been treated by paramedics and refused hospital treatment even though Rik's ears were still ringing and he had to continually ask people to repeat things for him.

The rest of the day had been a haze of activity and decision-making for the detective who was certain this was the worst day he had ever had as a cop or an adult. The day after his wedding, the day he had cancelled his honeymoon.

It was almost midnight when he eventually sat down, breathed out and looked across at Donaldson, who had been truly amazing throughout and Rik was certain he could not have made it without the American by his side.

They were in the dining room of the Tawny Owl.

'Hell,' Rik said.

Donaldson nodded. 'Yup.'

'Thank you,' Rik said simply.

'Love to say it's been a pleasure, but you're welcome anyway.'

They looked at each other.

'Have I missed anything?'

Donaldson sat back, pondering, then shrugged, 'Dunno.'

As much as Rik Dean would like to have said he had quickly regained his bearings and senses after the explosion, in reality it was probably an hour before he really began to understand what had happened. He could never have imagined in his wildest nightmares how confusing it could have been and he had thought about front-line soldiers who somehow battled through shit like that every day in combat.

Being close to an explosion fucked your brain, no doubt about it.

So an hour after the blast, Rik was sitting in the back of an ambulance with Donaldson opposite. Rik was being attended by a burly paramedic called Matt whilst the American was treated by a pretty lady paramedic who, whilst delicately swabbing his hands, kept giving him big dopey come-to-bed eyes.

Also, by that time, a crime-scene van had trundled up, a fresh CSI and forensic team were at work and two pairs of authorized firearms officers were guarding the perimeter as the CSIs erected barriers, ran crime-scene tape from tree to tree, put up tents and started up emergency generators for the lighting that would be needed. This was going to be a long day and night and a lot of brews were also going to be needed.

All these resources, plus a growing number of detectives and uniformed personnel, plus the bomb squad, had been arranged by DS Jess Makin who had been constantly on the phone, battling an unreliable signal. But she had persisted and succeeded.

'Really, you should let us take you to hospital,' Rik's male paramedic encouraged him.

'Don't think so,' Rik grunted. The prospect of being over a dozen miles away did not appeal to him. He knew he had to stay on the scene and could not waste time. 'Just plaster me up and let me get on with it.'

'It's possible you could have concussion,' Matt warned as he shone a torch beam into Rik's eyes. The intensity of the light gave him an instant headache. 'Or worse.'

'I'll be fine.'

'So should you,' Donaldson's paramedic said. Her name tag said Penny. 'Go to hospital that is.' Her eyes were really shining at him.

Rik witnessed this and it was at that moment he understood what Henry Christie had meant when describing Donaldson in very envious tones that 'women all simply want to go to bed with the good-looking Yankee bastard.'

Rik even managed a wry smile. Henry had been right.

'Boss?'

Rik turned to the voice. Jess Makin was at the ambulance steps with a notebook. She looked stressed but very much in control and Rik knew and appreciated what a brilliant job she had done so far.

'Hi . . . Where are we up to?' he asked.

'The chief constable's been informed but he's away on a conference so the deputy chief has turned out. I've called out the local mountain-rescue team for advice about searching et cetera and HQ Ops are pulling together two search teams plus two firearms teams and a couple of PSU serials for the search itself.'

'Good stuff.'

She continued, 'The media are on to it, big style.'

'Only to be expected.'

'And the helicopter is on standby but they don't want to turn out until they have a proper briefing, just in case they have to go straight back and fuel up again.'

Rik narrowed his eyes as something dawned on him. 'I thought I'd heard a helicopter.'

'You did, the air ambulance.'

'For . . .?'

'Ah . . . well,' Makin said hesitantly and emitted a little emotional gasp.

'What is it?' Rik asked.

'It's Henry Christie, sir . . . not good news.'

Jake was glad he had the foresight to ensure the air ambulance was on standby. It arrived in less than ten minutes from its base at Warton and homed in on Jake's position via the GPS application on his PR.

It was with relief he heard the whump of the rotor blades and then, miraculously, the helicopter was overhead. Fortunately where Jake had found Henry was at a point where the river valley widened and the very experienced pilot was able to touch down carefully on a slightly raised area of stones and pebbles.

Jake cowered as it edged tentatively down and then two paramedics leapt out just before the wheels touched. The pilot did land, but kept the rotors spinning to keep the full weight off the ground.

The paramedics quickly assembled a stretcher after a quick examination, lifted Henry on to it and made their way back to the copter and slid him on board. Almost instantly it began to rise out of the gulley, reached a height well above the hills, tilted and sped south.

Jake watched it disappear then began to trudge back down to the damaged car, wondering what he was going to say to Alison, a prospect that made him stop, wipe his brow and bend over to scoop up handfuls of fresh, cold, ultra-clean water and sluice his head with it.

Sitting in the back of the ambulance following the explosion, Rik knew nothing of these events. The last thing he'd known was that Jake had found Henry's car and he wasn't in it.

'Jake radioed me just as the grenade went off,' Makin explained. 'Then I got a bit busy myself.'

'Understandable.' Rik paused. 'So where are we?' he asked again.

Makin briefed him and Donaldson on as much as she knew of the Henry Christie situation and concluded, 'But the truth is, that's all I know. We haven't heard anything from the hospital.'

She explained Henry had been flown to Royal Preston Hospital (RPH), where there was a helipad and the necessary set-up to deal quickly with patients arriving by air.

'What did Jake say about Henry's condition?'

'He thought he was dead at first, then saw some signs of life, but that he is badly injured from the accident – and he thought he'd also been shot.'

'Shot?' Rik exclaimed.

'Seems to have a bullet wound in his right bicep,' Makin said. 'That's only Jake's interpretation of what he saw, but there were bullet holes in the rear window of the car and shell casings on the road where it went over the edge.'

'What the hell's all that about?' Rik mused.

The explosion really had rocked his brain.

Jake wished he'd had the foresight to cadge a lift in the air ambulance up onto the road because his only quick way back up was by rope. However, by the time he got back to the Navara, more traffic cops had appeared and he was heaved up by three of them, who quizzed him incessantly. The road-crash investigator was particularly probing and was keen to get down to the vehicle and have a closer look with the CSI.

'Be my guest,' Jake said and both were lowered by rope.

Jake sat on the low wall by the roadside and waited for a signal to appear on his phone, then called Alison, knowing this would be one of the most difficult phone calls he had ever made in his life.

'I don't necessarily see a connection,' Karl Donaldson said. It was just after midnight and into the next day as he and Rik tried to get their collective, flagging brainpower around the day's events. They were in the Tawny Owl dining room. 'In fact, I don't think there is one. Something happened to Henry on that road that we have no answers to as yet . . . like Tod, maybe he stumbled into something bad.'

Rik nodded. 'I think we have two separate investigations here. The guy attempting to take Ginny being the same one who killed Tod and Ray Bower, our CSI – and us. The only connection is Henry himself and I think that's just accidental.'

Donaldson agreed.

Rik had a desolate look on his face. He had cancelled his honeymoon with no argument from Lisa, his wife, Henry's sister. She was presently in the bar with Karen, Donaldson's wife, and Anna Niven, Jake's wife, all awaiting news of Henry.

Alison and Ginny had been whisked by a traffic car from Lancaster Infirmary down to Preston where Henry was being treated and she was keeping in touch from there. At Alison's request, and because she now worked full time at the pub, Anna Niven had assumed control of the keys and had closed at the end of the day, shooing many of the regulars out at eleven thirty p.m. It was doubtful at this moment if the pub would reopen to the public the next day, but Anna was determined it would.

Alison had told Rik that the facilities of the Owl were available to him and his officers for the next few days and had instructed the chef to come in and help out with food and drink for the troops by putting on a breakfast buffet and packed lunches and constant hot water for brews.

She would be home when she would be home.

However long it took.

A mobile incident room had been set up on the car park and

Rik intended to run the concurrent investigations from there, rather than at Lancaster where the nearest office facilities were. He had told staff to get around the phone signal problem, whatever it took.

DS Makin walked into the dining room, clearly flagging on her feet as were the rest of them. Rik had offered her a room at the Tawny Owl if she needed it, but she had declined the offer. She wanted her own shower, bed and a change of clothes. Even so she had stayed on to help set up the mobile incident room for a real push that would begin in the morning with a proper large-scale search for the offender.

'Hi, Jess,' Rik said.

She nodded and took a seat at the table. There were two sheets of paper in her hand, a printout from the Police National Computer and one from the National Fingerprint Database.

She looked puzzled.

'What's that?' Rik asked.

'Well, odd thing,' she said. 'Obviously we've checked the camper van on PNC and there is no registered owner, which is not that unusual. Someone will follow that up tomorrow morning with previous owners et cetera. There's nothing back from the DNA database yet.' She sighed and stuck out her bottom lip. 'But this' – she held up the printout from the fingerprint database – 'is the strange thing. We've run all the partial prints we found in Ginny's room, no full ones, but what were lifted from the syringe and the gaffer tape, and all of them were enough to get an identity of anyone on the system, though not enough for a court.'

'Yes, yes.' Rik was feeling sore, irritable and exhausted. He was holding a cold wet towel to his facial burns and was almost overdosing on paracetamol and ibuprofen, the effects of which were wearing thin. He needed something much stronger.

'We got a response,' Makin said.

Donaldson and Rik leaned eagerly toward her.

'Surely that's good?' Rik said. 'But the expression on your face says not so.'

She narrowed her eyes. 'They're blocked.'

'What do you mean, blocked?' Rik demanded.

'I mean there is a match on file but for some reason the system will not tell us who . . . There is a London phone number to ring and reference number to quote for assistance.'

'I take it, hope, you've rung it.'

She nodded. 'No reply, goes straight to voicemail, on which I've left a message. And, no, there is no indication who I'm actually phoning.'

'Blocked fingerprint ID?' Rik said, screwing up his nose. 'Don't like the sound of that.'

The three of them, all experiencing brain freeze, looked helplessly at each other, but then they all turned their heads at exactly the same time as Karen, Lisa and Anna appeared at the dining-room door with expressions of horror on their faces. Anna was clutching a mobile phone.

TWELVE

Although Jake Niven was correct when he checked Henry Christie's vital signs – his heart was still beating, he was still breathing – things changed dramatically almost as soon as the air ambulance lifted away from the river bed and tilted to fly south.

His heart stopped.

The paramedic treating him responded instantly and while his colleague prepped the defibrillator pads he applied CPR, heaving on the centre of Henry's chest with one hand above the other. When the pads were charged they were applied and discharged, sending a shockwave across his heart that jerked him like a cow-prod.

But did not restart his heart.

They were charged again and reapplied, jerking him like a monster in a Frankenstein movie, then the straight line on the monitor became a series of steep mountain crests as his heart began to beat strongly again.

The helicopter banked and the two paramedics eyed each other with relief and got on with treating Henry's other injuries.

The air ambulance landed at RPH ten minutes later, greeted

by the already alerted crash team. Two minutes later Henry was in the emergency treatment room surrounded by doctors and nurses.

A traffic car picked Alison and Ginny up from Lancaster Royal Infirmary and blue-lighted them south via the A6 and M6 to RPH, where they then had to wait tremulously for news.

Alison did manage to glimpse Henry once because she forced her way into the ETR and almost collapsed with the shock of just how bad he looked. If she hadn't been told different, she would have said he was dead. A nurse gripped her gently and steered her back to the waiting room and promised to keep her updated of any developments.

It was already a long day, one which now seemed likely to stretch to infinity.

Ginny – ever resourceful and recovering all the time from her own ordeal – kept Alison plied with liquids, although she could not entice her stepmother to actually eat anything.

Late into the evening, the consultant who had been in charge of Henry from admittance came to see Alison.

After removing his surgical gloves, he shook hands and introduced himself as Mr Basheer, then sat alongside her.

'I believe you're Mr Christie's partner,' he said.

She nodded.

Basheer paused.

Many years ago Alison had been a medic in the British Army and served in several fields of conflict, including Afghanistan, where her husband Jack had been killed. She saw the same look on Dr Basheer's face as she had on many army doctors about to deliver bad news.

She swallowed and braced herself, but was unable to look the doctor in the eyes.

'He is badly injured, as you've seen yourself. I've been briefed about the circumstances of the accident in which he was involved. He has been shot and a bullet has torn quite a big chunk out of the rear of his right bicep before exiting. It is not a life-threatening injury and I have sealed the wound.' He sighed: that was the good news portion, and Alison knew it. 'He has also sustained quite severe head injuries. I cannot tell you how severe, unfortunately, until the swellings have gone down, but I can tell you he does have a fractured skull.'

Alison gasped. Ginny gripped her arm.

'As far as fractures go, it looks minor . . .'

'But?' Alison said.

'We don't know the condition of his brain yet. My plan is to keep him stable and let everything settle and then see where we are. There are other internal injuries, too, and I am investigating them. He will need twenty-four-hour monitoring for at least two days, firstly in intensive care.' He paused again. 'At the moment, he is in a critical condition.'

Alison closed her eyes in despair and did not initially see the worried-looking nurse rush into the waiting room. She opened her eyes when she heard the words, 'Mr Basheer, please come quickly.'

Alison recognized the nurse as the one who had brought her back into the waiting room earlier.

'Quickly,' the nurse stressed.

Basheer hurried away.

Following the harrowing phone call from Ginny bringing everyone up to date with Henry's condition and the fact the doctor had been called urgently back in to see him, Karen, Donaldson's wife, after speaking to Ginny, volunteered to drive to the hospital to be there to bring back Alison and Ginny in the Jeep when they were ready.

Rik Dean, Donaldson and Makin retired to the front steps of the pub, which was becoming the gathering area. It was well after midnight, but the air was still tepid and pleasant, quite possible to sit out without coats, drinking the whisky that Donaldson had pilfered from the bar. They were now waiting to see why the doctor had been dragged back so urgently.

They had been joined by Jake Niven, who brought them up to date with his hypothesis surrounding Henry's accident, in which he was certain it wasn't an accident, but a deliberate attempt to kill Henry, as a result of which Rik Dean had asked Preston police to get an officer to the hospital to keep a watch on Henry and be there when he either woke up or died.

The medical confirmation of a bullet wound in Henry's upper arm made it more than conjecture.

The 'why' pertaining to that scenario had yet to be established.

In backtracking Henry's movements, Jake had visited Lord Chalmers' house but had got no further than the front gate because there was no reply either to his repeated finger-stabbing of the intercom button or calling Chalmers' home number, which he'd managed to acquire from the Tawny Owl phone book.

Jake was as exhausted as any of them. He had been in regular contact throughout with Ginny and Alison for updates on Henry, which had been worryingly few and far between – and the toll was getting to him.

He sat out with the others mulling over the day as the other two reflected on theirs. Jake was focused on trying to piece together Henry's travels after he'd left the Tawny Owl in Alison's Navara.

'If we say Henry went to see his good lordship, and we assume he did, then the next assumption is that he conducted his business, then left – meaning he left Brown Syke ahead of Chalmers. Now I can't get a reply from the house to confirm it, but it is logical.'

'And an assumption,' Rik reiterated.

'But if it is right, and presuming Chalmers left by road, wouldn't he have come across Henry's "accident"?' Jake twitched the first and second fingers of both hands to represent air speech marks around the word 'accident'. 'And if he did, why didn't he stop, help, report it, or whatever? Or do lords not do things like that? Help plebs? And obviously we don't know the exact time Henry's car went off the road, but it couldn't be long after that Dr Lott drove in the opposite direction and found it. He tells me he didn't see any other vehicles on the road, by the way.'

Jake shook his head. His brain was in meltdown and despite the fact his liver was still recovering from the assault he had suffered many months ago, and he'd had too much to drink at Rik's wedding, he said, 'I could do with a shot of that firewater,' and pointed to the bottle of Bell's.

Donaldson reached for the bottle, but as he did, Anna reappeared from inside the pub, once more clutching the phone and followed by the other two ladies.

'It's Ginny,' she said.

Henry had come out of surgery that had lasted just short of ninety minutes, during which Alison had been sick several times.

'Please live,' she had intoned whilst walking trance-like through the hospital corridors. 'Please live.'

Ginny had walked with her, holding her hand.

Other than what Alison was muttering, they said nothing to each other, wrapped up in their own thoughts.

Mr Basheer found them in the waiting room, where they had just sat down. Alison shot back to her feet, her hand cupped fearfully over her mouth.

Basheer laid his hand on her arm and gripped her gently, looking deep into her eyes. His face was serious, but then broke into a smile. 'He had a bleed on the brain which we were unable to see initially, so I have operated on him, drained excess fluids and sealed the bleed successfully.'

Alison waited.

'He's doing all right. Still critical but stable.'

'Right, right,' Alison said, taking it in. 'What happens now?'

'We wait, we monitor, we care,' he said, words that sounded corny but which he meant sincerely.

'Thank you, thank you so much.' Alison sank to her knees as all her strength inside her drained away.

Donaldson took the phone away from his ear, closed his eyes, blew out his cheeks, opened his eyes, looked at Rik, Jake, Makin (who still had not gone home), Lisa and Anna, and said, 'Fuck me.' He gave them the update, which made Rik and Jake jump up and punch the air high and low in relief. Even Makin, who did not know Henry, jumped to her feet and did a little dance.

Donaldson picked up the whisky and refilled all the glasses, including one for Jake. He gestured to Makin. 'Want one?'

'You know, I will,' she said weakly. 'I'll get a glass.'

She returned a few moments later and held the glass, into which Donaldson tipped a generous measure of the spirit. She took a sip, cringed, then said, 'Is the offer of accommodation still there?'

Rik said, 'Yeah, we can sort it.'

'In that case . . .' She tipped the rest of the liquor down her throat in one and held out the glass again. Donaldson refilled it and she sipped this one. 'I've been in these clothes for eighteen hours and my underwear is rubbing like mad, so I guess I'll just have to rinse it in the sink, won't I?'

'I'll drink to that,' Donaldson said.

Rik plonked himself heavily on the wall again and said, 'Gonna be a long day tomorrow.'

He tipped the last of his drink down his gullet, stood up, nodded and said, 'I'm back to the bridal suite, where my bed awaits.' He walked into the pub and collected Lisa, before sticking his head back out the door again and saying, 'Seven a.m., guys . . . gal.'

'Gonna be a honeymoon they'll talk about at dinner parties for years to come,' Donaldson chuckled.

'I need to go, too,' Jake said and made his way into the pub to see Anna, who was in the process of locking up the bar for the night.

Jess Makin and Karl Donaldson sat side by side on the wall, sipping the last of their whiskies.

'You know Henry well?' Makin probed.

'Twenty years, I guess. First met him way back when I was a field agent. We've worked together a few times since and we're good buddies but I don't get to see as much of him these days. Reckon that's how life is.' He shrugged philosophically.

'Was he a good detective?' Makin asked. 'I never came across him, unfortunately, but I heard a lot about him. Bit of a legend.'

'He had his moments. The thing was, what drove him, he fought for the dead, believed that was his lot in life. No matter how stupid he was, or cowardly, or brave, or intuitive or dumb, that was the underlying principle that drove him.'

'And what about you?'

'Me? As Clint Eastwood once described a guy in a film, I'm firmly in the category of pen-pushing asshole. I sit in an office, fiddle about with intelligence. That's about it.'

'But you were once a field agent?'

'Yeah,' he drawled, 'too goddam dangerous for me.'

She smiled, knowing he was lying.

'What about you?' he asked.

Even in the darkness, Donaldson could tell she had coloured up.

'Just wanted to be a cop because it seemed a good idea at the time. Now I just want to help victims and nail offenders.'

'Sounds dandy to me.'

'I'd like to be like Mr Christie eventually, an SIO.' She finished her drink. 'Maybe I'll go to bed . . . Good night.'

'I'll just wait on a while,' Donaldson said. 'Night, y'all.'

He sat out and poured himself another drink. A short while later, Jake and Anna walked past on their way home and Anna told Donaldson to close the pub door behind him when he went to bed. He said he would.

Donaldson stood up stiffly when he saw the headlights coming into the village, recognized the sound of the engine – his Jeep. Karen pulled up at the bottom of the steps. Alison, Ginny and Karen climbed out, past exhaustion.

Donaldson hugged his wife, then Alison and Ginny, who both felt as weak as twigs in his arms.

'C'mon, Mum,' Ginny said and took Alison's arm to lead her away to bed. Both looked like pale ghosts, their eyes sunk deep in their sockets.

Alison shook her off and spoke to the American. 'What do you know about the man who tried to kidnap Ginny? Some things must have come to light . . . I know horrible things have happened.'

'We don't know much,' Donaldson admitted. 'I think he's military or ex-military, but those are my own thoughts.' He saw Alison blink at this news and a strange look came over her features, a look he did not quite comprehend.

'Any fingerprints? DNA?' she asked.

'There's DNA from some things found in Ginny's room. It's been fast-tracked for analysis but that could take a few days. That's just how it is,' he shrugged off her look of disbelief.

'Fingerprints?'

'Some partial prints were lifted.' He hesitated, not sure if it was his remit to tell her the result of that. 'Rik should know in the morning,' he decided to tell her.

Her mouth twisted unhappily.

'How's Henry?' he asked.

She tried, but found she could not answer. 'I . . . he . . . er . . .'

Ginny interjected for her. 'He's heavily sedated and we won't know for a while.'

'For sedated, read coma,' Alison said bluntly.

'Mum, we need to get you to bed. Let's both get some sleep and then first thing we'll go back to Preston.'

Alison nodded compliantly. She kissed Donaldson on the cheek and set off inside. Ginny paused by him. 'I know this is a big ask, but would you sleep in our living room on the settee? It's just . . .'

'Yeah, sure I will,' he said. 'And I'll lock up.'

'We'll feel safer,' Ginny finished, hugged him and then followed Alison into the pub leaving Donaldson with Karen.

He complained, 'I thought English villages were supposed to be idyllic.'

'They are – until a vicious killer comes to town,' Karen said.

'Yeah,' Donaldson said, turned and looked across the dark village green and the dark mass of woodland beyond the stream. 'Where are you, you bastard, and who are you?' he asked the night.

Donaldson locked the front doors of the pub, then walked slowly around the outside of the old part of the building with a torch, checking doors, windows and fire exits. The window in the gents' toilet through which the intruder had entered had now been nailed shut from the inside, but even so he checked it thoroughly, giving it a good push and pull. Then he flicked off the torch and stepped into shadow by the building line, let his eyes adjust and simply stood there watching and listening wishing he had night-vision goggles to penetrate the darkness. He was sure that if the intruder was from the sort of background he believed him to be, then he would be armed with such basic equipment and could now very easily be observing Donaldson's antics, maybe even with a rifle aimed at his heart.

Just in case he was, Donaldson gave him a middle finger.

Then, not having seen or heard anything untoward, he made his way to the front door, let himself in, checked everything internally, including the locked door to the new annexe. As all the bedrooms in there were empty, Donaldson made extra certain the door was secure because he thought the annexe was a weak spot.

Satisfied, he made his way into the owner's accommodation where, hopefully, Alison and Ginny were now asleep.

He went into the lounge, dragged an armchair to the door and after making himself a coffee, he sat in the doorway so he had a view of the whole length of the corridor and the doors to the bedrooms opposite.

He was determined to keep awake until the two ladies surfaced in the morning, then he would catch up on his own sleep.

At that moment, Major Smith was still at his cramped desk in his office in Hereford.

Behind him, the door to his office safe was open, the safe empty, because the single A4 folder which it had contained was on his desk. It was marked 'Top Secret', as though stamping those words on it would deter anyone in possession of it from reading it.

Smith opened the folder and extracted the contents.

He adjusted his desk light and looked at the photograph of the man pinned to the top right-hand corner of the cover sheet.

The file was simply entitled, 'Codename Stiletto'.

Smith actually did not need to read any of the contents. He knew them well.

With a dithering hand, he picked up his desk phone and dialled a London number which was etched in his brain.

THIRTEEN

'He's in exactly the same condition we left him,' Alison said to Rik Dean and Karl Donaldson. She had been on the phone to the hospital for an update on Henry in the intensive-care unit. 'If he remains stable they may move him to a ward . . . I dunno,' she shrugged. She had managed three hours of restless sleep, but it had helped her achieve some balance.

It was seven a.m. She was in the dining room, talking to Rik and Donaldson. Rik was smearing his burned face with antiseptic cream.

From settling down, the night had been quiet, without incident and Donaldson had not slept in the chair and he did not want to even now, even though he knew he must.

'We're going to go back down to sit with him. We'll use Ginny's car seeing as Henry's still has four flat tyres, but I've got a garage coming out to fix them this morning.' She looked at Rik. 'As I said, I'll happily feed your staff for a couple of days. I've told chef what to do, but he will need to know numbers.'

'I'll keep him informed,' Rik said. 'And thanks.'

'I've decided to keep the place open for business, though. It might sound mercenary but we can't afford not to, so the pub'll be open from now, as usual. I've left messages with staff and Anna will manage it.' She sighed, almost wilted. 'We're setting off in a couple of minutes.'

'I'll get a car to follow you down,' Rik offered.

She shook her head. 'No, don't, we'll be fine . . . you need as many people up here as possible to find the man who almost took Ginny.' Her voice cracked. 'And killed Tod and your crime-scene man. He needs catching – and so does whoever forced Henry off the road.' She looked challengingly at Rik. 'I don't envy you, because I'll be harassing you every step of the way, you know?'

'Yup. And I promise I will do everything in my power to get those results.'

She softened. 'I know you will.'

'Keep me informed about Henry, please,' Rik asked. 'There will be a police presence at the hospital, but I want to hear from you personally, OK? I'm still concerned that man is out there and he hasn't finished what he started.'

She nodded. 'We'll be OK.'

They watched the two ladies drive away in Ginny's battered Fiat Punto, then eyed each other.

'You need sleep,' Rik told Donaldson.

'I'll sleep when I'm dead,' the American said. 'I'll be OK. I'm on drugs . . . well, caffeine at least.'

'Did I say thanks for saving my life yesterday?' Rik asked.

'By using you as a human shield?'

'That too.'

'Yes – but you can say it again.'

There was an awkward moment, broken when they gave each other's shoulder a manly punch. They would probably have embraced, but fortunately the first of a stream of police vehicles arrived on the car park next to the mobile incident room and Rik knew he had somehow to get his head around some serious deployments, PDQ.

Smith tried to avoid London if at all possible, but the nature of his job often brought him into the capital, which he despised, not only for its overcrowding and rudeness but also because of its sordid underbelly, an example of which he was about to meet.

To be fair, the morning was glorious and his journey down from Hereford to Watford, where he parked his car and caught a train into the city, had been pleasant enough. He was now standing on Westminster Bridge close to the Victoria Embankment looking down the Thames at the London Eye on his right and Hungerford Bridge dead ahead. And the river looked well as he leaned on the railings. He turned around and looked up to the top of Big Ben and the Houses of Parliament, wondering how easy it would be to blow the whole lot to smithereens these days. Pretty easy, he assumed, for someone determined enough.

He watched the big hand move on to eight a.m. and the clock began to strike just as a rotund, small, suited man walked past him, tapped him on the shoulder and said, 'With me.'

Smith dropped in a few steps behind and followed this man, who he believed to be called Jenkins, although this could be right or wrong, he did not know. What he did know was that this chubby, shadowy guy operated across all levels of the government, the security services, the military, and had the ear of the Prime Minister and several key members of the Cabinet.

He was a man who wielded power and influence and owned people's lives.

Smith trudged behind him all the way up Whitehall, past Downing Street and up to Trafalgar Square (where Smith gave Nelson and his four lions a respectful nod), before Jenkins plunged into the crypt underneath the church of St Martins-in-the-Field where there was an excellent, fairly inexpensive underground cafe.

Smith inhaled the aroma of cooked breakfasts, ordered one

and joined Jenkins at a table where he was already sipping his coffee, awaiting a full English.

Smith slid in across from him.

'I like this place,' Jenkins announced, looking up and around at the vaulted ceilings. 'Just off the beaten track for the likes of us – and not too costly.'

'Yeah,' Smith said, 'a crypt. Very appropriate.'

Their breakfasts arrived – service was always quick – and after they had buttered their toasts and forked a few mouthfuls of scrambled eggs into their mouths, Smith said, 'You read the email?'

Jenkins nodded. 'Stiletto has surfaced and is causing bloody mayhem by all accounts.'

'You know more than me,' Smith confessed.

'I am connected,' he smiled. 'Lancashire Constabulary seem to be his hosts for the moment.'

'OK . . . what are we going to do?' Smith asked. Without enthusiasm he sliced a sausage and placed it in his mouth. He was very hungry but did not feel like eating.

'You have his file?'

Smith reached into the rucksack he'd been carrying over his shoulder and extracted the folder he had removed from his safe. He slid it across to Jenkins who skim-read it whilst shovelling the food into his mouth with gusto, then pushed it back to Smith with his fingernails.

'What has he done?' Smith asked.

'Bad, very bad things,' Jenkins said and briefly explained.

'And the people up in Lancashire, the cops, the public, they don't know who or what they're dealing with?'

'Clueless,' Jenkins said, slurping his coffee.

'Then they need to know.'

Jenkins almost choked and his chubby face screwed up in horror at the thought. 'I'm not sure they do.'

'He's killing people, Mr Jenkins.'

Jenkins gave a helpless, couldn't care less shrug.

Smith pushed another section of sausage into his mouth and glared at this man.

'There are people up there who need explanations,' Smith insisted, 'and now we know where he is we can take appropriate action.'

Jenkins still winced. He took a sip of his coffee and thought about things.

'Actually, we might not be able to avoid having to make explanations,' Smith persisted. 'The very fact that his fingerprints and DNA are blocked on the system will ensure people up there will be knocking on your door, eventually.'

'My door? I don't think so . . . and why was he not wiped from this system anyway.' He pointed his fork accusingly at Smith. 'That's a bit of an oversight, isn't it?'

'Whatever.' Smith was not intimidated.

'However, you may have a point.' Jenkins started to mull things over. Smith could only speculate what the hell was going on in those twisted brain cells of his.

'OK, first of all,' he said at length, 'a lid needs to be kept very firmly on this. People up there do need some form of explanation but not necessarily everything. We need to manage this situation, otherwise it will reflect badly on us and we do not want that. So,' again he organized his thinking, 'we tell them what they need to know, we offer them assistance, but ultimately we deal with the situation in our own way.'

Jenkins placed his fork down, pointed a stubby forefinger at Smith, cocked his thumb and said, 'Bang!'

Smith sighed. 'And how do you propose to do that?'

'We will order people to comply. We will assist and direct the manhunt and we will conclude it for them in our way, then it will all be buried in the manner in which I am incredibly skilled. How many identities does Stiletto have? Five, six?'

'Six.' Smith said dully. Jenkins was referring to undercover identities.

'Therefore the fallout, if any, will relate to one of those and we will come out of this with our shit shining, as we do.'

Smith's face showed how unimpressed he was and how he fucking hated it. 'Only if we get our hands on him first.'

'That is something you and I shall ensure happens.'

'We need people on the ground for that.'

Jenkins grinned like an overweight wolf. 'It just so happens we have a team already operating "oop newerth",' he said, trying to emulate a Lancashire accent, 'wherever the north is.'

'What? What do you mean?' Smith demanded. 'What team?'

'RedFour?' Jenkins asked pointedly, still smiling. 'Heard of that?'

Smith's jaw rolled. Of course he'd heard of it, he'd once been part of it, as Jenkins knew well.

Rik Dean sat in the mobile incident room and looked at the dry wipe board on the wall on which he had brainstormed his split investigative strategy. He took a photo of it with his smart-phone just in case some vital part was accidentally erased by some numbskull.

He had decided to go for two approaches.

With regard to the attempted abduction of Ginny and the subsequent deaths, a forensic team was still working the crime scene in the woods, and a search team under the direction of an experienced Ops inspector, coupled with the local mountain-rescue team and several firearms officers, was just beginning a structured search of the area surrounding the blast and killing area.

Fewer resources were being used in regard to the incident involving Henry Christie, but a forensic team was at the crash point and a crane was en route, provided by a local company, to lift the Navara out of the river and onto a recovery truck.

A couple of pairs of detectives were canvassing the inhabitants of the village to find if anyone had seen anyone or anything mysterious or out of the ordinary recently.

The two bodies from the woods – Tod and the CSI – which were still in situ would be taken to the mortuary at the infirmary in Lancaster where post-mortem examinations were scheduled to be carried out later in the afternoon. Tod's dog, Nursey, was also being taken there for that purpose. Jake Niven had already spent time with Tod's parents, who lived in Thornwell, the next village along. Karl Donaldson had volunteered to tag along with him, having been the one to find Tod's body.

Everybody was 'out doing' and Rik was looking at his newly acquired A4 notepad, which would become the murder book, a document required to be kept by every SIO on a murder invest-igation. He only hoped that he would not have to start a second book for Henry Christie.

He had already written quite a lot. From the moment Henry

had been assaulted in the car park, to Ginny's attempted abduction, to Donaldson out for a run and encountering Tod's body; then his own visit to the scene and the next incident and killing. At the top of the first page, as ever, he had scribbled his favourite, '*5WH*', and then under that, '*Victim/Location/Offender*', then the old murder enquiry chestnut, '*Find out how they lived, find out why they died.*' All good principles to be constantly reminded of, but he did believe that the inciting incident in all this, the key to it, was the attempted kidnapping. He knew this was the crux and the killings were just very bad luck.

He re-read all his words, then tapped his forehead with his knuckles. 'C'mon, mate, wake up,' he told himself.

His phone rang. It was the chief constable's office.

'Detective Superintendent Dean, can I help you?' he answered in his most businesslike manner, but did not do what Henry Christie had often done in similar circumstances: stand to attention and salute.

Her hands were in front of her, palms together as though in prayer, her fingertips under her chin as she whispered, 'Come on, my love, pull through this . . . We've got a wedding to arrange, if you remember . . . I know it sounds selfish, but I don't want to go on without you . . . I love you so much . . .'

Henry did not stir.

He looked beyond a mess. His head was almost twice the size it should have been, his face horribly bruised and cut. A drain ran from his skull into a plastic bottle rigged to the side of the bed. He had three cannulas in his arms, two tapped into the backs of his hands, one on an inner elbow, feeding something into him from saline to morphine and vitamins. He was also connected to a device monitoring his vital signs, including brain activity.

His blood pressure was verging on worryingly low, his heart-rate just acceptable.

'So much,' Alison whispered.

They were in a single room off the intensive-care unit, but staff were making him ready for a transfer to the critical-care unit.

Space had to be made.

Others would need to come in after him.

He was in the sausage machine that was the NHS.

Ginny came in bearing two mugs of tea provided by the nursing staff.

'Anything?' she asked. She had only been away five minutes.

Alison shook her head tightly. She took the tea and sipped it, her eyes constantly focused on Henry's face.

His eyelids flickered.

Alison stiffened.

But the eyes did not open.

Ginny laid a hand across her shoulder and squeezed gently. 'He'll come out of it,' she reassured Alison, then sat down next to her.

Alison looked at her and forced a tight smile. 'How are you feeling?'

'I'm OK. Feel a bit of a cheat – I slept through it all.' She laughed without humour.

'It's a good job Henry heard something.'

'Yeah . . . yeah.' Ginny gripped her mug to stop herself from shaking.

'Do you remember anything at all? Do you remember him saying anything to you?'

'I've tried, mum, but no . . . but yet I think there is something. I can't quite . . .' She shook her head.

'Never mind. I'm sure it'll come back at some stage.' Alison looked at her stepdaughter, hoping she was wrong in what she herself was thinking. 'Look, you don't have to stay . . . why don't you go to the cash and carry? We have to keep the place going, even though I just want to shut it all down and run away. You know what we need . . . the wedding depleted a lot of the basic stock which we were going to replenish today. You've got the business card. Do that, eh? Then come back. If anything happens in the meantime, I'll call you. If nothing's changed, we'll get something to eat from Booth's across the road.' She was referring to the supermarket opposite the hospital, which also had a cafe.

'OK.' Ginny said reluctantly. 'I'll have my brew first.'

Rik Dean was very reluctant to leave his post, but a summons from the chief constable was not something he had the courage to refuse.

Jess Makin had just returned from a quick journey home and

back for a clothes change and he left her in charge of the MIR, much to her delight and consternation.

'I've been ordered to attend the dream factory to see Papa Smurf,' he said. 'I'm thinking he wants an update in person.'

'Understood, sir.'

He went, jumping into his VW Golf. Makin watched him drive away, then turned back to the MIR, staffed for the moment by a single civvy who was working at the computer, trying to set up the HOLMES network, the Home Office Large and Major Enquiry System brought in following large, cumbersome, badly run police investigations in the 1970s.

The man at the computer turned to Makin. 'Sarge, don't know if you need to know this,' he said, pressed the print key and a sheet of paper clattered off the printer.

Makin snatched it before it hit the floor.

It was simply the report of a stolen van from the adjoining village of Thornwell, a backwater, even sleepier than Kendleton. A place where, usually, very little happened. Not a place from which vans are stolen. Usually.

'Circulate it, let everyone know.' She handed the sheet back to the man, frowning, wondering if there was any connection to what was going on.

The MIR was equipped with radio equipment and a few moments later, details of the stolen van, a ten-year-old Ford Transit, had been circulated to all patrols.

Makin read the report again. The owner of the van had phoned it in to control room at headquarters and no actual deployment had been made, so no one had been to see the owner about it and the report, like so many others, was just recorded for insurance purposes mainly.

Such was the way of the new world when victims of everyday crime would often never even see a cop at their door.

Makin thought it might be worthwhile in this case.

It took Rik Dean forty-five minutes to reach headquarters from Kendleton. He pulled up in a space outside the main entrance, glanced very briefly at the military helicopter on the helipad and thought nothing of it, then quickly badged his way inside, giving the lady behind the reception desk a nod. He went up on to the middle floor of the building on which the chief's office was situated. Mostly – if he could – Rik avoided all contact with the chief and his deputy, although it was hard to stay out of the way of the assistant chiefs, who were more hands-on. He recalled that Henry Christie seemed to have spent a lot of time – unwillingly – ducking in and out of the – then – chief's office, a man called Robert Fanshaw-Bayley (RIP).

Rik poked his head into the outer office (there was no direct route off the corridor into the chief's office for minions), which housed secretaries and the chief's staff officer, a jumped-up chief inspector called Riley, who beckoned Rik to enter, then pointed to the big, closed, oak door to the chief's domain.

'Just an update?' Rik asked Riley, before knocking.

'Don't think so. Some shenanigans happening,' Riley said under his breath.

Words Rik did not necessarily wish to hear.

'Just go in,' Riley added. 'You're expected.'

Rik knocked but still waited for the 'Enter' call before pushing open the heavy door and stepping through.

The chief constable's face looked serious and strained as he gestured for Rik to join him and the other two men wearing visitors' badges at the conference table in his large office. It dawned very quickly on Rik why the grey helicopter was outside. These guys had arrived in it.

'Morning, sir,' he said to the chief.

'Superintendent.'

'I'm assuming you want an update on the progress of matters up in Kendleton?'

'No, actually . . . but this does concern those matters.' The chief's sharp eyes flicked towards the two men. 'May I introduce . . .'

The less military looking one of the two raised a quick hand to interject and cut the chief dead. He said, 'No need for introductions, Chief Constable,' with an arrogant tone. 'All the superintendent needs to know is that myself and my colleague are from . . . certain government departments and that we are here to assist his investigation.'

'Oh, OK,' Rik said, but did not say anything else. He knew

when to keep his mouth shut and intuitively realized this was one of those situations.

Eventually and reluctantly, Ginny left Alison alone with Henry and made her way to the front entrance of the hospital, where she took a deep breath of fresh air from a day that was beginning to warm up but was also becoming close, possibly thundery.

'Right,' she said, 'cash and carry.'

Turning right, and avoiding a couple of patients who, whilst still attached to drips, had sneaked out for a quick cigarette, she walked towards the visitors' car park on East Drive, about a three-minute walk away. When she and Alison had arrived, the car park closest to the main entrance was already full and they had to drive around all the others before finding a space. All very frustrating but a fact of life for the NHS. Parking at a hospital never seemed easy or free.

She passed a pay station on the way and inserted the required three pounds before getting to her car.

Her mind was full of what had happened to her the night before and also about Henry and Alison, the two people she loved most in the world. Life seemed so unfair. They had done nothing to deserve any of this. They were good people, making their way in life, forging ahead but not treading on others on the way.

'It's shit,' she said out loud to no one in particular as she crossed the pedestrian walkway into the car park and tried to remember where she'd bloody well left her Punto.

The car park was still almost full and one poor guy in a van was creeping slowly around, looking for a space, or for someone to leave.

She waved her ticket at him and pointed to her car. 'I'm going,' she mouthed and saw his thumbs-up gesture. She walked on, passing a couple of empty places, but did not really think very much about them. She got to her car, parked nose-in to the space. She was at the driver's door fumbling with her keys – this was a pre-remote-locking Punto – when the man in the van drew up, his window wound down.

'I won't be a tick,' she said.

He smiled. Ginny turned her back to him as she opened the

driver's door, just vaguely aware of the van driver opening his door, which was slightly odd.

It suddenly unsettled her. The question: why did he need to park here? Why not in one of the other bays? Or was paranoia setting in?

She peeped over her shoulder.

The man had gone to the back of his van and had opened one of the rear doors.

Ginny was about to ease herself into her car when a hand clamped over her mouth and suddenly she could not breathe.

There was a sharp pricking sensation in the side of her neck. She knew what it was: a syringe. She felt the warm flood of liquid in her vein and instantly went limp, everything turned a dark, misty grey, then black and she knew nothing else.

'You have a very dangerous man operating in your area,' Smith – not introduced, but prompted by the other man, Jenkins, also not introduced – said to Rik Dean.

'Tell me about it,' Rik grunted.

He had taken an instant dislike to these men in the chief constable's office and was fidgeting uncomfortably.

'We intend to,' Jenkins said with a patronizing smile. In his mind, Rik had christened him 'The Plump One'. The other, more military one, rugged, older and quite handsome, he had nicknamed 'Clint'.

'I assume I'm going to hear about why this man's fingerprints were blocked on the system?' Rik said. 'And although we haven't heard anything about DNA, I also assume that is going to suffer the same fate?'

Smith – 'Clint', the man who seemed more normal than the other, dipped his eyes, looking a little embarrassed, but even so said, 'Actually we can't tell you very much, I'm afraid.'

'I think you need to be telling me everything,' Rik said and added, 'Actually.'

The belittling smile on the pudgy man's face remained intact as he said, 'For the sake of, shall we say, ease, let us call this man Jones.'

'Why don't we call him by his real name?'

'Because you do not need to know it, but to be fair to you,'

Jenkins said, making Rik snarl in disbelief, 'I will give you some background, some context in order to help you understand our position.'

'I'm all ears.'

'Superintendent Dean!' the chief chastised him.

'Weeell,' Rik said elongating the word to show his irritation. 'What's going on here, boss? Yeah, I get it, this guy is dangerous, very dangerous. He's killed two innocent men and we suspect him of trying to abduct an equally innocent girl, plus' – Rik jerked a finger in the direction of his own seared face – 'he almost killed me and my friend.' He glared at Jenkins, who remained unbowed. 'Tell me everything you know about this man, not least why he is up here on my patch, killing people, kidnapping people . . . He hasn't just turned up by accident.'

'No,' Jenkins said resolutely. 'I will tell you some things and that will have to suffice because, as corny as this sounds, this man – Jones – is, was, a state asset and anything concerning him is a matter of state security.'

'State asset? What does that mean?'

'Jones is someone who kills people on the orders of the government,' Jenkins said brutally.

'His codename is Stiletto but he is often referred to as Blade,' Smith said, 'and our problem is that' – he tapped his temple – 'post-traumatic stress disorder . . . he's gone rogue.'

Everything was ready for Henry's transfer to the critical-care unit which meant a long-ish trip along ground-floor corridors, then down in a lift to the lower ground floor on which the unit was located.

Alison watched nervously as they prepared him.

Although she had been an army nurse in a previous life, she wasn't watching the nurses with a professional eye. Her mind was in too much turmoil for that.

Finally when he was ready, two porters entered the room and manoeuvred Henry across to a trolley.

They smiled and chatted to each other, trying to keep it light, and even made some humorous comment to Alison that flipped straight over her head.

She stepped into the corridor to give the porters more space and did half-notice a man lurking further along the corridor next to a confectionery dispenser, but thought nothing about him. There were plenty of weird characters knocking around the hospital.

The porters rolled Henry out.

A tear trickled from Alison's eye, tracing a line down her cheek. He looked so poorly.

Once more she prayed silently.

As the trolley moved away, she sighed, began to follow and then suddenly realized she was bursting for a pee as she passed the door to the ladies' toilet.

She stopped, backtracked, and entered the loo.

'Sometimes it happens,' Jenkins said blandly, making Rik want to punch him in his pudgy faceless face, although if he did, he knew the very physically dangerous other man, Clint, would probably tear his limbs off.

'Shit happens. Go on, tell me.'

'It got to him, eventually . . . which is a shame because he was, is, very good, but things started to go wrong when he was involved in a mass killing in West Africa. That was when we began to question his judgement, you know, when the flies buzzed and the bodies burned and stank.' Jenkins glanced at Smith.

Smith continued for him. 'Two more occasions after that and we decided to withdraw him from active service and for a full psychological evaluation. We discovered he had gone over the edge, lost his perspective, his logical reasoning, the ability to think critically and although we tried to deal with him in a secure establishment, he . . . uh . . . escaped.' Smith paused. 'Strangled two nurses.'

'Shit,' Rik said. 'So why the fuck has he turned up in Lancashire?'

'I can't tell you that,' Smith said. 'But we will help you track him down.'

Rik would not have been surprised if the word 'WANKER' had appeared on his forehead, because that is exactly what he was thinking.

'And you propose to do that how?' he asked.

'We have assets in the region,' the Plump One said.

'Ahh, more assets,' Rik said sarcastically.

There was an urgent knock on the chief's door. At the same time, Rik took his mobile phone out and glanced at the screen. It had been on 'discreet vibrate' and for the last minute or two he had felt it pulsating like mad in his pocket. It showed ten missed calls, four texts and two voice messages.

'Sorry to interrupt.' The chief's staff officer shoved his head through the door.

The chief sighed irritably. 'We're busy, Chief Inspector.'

'I know, sir, and I'm sorry . . . it's just . . .' He nodded towards Rik.

Rik tore out of the chief's office with his phone clamped to his ear, ran along the corridor, then swarmed down the stairs.

'I'm on my way, Jess . . .'

He hurtled through the foyer and out of the revolving doors, which could not go fast enough for him.

'Ten minutes at most,' he said breathlessly as he jumped into his car and threw the phone across to the passenger seat, reversing with a squeal of tyres out of his spot.

'Shit,' he said, 'Shit, shit, shit, shit.'

FOURTEEN

'I pronounced life extinct in situ,' the consultant, Mr Basheer, said to Rik Dean. 'I knew you would rather see that, as awful as it sounds . . . crime scene and all that. I can't say evidence has not been contaminated because a lot of people, including myself, have been in and out, although I have tried to restrict numbers.

'OK, OK, just show me.'

Rik had pulled up in the ambulance bay and abandoned his car there. The doctor had been waiting for him, explaining everything as he hurriedly led him along the corridor in the emergency department.

Rik could already feel the palpitations of his heart and they dryness of his throat as he ducked under the crime-scene tape stretched across the corridor. He flashed his warrant card at a white-faced bobby.

Twenty metres further along the corridor, another uniformed cop was standing by the door to the ladies' toilet. Rik strutted past a local detective sergeant, not wanting any eye contact because he wanted to be cold, focused, and be able to hold himself together for this one. He had to, had to . . .

The toilet door had been wedged open.

This is where Rik stopped abruptly.

'My God,' he said, swallowing back the nausea.

It was only a small room, a ladies' loo, two side-by-side cubicles, one wash basin, waste bin, hand drier, baby-changing facility.

It had happened in the first cubicle on the left.

They were the sort of cubicles with a gap at the bottom, a gap at the top, made of laminated wood, not offering a great deal of privacy.

One of her feet stuck out at a strange angle through the side gap. The other was poking out through the opposite gap.

Rik even recognized the slip-on shoes.

His fists bunched as his eyes took in the huge amount of fresh blood covering the tiled floor in which her legs lay.

He swallowed again.

Keep it together.

There were footprints in the blood. Doctors, nurses, the general public – contamination already an issue but understandable.

Even so, Rik sidestepped and overstepped as much as he could until he manoeuvred himself into a position to see straight into the cubicle and the full horror that awaited his eyes.

She sat twisted at some grotesque angle. Her legs were sticking out under the cubicle sides, her back against the toilet, and her head lolling back, almost severed from her body, a huge gaping, bloody cut. The blood fountains from her severed veins having splattered up and high on the inner cubicle sides, still dripping, still warm, still smelling.

Rik knew he was going to lose it.

Tears welled in his eyes, misting his vision.

He rubbed them away with the back of his hands, took firm control of his breathing.

The consultant was still with him, standing just behind. 'You knew her?'

Even from that angle, Rik's body language was easy to read as his shoulders shook.

'She was a friend, a good friend.'

'I'm sorry.'

'Not half as fucking sorry as I am,' Rik blinked. 'Where is her daughter?'

'What do you mean?'

'She was here with her daughter, Ginny.'

'I don't know where she is,' the doctor said. 'I think she'd gone.'

'Is Henry Christie all right?'

'Yes . . . he's in the critical-care unit.'

'Good, good . . . So where is Ginny?'

Rik's headache was phenomenal.

He was sitting with a pen and pad in front of him, struggling to write a single word of his new and ongoing investigative strategy. He was in a conference room at police HQ. Several high-ranking detectives were due to join him in half an hour and with them he was going to map out the way forward.

But just at the moment he had nothing. In local parlance he was having a shed collapse, his brain in meltdown, not working.

He placed down his pen and interlocked his fingers.

'I didn't protect her,' he said out loud. 'Fuck,' he sighed and rubbed his forehead, then drew his hands down his face, stretching and distorting his features.

The image of Alison's mutilated body was stuck in his brain and the horrific, sordid way she had died. In a fucking toilet cubicle. Throat severed, hacked open, exposing the muscle, gristle of the larynx.

He was in a rage, furious that the police presence he had ordered, expected, at the hospital had not even shown up. There had been an oversight, he'd been told by some snivelling, shithead of a patrol sergeant – whose head would roll, Rik had decided.

He swore again.

It was almost midnight, but Rik did not care any more.

From now on this was going to be a twenty-four hours a day, seven days a week investigation until that bastard was caught and nailed to the wall, whoever he was.

Jake Niven had taken over the vigil at Henry's bedside from Karl Donaldson.

They had decided on six-hour shifts, so one of them, someone he knew, would be there the moment he woke up from what the doctors were calling a mild coma. All his vital signs were good. The skull fracture was hairline, almost non-existent, but was there. There was now no bleeding, no excess fluids on the brain, and after four days the swellings were reducing bit by bit.

He seemed to have gone on standby mode, self-repair, and would switch back on when his body was good and ready.

It was possible to jerk him out of it with drugs, the doctors said, but no one wanted to do this. It had . . . complications.

Best to let nature run its course.

Until that happened, all the people around him would take their turn to be with him.

Karl Donaldson had gone straight back to work alongside Rik Dean on the investigation. The American's attachment was now official, sanctioned for the time being by the FBI and the US Embassy.

Jake stood at the foot of Henry's bed, hands in pockets, looking at the patient.

He had so much to be grateful to Henry for, someone he had not even really known until quite recently, but who had become a close, dear friend.

Jake's face creased with emotion, and not for the first time whilst standing at the bed.

'Come on, you old warhorse,' he whispered.

Then he stopped speaking and thought forlornly, what would be there for Henry when he did wake up? If he wasn't brain damaged (which wasn't a certainty), then found out Alison had been murdered, Ginny was still missing, maybe also murdered. Even if this killer was captured, that would not bring Alison back. Henry's planned future as a good husband (Henry had confessed some terrible things about his past and not having been the husband he should have been to his late wife, something he wanted to rectify with Alison) and 'mine host' at the Tawny Owl was effectively over. Jake conjectured if Henry would be able to deal with it.

He had his doubts.

He walked around the bed, located in a single room in the CCU, and sat in the armchair that had been imported from somewhere.

The uniformed cop on duty outside the room opened the door and poked his head through. Rik had now insisted on a twenty-four-hour guard for Henry following the debacle with Alison, although even he did not have the muscle to make it an armed guard, which he would have preferred.

'Mind if I get a coffee and sarnie? I'll be back in five,' the officer requested.

'No probs, I'm not going anywhere.'

Jake settled comfortably, wondered how it would all pan out, these live changing, life-ending events over the last few days.

He knew the murder investigation – now triple (plus dog) – was one of those all hands to the tiller kind of things, but also that not much progress was being made. It was approaching the critical seventy-two hours stage where if there was no break-through, then it could be a very long slog, a fact that related to all murder enquiries.

Extensive searches had taken place over some sections of moorland without success, as clearly the killer had moved on using a van he had stolen from Thornwell, then somehow followed Alison and Ginny to RPH where he had butchered Alison and kidnapped Ginny, whose fate still remained unknown.

The police knew she had been kidnapped because the event had been captured by a security camera scanning the East Drive car park and had shown her being taken by a man wearing a baseball cap to cover his face and using the stolen van, the registered number of which had been clearly caught on camera.

The vehicle had since been found abandoned and burnt out in a field near a council estate in Preston.

And there the investigation had run into a cul-de-sac.

Jake knew there were aspects of it he was not privy to – such as why what looked like an SAS team assisted with the search; and at a couple of briefings he had managed to attend, why there were some unidentified, faceless guys hanging around in the background. He'd also heard some cryptic murmurings between Rik and Donaldson that he didn't understand. Neither man was happy about something that was going on, but obviously Jake didn't need to know what.

And then there was Henry – almost forgotten because of everything else.

He could have died, probably would have if Dr Lott hadn't been going brown-trouting that morning and seen the hole in the wall.

Jake seemed to have been given what became known as the 'Henry thing' on his lap to sort, clearly a very serious occurrence, but because it had been so far impossible to ascertain exactly what had happened it had all taken second place, gone into limbo, which he kind of understood.

But he did know some things for certain.

Henry had been shot at.

Henry had been run off the road, tupped by another vehicle, a black one from the paint samples, with a damaged front light.

Henry had then been shot at from the road and somehow he had clambered or been thrown out of the Navara and despite his injuries, maybe spurred on by the primitive urge of self-preservation, he had scrambled away from the wreck, probably under fire, and taken refuge upstream behind a large rock.

Jake glanced at Henry. 'How the hell did you pull that off, mate?' he asked him out loud.

Jake believed that Dr Lott's appearance had saved Henry's life. Although the doctor had not seen anything, Henry's assailants must have seen or heard his approach, slapped a quick reverse in and managed to leave the scene. Jake, however, could not work out where they had gone; possibly off-road to escape.

He still had not been able to contact Lord Chalmers about Henry's visit that morning. It seemed the good lord had gone on an extended holiday, supposedly incognito on a yacht in the Indian Ocean and was uncontactable . . . another thing that did not sit easy with Jake. The only route to and from Brown Syke was via the road, so surely he would have seen the crashed car, or had he just ignored it, or had he left by plane from his little airstrip?

Jake shook his head with frustration. Too many things unanswered, but he was determined to get to the bottom of it all.

At least there was some good scientific evidence.

The empty shells by the roadside were all 9mm, and being analysed by the ballistics people at the lab in Huntingdon. He was waiting the result of forensics on the paint and glass samples from the Navara and those he'd found on the road and was hopeful he would find out what make and model of vehicle they were from.

Jake looked quickly at Henry.

Had he just moved?

Did his eyelids flutter?

Jake relaxed. Maybe not.

'I'll tell you what you can do,' Rik Dean said into the face of the man with no face – Jenkins, the mystery man from London. 'You can fuck right off. You clearly know who the murderer is and you want me to play your stupid games just so you don't end up with egg all over your pin-striped shoulders.'

'You should understand our position, which, as I have stressed previously, is one of national security,' Jenkins said blandly. He still had not been formally introduced to Rik, nor had the other mystery guy, Smith, who hovered around like a bodyguard. 'I am more than happy to furnish you with details . . . of a man . . . so you can reassure the general public that the offender has been identified and is being hunted down.' He paused. 'And when you catch him, we will have him back, thank you.'

Rik had two sheets of paper in his hand, containing details of a man called David Jones and a grainy passport-sized photograph in the top corner.

He knew he was looking at details, sparse ones at that, of an undercover alias, a legend, and that quite possibly the photograph wasn't even the correct one.

'I am not playing a game with the public or anyone else,' Rik said. He waved the papers in front of Jenkins, then screwed them up and threw them into a litter bin.

The three men were in the first-floor function room of the

Tawny Owl, the one in which Rik's marriage to Lisa had taken place only a few days earlier but felt much longer. In under an hour he was due to deliver a press conference at this location and various members of the media were beginning to arrive and set up.

The room had been arranged by Anna, Jake's wife, who had effectively taken over the day-to-day running of the pub for the time being, although how long that could continue was open to question. Not long, was the likely answer. There were rows of chairs and a table on the stage at the front of the room for Rik and the chief constable.

'You will not divulge anything you might have learned in the last few days,' Jenkins warned him.

'You mean about government-sponsored hit squads and mad assassins on the loose?'

Jenkins jerked his head. 'If you do' – he slipped a fat finger across his throat in a gesture that did not even register in its irony with him – 'your career is finito, and that's a promise.'

Rik glowered at him, then moved aside as a BBC news crew came through the door to set up their cameras.

'I'll tell you what I will do,' Rik said.

Jenkins waited.

'I will make no reference to you or this shit' – he pointed to the waste basket – 'and I'll tell the world that we have no idea who we are chasing, that fingerprint and DNA have not assisted, and that we will simply have to catch this brutal, dangerous offender by good old-fashioned detective work and when I hunt this man down, which I will, I will display him for all to see, and if that fucks you up, so be it.'

He resisted the temptation to flick Jenkins' nose.

Jake was eager to attend the press conference. He was replaced by Lisa at Henry's bedside. She looked as jaded as anyone and when she sat by the bed, immediately closed her eyes.

Jake headed up the motorway, joining the M6 at the Broughton interchange, heading north, coming off at junction 34 before veering off the A583 after the village of Caton and heading towards Kendleton. Unusually, and obviously because of the press conference, the narrow roads were much busier than normal.

He settled his not very quick Land Rover behind an equally sluggish TV truck, happy to chug along.

Suddenly two black Range Rovers appeared in his rear-view mirror, right up close to his back bumper and not backing off despite the police livery. They seemed to be occupied by the large, dark shapes of men.

The roads were twisty-turny but there was just one section where there was a decently long straight stretch just before the drop down into Kendleton, but because the road was narrow with quite deep drainage dykes on either side, few overtakes were ever attempted.

Not something that seemed to bother the drivers of the Range Rovers. Both veered out and with their offside wheels mounting the narrow grass verges and their horns sounding, they forced their way past Jake, then the TV truck, then they were gone.

'Gonna have words with you guys,' Jake said softly.

When he reached the village, the Tawny Owl car park was crammed with cop cars, media-liveried vehicles, trucks with satellite dishes on their roofs and a lot of people milling about, some reporters already speaking to camera.

The Range Rovers had been abandoned illegally on the grass verge outside the car park and one was parked at such a jaunty angle that other cars had to mount the kerb opposite to pass.

Jake parked further down the village in front of the butcher's shop.

He was immediately accosted by the butcher, Don Singleton, a good friend of Dr Lott, a Tawny Owl regular and friend of Henry and Alison. He supplied the pub with all its superb meat.

'Jake,' he called.

'Hiya, Don.'

The red-faced man, the epitome of a country butcher, came out of the shop wiping his hands on a blood-stained apron. 'You been t'see Henry?' Jake nodded. 'Anything?' the butcher asked hopefully. Jake shook his head sadly. 'You know, the whole village is devastated by all this. We really took Alison and Ginny, and then Henry to our hearts. They're part of the community. She didn't deserve this, she was a good person.'

'I know, Don, she was.' He patted the butcher on the shoulder, then walked towards the Owl, passing the two Range Rovers, wondering who they belonged to. Inside, folk were being directed up to the function room. Jake shouted across everyone's heads. 'Excuse me, people, I need to know who owns the black Range Rovers outside. They're causing an obstruction and I'm afraid if they aren't moved immediately, I'll tow them away.'

Two hard-faced men shouldered their way against the flow of people.

Jake eyed them.

Instantly he knew the type. Men who lived by violence. He could sense it in their movements and expressions.

'You the owners?' he asked.

'What the fuck d'you think you're playing at?' the first one said. He was muscled, but lithe, like a proper athlete.

'I'm just keeping the traffic flowing . . . doing my job, in other words. Busy day in town today.'

'Arsehole,' the man said. They split around Jake, going outside. He followed.

They went to their vehicles and though only one was really causing a problem, they moved further down the road.

'Thanks, guys, much appreciated,' Jake said as they re-entered the pub.

They eyed him disrespectfully but said nothing as they bypassed him. Jake watched them for a moment, then strolled down to the Range Rovers and called in the registration numbers for a PNC check.

The comms operator asked him to reconfirm the numbers which he did, then was told, 'Both vehicles blocked on PNC, Jake. You should phone me for details, I have a number you need to ring.'

'Roger,' Jake said. It wasn't totally unusual to check cars that were blocked – all police undercover cars were, as well as some military vehicles. But with what, admittedly little, Jake knew about some of the shady characters knocking about around this investigation like they had bad smells under their noses, maybe these guys were connected. He shrugged mentally: none of his business. But as he walked away, something on one of the cars caught his eye.

He stopped, took out his penknife and unfolded it.

By the time he had finished he just about managed to edge into the function room where the briefing was about to start.

Rik Dean was on stage sitting alongside the chief constable.

He adjusted the microphone in front of him. 'Thank you all for coming,' he began. 'I know this is off the beaten track and it may be inconvenient to you, but I felt that having a press conference out here would serve to tell you all exactly what the investigation of Alison Marsh and the abduction of her daughter, Ginny, means to this community . . . These events have torn a huge hole in the heart in this village . . .'

'My God, he's actually pretty good,' Jake said to himself. Rik looked tired but ultra-determined and Jake thought this enquiry was in pretty good hands. Rik seemed to have stepped up to the bar with this one.

FIFTEEN

The press briefing, including the many questions that followed, lasted almost an hour. The assembled media folk began to disperse.

Jake stood aside as they filtered out and watched for the drivers of the Range Rovers to leave. They had spent the briefing in the back corner of the room with the other two individuals Jake had seen knocking about before.

He followed them out as they shouldered their way through the crowd. When they emerged into sunlight, each slid on very cool-looking aviator-style sunglasses, hiding their eye, their identities.

'Gents,' he called.

Neither acknowledged him, but headed down the steps towards their cars. Jake hurried after them and caught up as they stopped for a chat amongst themselves.

'Gents,' he said.

This time they looked but did not speak.

'I need a few details, I'm afraid,' he said.

The one he had first spoken to, the one lithe and muscular, said, 'What do you mean, officer?'

'I need to see your driving licences or failing that I'll give you both a producer and you can take all your documents into a police station of your own choice within five days. Either way.' Jake smiled.

'Why?'

'Because you are the drivers of motor vehicles on a public road and under the Road Traffic Act I have the power to see and check such documents and I'm now exercising that power.' Jake kept smiling.

'I don't think so,' the man said.

'I do think so,' Jake continued pleasantly. 'And if you refuse to furnish your details I'll arrest you. Simple.'

'On what charge?'

'Oh, I thought I'd said. *Failing to provide details.* Did I not make myself clear?' Jake said. His tone of voice was beginning to lose its pleasant edge. 'Plus I think this vehicle' – he pointed to one of the Range Rovers – 'was involved in a serious road-traffic accident.'

'Utter cock,' the man said. 'What makes you say that?'

Jake was about to respond when he heard Rik Dean behind him say, 'Jake, what's going on here?'

Rik, plus his two shady mates, Jenkins and Smith, were approaching him.

'I'm just trying to elicit details of these men in relation to a car accident I'm dealing with, boss,' he said, arching his eyebrows. 'You know the one I mean . . . but they're being awkward.'

Jenkins said to Rik, 'Call off your bloodhound, Superintendent.'

'He's investigating a serious accident involving a retired police officer. I'm sure he's just doing his job.'

'His job does not include these men,' Jenkins said. 'Pull him off.'

Rik jerked his thumb at Jake, who physically backed off, confused.

Jenkins nodded at the two men, who climbed into the Range Rovers and started the engines, which growled like lions.

Jenkins nodded haughtily at Rik, then strutted away with Smith in tow.

Rik sidled up to the unhappy Jake. He was just as unhappy.

'Hope you don't mind me asking, boss, but what was that all about?'

'Spooks and assassins,' Rik said.

'The guy in the suit being the spook,' Jake guessed.

'And the other guy being the assassin,' Rik concluded. 'Secrets and lies, and perversion of justice, but don't get me started,' he muttered. 'And anyway, why were you talking to the Mitchell brothers?' he asked, making reference to a pair of roguish brothers from a TV soap opera.

'I think they were involved in Henry's so-called accident.'

'Clutching at straws?' Rik asked.

'No,' Jake said with certainty. 'If you've got a second . . .'

He beckoned Rik to accompany him to his Land Rover where he took something from the front seat.

'Couple of things.' Jake took out his mobile phone and opened the photo file. The last dozen pictures were of the two black Range Rovers, but predominantly one of them, the one with evidence of damage on the front bumper. He let Rik slide through these, then showed him what he had just taken from the front seat of his car. 'I took the photos and also took the liberty of taking paint samples from the front bumper. Black, of course, but also some flecks of white paint, the colour of Alison's Navara.'

He then handed Rik a clear, sealed evidence bag containing the shavings he'd pared off the car, black, white and undercoat.

'I'm no scientist, but I do know black paint was on the back of the Navara and on the road. I'll bet it matches. And not only that . . .' He reached back into the car and pulled out another evidence envelope containing some tiny cubes of broken glass. 'The front nearside fog lamp was broken. I took this sample from the Range Rover. There were bits of broken glass on the road where Henry went over the edge like this. Forensic will match it, I'm certain.'

'Shit,' Rik said.

'For certain it's the one that forced Henry off the road.'

'Have you checked it on PNC?'

'Yep – blocked.'

'Oh, what a surprise . . . What the hell had Henry got himself into?'

Jake shrugged. 'Dunno. I can only assume Lord Chalmers is involved somewhere along the line, but he's proving to be elusive, which is a sign itself. Look, boss,' he said plaintively, 'I don't know who those guys are but they're clearly a nasty bunch. They must know Henry is still alive – unwell, but alive – and if they do want him dead for some reason we haven't yet worked out, he's a bit of a sitting duck.'

'And talking of Henry, how was he?'

They reconvened at the Travelodge located on the M6 services south of Lancaster. The hotel was itself on the northbound side of the services, historically known as Forton Services, now renamed as Lancaster Services so travellers knew exactly where they were in the world. To access the hotel travelling south, they exited onto the southbound side, then drove across the motorway bridge.

They gathered in one of the small conference rooms.

Jenkins glowered at the men who had been driving the Range Rovers.

'Fucking idiots,' he blasted. 'Do not make the mistake of thinking the cops up here are hillbillies. They're professionals, supposedly just like you,' he said with contempt. 'And if we don't watch it, they'll have you.'

'Us, don't you mean?' one of them said. His name was Sandy Barnes.

'No, I mean *you*,' Jenkins retorted. 'You told me there were no witnesses.'

'We were pretty sure the guy was dead. We had to pull out because another car was coming.'

'Pretty sure? Don't guys like you ensure things like that?' He shook his head. 'Fucking mess. We've got a nutter on the loose, who, incidentally, we need to eliminate and there's another witness still alive on a completely different issue . . .'

'Who we need to eliminate,' volunteered the other man, Dave Beck.

'Not only that,' Jenkins said, 'we still haven't recovered what you went up there for in the first place!'

'We can't find the plane,' Barnes whined. 'We're sure it came down, it must have, we shot the fuck out of it, but those are fucking big moors for just a handful of us to search . . . someone'll find it.'

'We need to be the ones to find it,' Jenkins corrected him. 'Not some other random fuckwit.'

'I have an idea,' Smith ventured. He'd been silent up to this point. They looked at him. 'I know we've had a few guys helping out with the searches for Stiletto, but why don't we organize a search-and-find operation of our own? Get our own resources in, scramble people and control it . . . no friggin' mountain-rescue people. Just us and do it under the guise of a training exercise. I can mobilize fifty men in two days.'

'Two days! Fuck me,' Jenkins said. 'The plane will be broken up and sold for scrap by that time.' He relented. 'OK, OK, it's a plan.'

'There's an exercise in the Beacons now. I'll just relocate it.'

'Do it,' Jenkins said and considered the two other men. 'And in the meantime, cover your tracks and kill that fucker in the hospital bed. That can't be too hard, can it? You walk in, put two bullets in his brain and then walk out. Hey presto! Then at least that side of it is locked down.'

Karl Donaldson sat by Henry Christie's bedside, having taken over the reins from Lisa. It was late in the day.

He had his laptop on his knee, trying to catch up with some of his own work as much as he could. Although his bosses had given him permission to help out, they were now getting twitchy, not least because a new terror cell had been identified in Brussels and they wanted him to start delving into possible US connections and threats. He had stalled and they understood, but he also understood his work was elsewhere, even if his heart and soul were up in Lancashire at the moment.

At least he could do some of his work via his laptop, just enough to appease the powers that be for at least another day.

Donaldson had enjoyed his catch-up with Henry on Rik Dean's wedding day, during which he and the ex-detective had a rare heart-to-heart about the future and what it held for them both. For Henry it was with Alison and Ginny and the Tawny Owl, and of course his two daughters, Jenny and Leanne, both of whom led very independent lives now. Henry hadn't left them behind and he confessed that being apart from them was very tough for him, but that he thought about them all the time and had learned to use Skype. Both understood he had to push on with his life now that Kate had gone.

In turn Donaldson had told Henry about his possible plans to relocate back to the US. He'd had a good innings as a legal attaché in London and loved it, but staff were always being trimmed and he thought he might be better off back in the States. It meant uprooting his family. Karen was up for it, but the children less so. They were in their teens and had a lot of friends they didn't want to leave.

It had been a good chat with an old friend and had been interrupted by Rik Dean, who had also now become an old pal. The three of them had been involved on a few cases over the years.

Donaldson accessed the FBI database via a special satellite link and clicked his way through a series of firewalls before arriving at his own desktop.

Discreetly he slightly adjusted the cordless, almost invisible earpiece tucked into his left ear.

Then he clicked the transmission button connected to the tiny microphone on his collar, acknowledging a contact call.

He was ready.

Rik Dean looked at the floor plan of Royal Preston Hospital and counted the number of green-arrowed entrance signs. He made it eighteen. Eighteen official ways in and out of a vast complex. Far too many to cover effectively.

The critical-care unit, where Henry had been admitted, was on the corridor known as Grey Street, on the lower ground floor, and could be accessed easily by anyone who knew the hospital layout and, like Rik, had a map he had downloaded from the internet.

Therefore sixteen entrances had not been covered, just the one off the car park outside the Rosemere Cancer Centre, which was further down the corridor from the CCU. The main entrance was also being covered, and that was it. All other resources were inconspicuously deployed in strategic positions close to the CCU itself.

Rik was sitting in the rear of a plain operations van the size of a personnel carrier but without windows and kitted out with an array of communications technology to run ops 'on plot'. The van was parked at the far end of the car park of Booths Supermarket opposite the hospital on Sharoe Green Lane.

Rik was with a firearms inspector, who was hands-on running the op, as well as Jake Niven.

Eight authorized firearms officers were deployed inside the hospital, secreted in various rooms but all kitted out in their uniforms consisting of dark-blue overalls, boots, ballistic vests and caps, all armed with H&K machine pistols and Glock hand-guns as well as tasers and the usual other accoutrements. There was no way Rik wanted any confusion about this. If they ended up challenging anybody, that person or persons had to know 100 per cent they were being confronted by an armed police officer who would shoot if necessary. The days of plain-clothed firearms officers were largely consigned to the past.

The comms van had four computer monitors being closely watched by a trained firearms support staff member. They were linked into the CCTV system within the hospital and each screen was split into four frames giving various views of car parks and hospital corridors, in particular, Grey Street.

Everything that was being seen or listened to was also being transmitted to the contact centre at headquarters control room, where the deputy chief constable was overseeing this operation – Gold Command – which he had also authorized.

Normally it would have required total concentration to watch all the images but as it was almost midnight the hospital was quiet, the only busy part being the emergency department which, as ever, was buzzing. Most corridors were deserted, just an occasional nurse walking along.

'This is just a one-off,' Rik said.

'I know, boss,' Jake Niven replied.

The operation had been his brainchild. Putting himself into the shoes of Henry's would-be killer, Rik supposed that if he were them and there was still a chance of killing Henry (for whatever reason that might be), he would go for it sooner rather than later. Henry was connected to a lot of tubes and wires, hadn't regained consciousness to finger them, and presented an easy target, not least because he couldn't move.

That was Jake's thinking.

'And if we catch them in the act, then they've got no wriggle room,' he said, 'and that way we start to find out why Henry is a target, unravel it all.'

Rik had gone for it, as had the deputy chief.

But – just as a one-off.

Running an armed police operation in a hospital was very contentious and hazardous and the police were nervous about it.

'Think they'll come?' Rik asked.

'Certain,' Jake said.

'Why so confident?'

'Because I saw it in their eyes.'

'Anything?'

It was an hour later and so far there had been nothing suspicious on the move. The question was asked by Jake of the guy monitoring the screens and radio channel. Jake already knew the answer.

'No,' the man replied. Jake had learned his first name was Trevor.

Jake leaned over his shoulder, scanned the screens.

'Getting late,' Rik Dean said and stretched wearily. He'd been sitting cramped up in a chair with his laptop on his knee, putting together a completely new investigative strategy – again. There was so much going on it was almost blowing his mind, not least the refusal of the man from the ministry to cough up details of the killer.

But Rik was determined to crush eggs into his face, whatever his name was.

And stick two fingers up the backside of national security.

He would relentlessly hunt the man down and then, maybe, go away on honeymoon.

'I'm off for a stroll,' Jake announced. 'Through the hospital.'

'Got your PR?' Rik asked.

'Yep.'

Jake slipped out of the rear doors and headed towards the hospital, crossing the road, then the main hospital car park, and entered the complex, not really having a plan, but trying to put himself into the minds of the men who might want to kill Henry Christie.

If they were going to come, how would they achieve it?

They would guess or know that Henry was likely to have some sort of guard and a full-on approach might not be the best option, but once they reached Henry's room it would be a different matter: the gloves would come off and they would blast away to their hearts' content.

So they would want to get in unnoticed, do the job, then get out as quickly as possible.

Jake took his downloaded copy of the RPH floorplan from his back jeans pocket as he stood in the main reception foyer. The corridor directly ahead, Blue Street, led to various departments and to the lifts or stairs which either went up to the general medical wards or down to the CCU and the Rosemere Centre.

To his right, Red Street, the corridor led to the emergency department.

Jake sighed.

If it was him . . . he would certainly want to be in and out as quickly as possible, and just on the off-chance of being blown out on the way in, he would want to be as incognito as possible – which did not include wearing the clothes he had seen the guys in before, the windcheaters and jeans.

He would want some form of camouflage.

'Anything?' he asked over his PR.

'Negative,' Trevor replied.

'Roger. Anything from anyone?'

He received negative responses.

They weren't going to come, he thought.

He set off along Blue Street, walking past the Day Care Unit, then Medical Illustration, passing through the crossroads with Green Street and ending up where the corridor widened and the lifts and stairs were located.

Nothing remotely suspicious.

It would be a quick job, he thought again.

In, do, out.

He'd already decided that.

Suddenly he felt naked without a gun. He had spent a lot of years as an authorized firearms officer on the response vehicle, armed every working day, until it had all gone wrong in such a dramatic fashion: the stupid affair with a colleague, the robbery in the jeweller's Anna got caught up in, and him having to shoot someone, take a life, and also lose his best friend who was gunned down in the same horrific incident. Henry Christie had saved his life and his marriage and those days were still with Jake many months later. He wondered if he would ever shake them off.

It meant he was no longer a firearms officer, and never would be again, but he did miss the feel of a gun and to have one at his waist just now would have been like a dummy with a baby. Reassuring.

He took the stairs down one level, lower ground floor, Grey Street. The cancer centre was at the far end, but before that was the CT scanner unit and the CCU, plus the reception area for the operating theatres on this level.

He looked along the corridor. All clear.

'Anything?' he asked again over the PR. 'Negative, PC Niven,' Trevor replied tersely.

'And fuck you, Trev,' Jake thought.

Beside him, the lift doors opened.

Jake stood to one side as two green-coated porters manoeuvred a trolley with a patient on board, linked to a drip.

They crashed the contraption a couple of times against the doors, but managed to straighten it up and push it towards theatre reception, the entrance to which was almost opposite the CCU.

Jake watched, uninterested – until two things clicked into place.

The porters were not very skilled at controlling the trolley.

Neither man had looked directly at Jake.

But then one peeked over his shoulder at the same time as Jake glanced into the lift from which they had just emerged and saw two crumpled bodies just in the second before the doors clamped shut.

'They're here,' Jake said coolly over his PR. 'Grey Street, approaching CCU, masquerading as hospital porters dressed in green, shoving a trolley.' He said that as he started to run and pick up pace.

The two men reacted.

The one actually pushing the trolley heaved it away from himself, sending it careening down the corridor, bouncing off the walls. He spun to Jake at the same time who saw the pistol in his right hand and also recognized him as the driver of the damaged Range Rover.

Jake threw himself to one side as the gun fired.

The other guy zig-zagged across the width of the corridor into the CCU as the one who had fired at Jake came back for him, gun held in both hands, moving quickly towards Jake in a combat stance.

From the CCU, Jake heard shooting.

'Shots fired,' he said into his PR.

The airwaves then became a rush of voices.

And the man with the gun came on remorselessly for Jake.

That was until two firearms officers stepped out from theatre reception, weapons drawn and challenged him from behind.

'Armed police, drop your weapon,' one shouted clearly.

Jake pressed himself against the wall, saw the look on the man's face, that delicious look of defeat as the Glock in his hand clattered to the floor and his hands rose in a gesture of submission. The AFOs came up cautiously, still warning him, still meaning it.

Jake gave the man the thumbs up and a victorious, 'Ha!' as he sprinted past him towards the CCU.

The shots he'd heard in there worried him.

He spun into the room to find the second guy pinned to the floor by Karl Donaldson, his weapon having been kicked away by one of the pair of AFOs who had been waiting there whilst the other one kept his weapon aimed steadily at the guy's head while Donaldson easily twisted his arms up behind his back, laid one wrist across the other and knelt on them before asking the AFO for handcuffs.

'The shots?' Jake asked.

Donaldson pointed to the bed. 'He managed to fire three before we grounded him,' he admitted.

Jake stepped over the prostrate man and went to the bed, slowly pulling back the covers. 'Good job we moved Henry and put this dummy in his place,' he said.

Donaldson eased himself to his feet and remarked, 'I'd hardly noticed the difference.'

*   *   *

Lisa Dean, née Christie, Henry's younger sister, now wife of Detective Superintendent Rik Dean, took the phone call from her husband. Her whole body sagged at the news, then she ended the call.

She re-entered the private room at Fulwood Hall Hospital and sat down next to Henry's bed, looking at her brother and reached for his hand.

'They would've got you, Henry,' she said, then reached for her paperback, a romantic novel she had planned to take on honeymoon to read by the pool. She wondered when that would happen.

She heard a cough and looked at Henry.

A kind of throaty noise from the back of his throat.

Did his eyes flutter?

She sat forwards. 'Henry?'

His eyes did open. They seemed sightless, unfocused. He blinked a few times then said croakily, 'Did they find the plane?' and closed his eyes again.

SIXTEEN

From complete blackness, just a hole that could have been deep space, with occasional terrifying flashes like the sun exploding, Henry surfaced very slowly into a new undersea whorl of hazy images, blurred lines and faces with distorted mouths out of which indistinguishable, meaningless noises emanated that meant absolutely nothing to his battered brain.

But he did understand the excruciating pain that seared around the perimeter of his cranium like one of those motorcycle daredevils in a circus, a pain that decelerated when, although he did not know this, morphine was pumped into his arm.

There were four days like this in which he grasped nothing at first, wasn't even sure if he was a human being, or what a human being even was; like trudging through a mangrove swamp with an alligator swimming alongside him with hungry eyes until, after one very long night of dreamless sleep, he awoke at eight a.m. and sat up under his own steam and said to a nurse,

'Scrambled egg on toast would be nice and an Americano, if at all possible.'

She smiled delightedly, plumped up his pillows, adjusted his bed and said, 'Coming right up, sir.'

He leaned back and emptied his bladder via the tube into a bag by his bedside and waited to be fed.

When the nurse returned with a tray of hot food as requested and placed it on the adjustable table, he said, 'Can you tell my wife-to-be I'll see her now?'

He saw the flinch of uncertainty on her face before she recovered and said, 'I'll see what I can do.'

He wolfed down the food, noting the Police and Community Support Officer standing outside the door to his private room, but could not quite get his swollen head around why that person was there or even why he himself was.

There was a vague memory of cars and gunfire but nothing concrete – other than he had got a very sore head and very sore right arm, neither of which made any sense.

A consultant turned up at nine-thirty a.m., sat Henry upright, probed around his head – *yes, that fucking hurt* – neck, shoulder and arm with a thick finger, muttered, nodded, then stood back.

'Can I go home?' Henry asked.

'Hardly.'

'What the hell's happened to me?'

'Essentially you were involved in a very serious road-traffic accident. The car you were driving overturned and you suffered a fractured skull, which you still have, although it is repairing nicely, and other injuries.'

Henry nodded gingerly. 'Essentially?' he enquired.

'Yes, essentially . . . now if you'll excuse me . . .'

'Oh, before you go, has my fiancée been told I'm back in the land of the living?'

'I'll check and see where we're up to on that score,' he said. Henry saw the same flinch flit cross the man's face as he'd seen on the nurse's, who then appeared by magic.

'Bed bath,' she announced.

'Nah,' he said, although severely tempted because she was a very pretty lady. 'I'd like to get up for a shower, if that's OK?'

'I'm sure it is.'

'Where am I, by the way?'

She told him.

'Oh, I'm impressed. I don't recall taking out private health care.'

The journey to the shower felt about the equivalent of a three-mile run and Henry was exhausted by the time he sat down in it but revelled in the sensation of hot water cascading over him, cleansing out the grit.

The nurse assisted him to towel off, then he told her he would shave himself.

He looked in the mirror and for a few moments, reeled in the shock of his reflection and said, 'Fuck me.' Then he shaved the field of stubble carefully away, making him wonder how long he had been here.

Lots of questions, not many answers, he thought.

His head was close-shaven and looked a complete mess, a criss-cross of cuts and abrasions, some stitching and still swollen and puffy, particularly around his right ear. He twisted to see if he could inspect his right arm, but it hurt his head to look down, and he didn't like what he saw anyway.

'If that's not a bullet wound,' he said to himself, 'I'll show my arse in ward 1.'

The shower room door opened and the nurse poked her head through. 'I heard voices.'

'So did I,' Henry said, 'so did I.'

'Well, I'm definitely not in heaven,' Henry said as he opened his eyes and saw Rik Dean sitting at his bedside with Karl Donaldson standing behind him. Rik had strange silvery burn marks on his face that puzzled Henry but not enough to make him be bothered to ask. He had fallen asleep after the shower and now, two hours later, it was quite hard to wake up again. 'You two look like the devil's disciples. Why the long faces? I have no idea why I'm here, but I'm alive, aren't I? That's got to be a plus, and I know who you are, so another plus.'

Neither man smiled.

'And I'm not paralysed, so what gives, as they say? And where the hell is my kept woman?'

*   *   *

It was the eyes, the expression on his face, that most affected Rik and Donaldson. The slow registering of facts, of the situation. The bereft look of utter loss and desolation, as though something inside him was emptying him into a vacuum of nothingness.

Rik began by saying, 'What exactly do you remember?'

He did not wish just to dump it all on Henry, but by the same token did not want to tell him anything other than the truth because that would be a path to confusion and misunderstanding, possibly false hope. But to begin, he had to know where Henry's mind was up to.

When the moment came, he knew he would have to be forthright and honest, then take it from there.

'I remember the murders,' Henry said, trying to think coherently.

'Oh, right, that's good,' Rik said, at which point Donaldson laid a hand on Rik's shoulders to shut him up and said, 'Which murders?'

'Which murders? Why, how many have there been?' Henry asked.

'Which ones are you on about?' Donaldson asked.

'One of Lord Chalmers' security guards and then Chalmers himself.'

Rik and Donaldson exchanged glances.

'You sure about this?' Rik asked. 'We don't know any of this – but we haven't been able to contact Chalmers anyway.'

'Because he's dead,' Henry said. 'So is one of his security guards and maybe his wife, because if that plane didn't crash, I'm a monkey's uncle.'

'What plane?' Rik and Donaldson said in unison.

'The one his wife was about to land in, but pulled up at the last moment and the killers strafed it as it went over their heads, just after they'd shot and killed Chalmers.'

'Which guys are these?'

'Two tough-looking army-like guys, turned up in black Range Rovers.'

Once more, Rik and Donaldson looked at each other.

'Could you ID these guys?'

Henry nodded. 'I'd give it a good go. Plus they were in cahoots with one of Chalmers' security guys. He's the one who put a bullet in the other security guy's head.'

Rik exhaled and said, 'Two guys, black Range Rovers?'

'Yep.'

'Then what?'

Henry pouted. 'Then nothing. Woke up in this place and that's all I know. Presumably some gaps in there?'

'Definitely gaps,' Rik agreed.

The detective superintendent steadied himself, got all his words into order and began to fill in those gaps for Henry. As he spoke, Donaldson edged around and perched on the side of the bed next to Henry, watching his old friend's face as those gaps became a story that reached a horrific conclusion.

The two men watched Henry's face as Rik finished talking and Henry digested the information in his already scrambled brain. He leaned back on his pillows and closed his eyes.

'This is true?' he said eventually, opening his eyes.

'I'm sorry, Henry, it is,' Rik said.

'Alison is dead and Ginny has been kidnapped and could well be dead also?' he said, trying to make sense of it.

His eyes closed tight again. A tear formed in the corner of both.

'Yes,' Rik said, knowing he had to make certain Henry understood it, that there was no mistake to be made.

Henry opened his eyes. 'OK, OK, can you leave me now?'

'Where is she?'

They were back with Henry, two hours later, and if it was possible, he looked even worse than before.

'Public mortuary, Royal Preston Hospital,' Rik told him.

'I want to see her.'

Donaldson's hand was under Henry's arm, helping him remain upright as three of them walked from Rik's car into the hospital entrance on East Drive, the one closest to the mortuary.

Alison's body was already laid out in the viewing room.

A muslin sheet covered the whole of her body and head.

A mortuary technician waited until Henry, flanked by Rik and Donaldson, looked at him and nodded. The technician reached for the corner of the sheet, but then Henry said, 'No.'

The man stopped.

'Can I do this?' Henry asked.

The MT nodded. 'Of course you can.'

'Thank you,' Henry said simply.

Donaldson removed his hand from Henry's left bicep. Henry reached out and took hold of the top corner of the thin sheet and began to peel it slowly back to reveal Alison's head and face. He folded it carefully across her shoulders and could see the new sewn-up, dreadful wound that had been inflicted on her neck. Her skin had a blue tinge to it, that of death. Henry had seen it on many corpses.

He had seen it on Kate.

Now he was seeing it on Alison.

He looked at her for a very long time, but said nothing aloud. He was going to have a private conversation with her in his own time and it would not be something anyone else would hear.

'Is this Alison Marsh?' Rik Dean said, fulfilling the requirements of proving an identity. 'She has no close family. You are it, Henry.'

'I can confirm this is my fiancée, Alison Marsh.'

Henry folded the sheet back across her face.

Karl Donaldson caught him as his knees buckled.

Henry's head thumped, his ears hissed, noises that seemed would never go away. They were there when he was awake and up, and when he lay down and closed his eyes to try to sleep, something he could rarely achieve. His skull pounded and hurt, as did every other part of his body.

He was unsure how he survived the following fortnight, which flashed by in a continuous series of scenes over which he seemed to have no control.

Things just happened.

He went along with them, still not truly understanding everything, like he was finding his way through a boggy minefield, doing things, saying things, saying yes or no to things, even though all those things seemed to be disconnected, unreal, yet also very connected and frighteningly real.

His mind was everywhere and nowhere.

At one point, having eventually been discharged from hospital and finding himself staying with Rik and Lisa in their new house in Blackpool, Rik whisked him off to Preston police station, to the identity parade suite where he was placed in front of a one-way mirror and asked if he could identify the men who had shot and murdered Lord Chalmers.

There were two parades.

Each time Henry picked one man from the line-ups. He was sure they were the ones, and also presumably the same guys who had then pursued him and forced him off the road – but he wasn't too positive about that bit because his stubborn memory refused to tell him anything beyond the murder of Chalmers and the strafing of the light aeroplane.

Occasionally there were flashes, nothing else.

Jake Niven was not given to blasphemy but when he saw the horrific scenes in the orangery at the back of Lord Chalmers' country house, his stomach immediately churned and he did say, 'Oh my effin' Lord.'

The bodies of Chalmers and his loyal security guard had been devoured by the two ravenous Dobermanns, torn apart as they grew hungry and desperate, having been left to roam the house, quickly reverting to wild dogs. The two bodies, it was assumed, had been moved from where they had been killed and then left for the dogs.

They had been ripped open like something from a horror movie, but by the time Jake and his colleagues forced an entry into the estate, then the house, there was very little left. Flesh had been eaten, bones had been gnawed and marrow licked out. There were the remnants of two rib cages, two skulls (empty, brains eaten) and thigh bones.

The stench was atrocious, death coupled with dog shit and dog vomit and also the bodily reek of the dogs themselves which had fought each other savagely and caused serious injuries to each other which became infected, smelly and gangrenous.

Their poor condition, however, did not prevent them from being ferocious and attacking the police, but having been fore-warned about the possibility of vicious dogs, dog-handlers wearing body armour and carrying dog-catching equipment had been pushed first through the door. A vet armed with a tranquilizer gun was also on hand.

Cornered and eventually caught on two heavy-duty catch poles, the dogs were dragged squirming and squealing, still fighting like devils, and placed in the rear of a dog van with two cages.

Only then did Jake and the others enter to find the flesh-strewn orangery.

Jake had left it to the others and retreated outside. He walked towards the airstrip where, according to Henry's account, Chalmers had stood on the runway and prevented a small plane from landing, but which was then shot at.

Henry had obviously been right about Chalmers and the security guard.

He was probably right about the aircraft, too.

The only problem being there was no record of any flight plans for such an aircraft on the day in question. Not that systems were infallible, planes did take off without submitting times and routes to the authorities. Jake had checked with the Civil Aviation Authority – no record – and also a few internet flight-tracking sites such as Flight Radar, which also had no records of such a flight.

Nor had any plane yet been found crashed on the moors.

Jake walked the full length of the runway, which had not had the grass mowed for a while and was fast becoming a meadow. When he got to the far end, he turned and walked back, imagining he was bringing a light plane in to land, even though he could not fly. He visualized the flight path in his mind's eye, coming in on final approach between the fells, just a dot in the distance at first, quickly growing as it got closer. Then, message received from the frantically waving Chalmers, pull up, don't land, and the pilot doing that at the last moment and then its belly being shot at.

Had the pilot been hit and wounded?

If so, how far had the plane gone?

Jake looked at the moors. There was an awful lot of space for a plane to ditch in and if it had it would eventually be found, but it was possible it could lie undetected for weeks, possibly even years, depending on where and how it came down.

If it had veered sideways into a tight, deep ravine, it could be a very long time before it was discovered.

Jake's mobile rang. He answered it, saying his name, though the unidentified caller had still asked, 'PC Niven?'

'Speaking. Can I help?' Jake was still working out trajectories as he spun around and looked at the hills.

It was a man's voice, a southern accent. 'I can't give you my name.'

'OK, but what can I do for you?'

'I know you spoke to the manager of Hyde Heath aerodrome yesterday.'

Jake suddenly concentrated. 'Yeah, that's right.' Rik had tasked him to find out more about the plane. He'd done some internet digging and found a photo of Lord and Lady Chalmers on the pages of some high-society journal, standing in front of a light plane on an airfield just outside London. There was a registration number on the plane, but Jake hadn't got very far with that, so he'd decided to phone the airfield in the picture just on the off-chance someone might know something, anything. He had spoken to a man called Dobson who categorically stated the plane had not ever, never, been on the airfield since that photo had been snapped. Neither did he know where it was now kept or flown from, had not seen Chalmers or his wife for years and it definitely DID NOT take off from the airfield at Hyde Heath on the day Rik asked about. He was blunt, aggressive and defensive, nervous, maybe, but Jake couldn't do much more than accept his word even if he didn't believe him.

'I overheard your conversation,' the man on the phone said. 'Well, Dobson's side of it.'

'OK,' Jake said, now interested.

'Look, mate, I don't know what's going on but I've been told to keep my mouth shut, or else.'

'OK, but who are you?' Jake asked.

'You don't need to know, but I can tell you that Lady Chalmers took off from Hyde Heath on the morning you're interested in.'

'How do you know?'

'I saw her. I saw her take a briefcase from a bloke in an Aston Martin, then take off.'

The call ended abruptly. Jake looked at his phone and thought, 'Aston Martin?'

SEVENTEEN

Rik looked across the expanse of the highly polished desk at the chief constable, having once more been summoned to his office. He hadn't had far to travel this time because he had been in his own office (previously Henry Christie's) over at the FMIT building, once an accommodation block for students at the training centre.

The chief was busy writing and had gestured for Rik to enter and sit down without even looking up.

Rik waited patiently, fingers interlocked, thumbs rotating, hating this petty rudeness.

Eventually the chief looked up and set down his bulbous fountain pen. He removed his glasses and rubbed his eyes. It had been a long day and was now eight p.m.

Rik wanted to get home.

Henry was still staying with him and Lisa and the day after would be Alison's funeral.

'Where are we up to?' the chief asked.

'Sorry, sir?'

'The shenanigans.'

'Enquiries are on-going.'

'What the fuck is that supposed to mean? Do not be cheeky with me.'

'Sorry, sir. OK, the murderer of Alison Marsh and the kidnapper and possible murderer of her daughter Ginny is still at large. We believe him to be one and the same person and we are trying desperately to identify him by our own means. Obviously this process could be speeded up if MI5 or SIS, or whoever they are, actually told us who this person is instead of playing games with us.' Rik paused, tried to get a grip on his rising fury. 'But I will identify and catch this man.

'Two men have been arrested for attempting to murder Henry Christie, who has since identified them as the murderers of Lord Chalmers, whose body was found at his house with his dead security guard, both having been eaten by his dogs, since destroyed, sadly. We have yet to trace Lady Chalmers but we believe she could be in a light plane that could have crashed in the Forest of Bowland. Search parties will be out again tomorrow, although I have heard that the army, the SAS no less, are running an operation on the moors, but I have no details of this. I do not know why Chalmers was murdered, but he was – by the men who tried to kill Henry in hospital.'

'Who were arrested during an armed operation of which I was not aware?'

'Yes, sir, but the deputy was.'

'Mmm,' he said dubiously, clearly unhappy about that. 'Anyway, how is Henry?'

'Not good.'

'Physically?'

'Recovering.'

'Mentally?'

'Struggling at the moment. He has lost everything.'

The chief looked past Rik's shoulder through the big window overlooking the helipad and sports pitches at the front of headquarters.

'So he's not a great witness?'

Rik Dean's insides suddenly became very chilly.

'He's a very good witness, actually.'

'Emotional, injured, not thinking straight . . . doesn't sound good to me,' the chief said. 'Any half-decent defence barrister would tear him to shreds, add that to R v. Turnbull with regards to identification.'

He was referring to a famous stated case which laid out everything that should be considered in relation to the visual identification of a suspect.

'I've covered it,' Rik said. It was basic stuff.

'He'll get shredded,' the chief said again. 'I've already heard the CPS is unhappy about it.'

'From who?'

'The CPS.'

'Look, boss, I don't know what's going on here and I don't think I want to, but I've got two killers in custody and I ain't letting them go.'

'Insufficient evidence. Bail them.'

'We don't even know for sure who they are yet. We can't bail someone we don't know.'

'Cut them loose, then.' The chief readjusted his glasses. 'Say bye bye to them without bail.'

'National security?' Rik asked.

'You got it in one.'

Rik stared at the man. 'How can that possibly be?'

'Just is. Release them and they will never cross your path again. We'll keep the investigation up and running for a decent length of time, then we'll pull the plug. Sometimes it happens,' the chief said off Rik's horrified expression. 'Sometimes we don't get a result. Play this as some kind of gangland killing, you know the score.'

'But it's not a gangland killing, is it? It's state-sanctioned murder as far as I can see.'

'Just do it.' This time the chief removed his spectacles. 'I don't like it either. Keep looking for the guy who killed Henry's fiancée and if you apprehend him, then he will be the person whose details you were given in that undercover legend, a loner, a loser, a pervert, a fantasist, a sad man acting alone.'

'But not who he actually is . . . a state assassin gone to the dark side of mental health.'

'Just do it, Superintendent. End of . . .'

Because of the difficulties in keeping the Tawny Owl open without Henry or Alison's presence, Rik and Donaldson, with Henry's consent, decided to close it down, hopefully temporarily, though that very much depended on Henry.

However, Alison's funeral procession began from the front door of the pub with her flower-festooned hearse and Henry, Rik, Lisa, Donaldson and Karen in the following car.

It seemed as though the whole village had turned out to pay their respects.

Henry sat numbly in the rear of the stretched limousine, staring at the head of the driver and beyond to the black-suited funeral director in the road, who, when the procession was ready, began to lead the funeral on foot to the edge of the village where he got into the hearse.

It was a slow journey to the crematorium in Lancaster.

*   *   *

Still in his funeral suit, but ripping open the shirt collar and discarding his tie, Henry slammed the front door of the Tawny Owl and walked through to the deserted bar area where he stood for a few minutes and turned in a circle to look around before going into the owner's accommodation area, having to tap in the four-digit entry code on the keypad next to the door that had also been used by the man who had killed Alison.

Ironically, Henry realized, the number had not yet been changed.

The living area was also deserted, exactly as it was when he had set out to see Lord Chalmers. This was the first time he had properly been back since being discharged from hospital. He had returned once with Lisa to get some changes of clothing, but had sat in her car, afraid to step inside.

Now he was back, with no idea of what the future would hold for him.

He had been kept at arm's length from the police investigation into Alison's death, Ginny's abduction, the Chalmers murder and also into the incidents in which he was personally involved, much of which he could still not recall anyway.

But it didn't change a thing.

Even if he could have recalled every detail, he would still be without Alison, still be wondering if Ginny was dead or alive.

He was alone.

He had good friends, good relatives – his daughters had been incredible, Lisa, amazingly, had been a rock – but that still did not stop him from being alone.

He understood the police stance on things. He would have done the same. There was nothing worse than pesky relatives. They had to be fed just enough to keep them happy, and that is what Rik was doing with him, but the other thing was that he knew Rik too well.

He could tell when he was holding something back.

Supposedly there was a name for the suspect (not shared), who was some kind of ex-military nut who had locked on to Alison and Ginny by pure chance. Yet when Rik was telling Henry this, he could tell there was more – but he had to accept that Rik was telling him all he could under the circumstances.

It was a balancing act an SIO frequently had to manage. Henry got that.

In respect of Lord Chalmers' murder and Henry's attempted murder, Rik was also reticent, talking about insufficient evidence, R v. Turnbull (which Henry knew backwards), a possible procedural hiccup in regards to the identity parades which might make them invalid. Rik did make vague allusions to Henry's delicate mental state in all this and that the CPS was looking very closely at it.

Henry could not understand what was meant by all this but he knew the accuracy of his evidence was in question; even more so when an SAS training unit on the fells found and recovered the remains of Lord Chalmers' plane and the body of Lady Chalmers. It seemed that human error was the reason for the crash and there was no evidence of shots having been fired at it as Henry had claimed, and Lady Chalmers had died from injuries sustained in the crash.

All things Henry had to accept.

That he thought he had seen something he hadn't. That his recollection of events was, at best, rubbish.

He went into the kitchen, found a clean mug, then came back out into the bar and spent some time cleaning his beloved coffee machine, refilling it with fresh beans, making a large Americano which he took outside then sat on the steps, looking out across the village green, as he had done on so many other occasions.

The coffee was good.

Alison had laughed at him taking a course as a barista, but she had eaten and drunk her words.

The cost of the course and the fancy machine was money well spent. He had become an expert 'grinder of the bean' as she often called him.

He smiled at the thought.

There was nothing special about Alison, other than she was an extraordinary person who had begun a new life in this village after the death of her husband. She had taken Ginny under her wing, never thought of deserting her, and both had started a new chapter in their lives.

And then Henry had appeared on the scene and entered this life, became a part of it.

His mouth tightened.

He took a sip of the coffee.

'Fuck,' he said.

Then his eyes caught a movement on the edge of the trees. The old red-deer stag Henry had christened 'Horace'. He was staring haughtily across at Henry, then with a condescending shake of the head, he turned and plunged into the woods.

'Even you came,' Henry said, raising his mug to the beast, to Alison, to Ginny. 'Cheers to you all.' He pushed himself up and went back into the pub, locking the doors behind him.

He walked through, room by room, inhaling the aroma of each space.

The private area, his and Alison's bedroom where he could smell Alison's perfume still; then Ginny's bedroom, picking up one of her hairbrushes and putting it back down. Then through the pub, the kitchens, the bars, dining room, and upstairs to the bedrooms and the function room used most recently for a press conference, still arranged as it was.

Henry stood on the low stage and went behind the table where Rik had addressed the media.

Even the waste bin was still there with some papers crumpled up in it.

Henry glanced in it, then reached down and picked the papers out, unscrewed and flattened them out.

At first he read with incomprehension, not sure what he was reading initially.

There was a grainy passport-sized photograph of a man's face in the top right-hand corner of the front sheet. Then just a list of straightforward details: name, date and place of birth, details of bank accounts, a national insurance number, details of a Nectar card even. Name of schools attended, qualifications attended, a list of dead-end menial jobs with big companies and some vague military details.

'An ex-military nut?' Henry thought.

He folded the papers neatly and slid them into his jacket pocket, then continued his walkabout going across into the new annexe.

'So how much am I going to get for you when I sell up?' he asked the building, because at that moment, all he wanted to do was get rid of it and run.

He needed another coffee, which he made with care, wondering if a career at Costa or Starbucks was on the cards as the coffee dripped through into the mug. 'Or maybe not,' he thought.

Once more he took it outside, sat on the steps.

His head was truly hurting now. He had been told he might have headaches for the rest of his life. Well, he'd thought, so be it.

Then he frowned, remembered a moment, a fleeting image, then it was gone.

Not so much a moment, but a look.

A look on Alison's face.

Then it dawned on Henry what it meant.

He took out the two sheets of paper he had found in the waste bin and placed his coffee on the wall.

What was the significance of this, he wondered.

'Henry?'

He raised his head and saw Jake Niven at the bottom of the steps, not having noticed him approach. Like Henry, Jake was still in his funeral suit, having attended with Anna and their two children.

'Jake,' Henry said.

'How you doing?'

Henry had to smile. 'Brilliant.'

'Thought so. Any of that coffee left?'

'Machine's on,' Henry gestured. 'You've seen me do it enough times. Help yourself.'

Jake was back five minutes later, mug in hand. He sat next to Henry and sipped the coffee.

'Don't say sorry again,' Henry warned him. 'Or it was a nice service.'

'I won't,' Jake promised. 'But, fuck!'

'Yeah,' Henry said, 'but fuck.'

Jake paused awkwardly, then said, 'I need to tell you something, Henry. You won't like it, but I suppose it's academic now.'

'Alison was having an affair with Dr Lott?'

'Well, obviously that as well, yeah . . .'

'Spit it out.'

'I know I'm only a mere pawn in this game, a mere PC who does what he's told to do, but you – you – now don't have any rules to stick to any more. No law, no procedure, no bosses . . . a lone wolf.'

'You're right. I've got nothing.'

'I don't mean that.'

'I know you don't. I just search for the double meaning in everything these days.'

'How's the head, the arm?'

'Head sore, arm sore.'

'Brain?'

'Scrambled as in eggs – how d'you think it is?'

Jake paused. 'I was asked to look into the last flight of Lord Chalmers' private plane, piloted by Lady Chalmers.'

'Mm.' Henry sounded disinterested.

'I couldn't find any actual take-off records or flight plans for that day, as though she never even took off. But I also found that all her previous flights were recorded, so it seems unlikely to me that she would take off without submitting a plan that day.'

'OK,' Henry said.

'So I phoned the private airfield where the plane was usually kept, stored or whatever it is they do with planes, because many of the previous flight plans were submitted via that airfield, a place called Hyde Heath, near London somewhere. I got told she definitely did not take off from there that day . . . except she did.'

Henry looked at Jake. Up to that point he'd been looking at the trees.

'I got an anonymous phone call from a guy who said he saw Lady Chalmers take off, said he saw a guy give her a briefcase, then she took off and the guy drove off in an Aston Martin.'

'Anonymous?'

'Obviously the guy works at the airfield cos he's been told to keep his trap shut and say he saw zilch. Could probably weed him out if I had to.'

'All very interesting . . . and it's scrambled my grey matter even more.'

'Thing is,' Jake said excitedly, 'when I was trying to locate private airstrips using the web, an unconnected news item came up about a murder near to Hyde Heath on that day. A guy in an Aston Martin. Police are looking for some men supposed to be in black Range Rovers who shot to death some sleazy ex-cop private eye called Brooks. Still unsolved. Guys in black Range Rovers,' he prompted Henry. 'I took it to Rik Dean who said, get this, "Forget it."'

Henry shrugged. 'How far away from Kendleton is Hyde Heath? Seems unlikely that—'

'I know where you're going . . . it's doable,' Jake said. 'They could have been up here just in time to meet the plane if roads were clear. Guess what – no accidents on any of the major motorways north on that morning.'

'Interesting,' Henry said.

'I didn't want to tell you this, but the guys you picked out of the line-up? They've walked, insufficient evidence – and we never even knew their identities.'

'Really?' Henry said, feeling a sudden chill but also a shimmer of excitement. 'What's the significance of this?' he said and showed Jake the sheets of paper from the bin. Jake read them, handed them back.

'Not for me to say.'

'Who, then?'

'Rik Dean.'

Henry nodded.

'Something else that's not for me to say,' Jake said.

'You know the SAS found the crashed plane up on the moors, yeah? It was fucking airlifted out by a Chinook and is supposedly in the hands of the CAA's air crash investigators . . . but it isn't, because I've tried to find it, just to see if there are any bullet holes in it like you said and if there is a briefcase in the inventory. I also tried to find Lady Chalmers' body so I could have a look at her, but apparently an army pathologist has carried out the PM and says she died of trauma from the crash and now she's been cremated.'

'What about Lord Chalmers' body and the security guy?'

'Oh, all done above board . . . Rumour says it's going to be put down to a burglary gone wrong.'

'He was assassinated,' Henry said.

'Yep – by gangsters unknown . . . and those paint samples I took from the Range Rover . . . they seem to have disappeared in the post. Just what the hell were the SAS doing on these moors, Henry? It all stinks to high heaven.' Jake looked hopefully at Henry. 'And as I said, you don't need to play by the rules any more, Henry.' He arched his eyebrows. 'Do you?'

EIGHTEEN

'Don't you come into my house shouting the odds,' Rik Dean blazed.

'I want to know what's happening,' Henry demanded.

'What do you mean, happening?'

'Why have they walked, for a start?'

'You know why, because your eyewitness testimony is unsound, fanciful, and there is no evidence to support it in terms of other witnesses or forensics. We got the wrong guys. Shit happens. Live with it.'

'Who were they?'

'Don't know, don't care.'

Rik stalked across his living room and flung himself miserably into an armchair. He looked as if he wished the world would swallow him whole.

He glared at Henry. 'It's what they say in American movies, Henry – above my paygrade, OK? I've been told what to do, and I'm doing it.'

'Does that include the investigation into Alison's murder?'

Rik contracted as though he'd been hit by a bullet.

Henry said coldly, 'I taught you better than that.'

Rik's raging eyes dropped in shame.

'You are an SIO, a senior investigating officer, Rik. You inherited my job, for fuck's sake. I thought you'd inherited my principles, too. These people who have died need justice and you're the one who has to seek it for them. That's what being an SIO is all about. I shouldn't have to tell you that.' Henry sat on the settee opposite. 'C'mon, tell me what the hell's happening.'

'No, Henry, I can't.'

'You know, if you get involved in something that backfires, you'll be the one hung out to dry, Rik. If there's some sort of cover-up going on, then you need to be squeaky clean, otherwise when the shit hits the fan, you can kiss your big fat pension pot goodbye.'

Henry closely watched the range of emotions and angst playing out across his friend's face.

'It's high up, Henry, too high for me,' he bleated.

'What's this, then?' Henry handed him a photocopy of the two sheets he had saved form the waste bin in the function room. He had kept the originals.

Rik took them from him and snorted derisively, then closed his eyes for a long moment before opening them and saying, 'If it's any consolation, Alison's death is not connected, as such, to Lord Chalmers.'

'I never thought it was . . . but what does "as such" mean?'

'I mean that some of the same people are involved' – here Rik pointed to the ceiling, 'up there, if you know what I mean, pulling the strings, but the two incidents are unconnected.'

Henry pointed to the papers. 'And that?'

Rik squirmed visibly. 'OK, OK, but this goes no further than this room.' He looked expectantly at Henry for that promise, but did not get it. Henry remained resolute. 'OK, OK . . . that's the name of the man who killed Alison.'

'You know who he is?' Henry was shocked.

'Yes . . . no . . . yes . . . shit . . . That's a legend, an under-cover alias and I've been told that if I ever track down this killer, which seems unlikely, I have to use this identity for him and a back-story will be concocted for him. I cannot ever reveal the true ID of Alison's killer, nor anything about him . . . not that I know who he is . . . and I suppose one way or the other it won't matter too much because the people who've told me all this will probably bring him to a sticky end somewhere along the line . . . I don't know how it'll pan out, Henry, I really don't know.' Rik was clearly at his wits' end. 'This is one of the legends of a guy who is a state-sponsored killer who has gone nuts, gone rogue and by pure chance, coinci-dence, or whatever, came across Alison and Ginny, got fixated on them . . . You know the rest. Either way, if I get him, they want him back.'

'Some coincidence,' Henry sneered. 'Is that something else you haven't learned? Have I not taught you? Coincidences are clues, coincidences are weakness in stories, they lead investiga-tors to the truth but sometimes if you believe a coincidence it smacks you in the face. It is no coincidence that this man turned up to abduct Ginny.'

'Why do you say that? I was assured it was.'

'And you believed it . . . You have so much to learn, my friend.'

'Why do you say different?'

'Because Alison knew who he was – and I think Ginny could still be alive.'

It was a fleeting moment. A flash of realization on Alison's face that Henry remembered, a frown, just as the paramedics were wheeling Ginny out to the ambulance in a time that now, to Henry, seemed a hundred years ago. It was after Henry had asked her if she thought anything was going on in Ginny's life that neither of them knew about. Alison had answered truthfully that she didn't know and then there had been the lines on her forehead, the eyebrows coming together, and then it had gone.

Henry had seen it.

Now he knew what it meant.

Alison knew who the intruder was.

'What,' Rik said cynically, 'based on a fleeting facial expression?'

'A picture paints a thousand words,' Henry argued.

'So do you, or Alison, or Ginny, know of a state-sponsored assassin gone on the loose?'

'Fuck off, Rik, of course not. It's someone close to home.'

They were sitting on garden chairs on the rear decking in Rik's back garden, drinking ever more coffee. Henry had calmed down a little, so had Rik.

'So where do we go from here?' Rik asked.

'I'm assuming the DNA samples taken from Ginny's room met the same fate as the fingerprints? Blocked, in other words?'

Rik nodded.

'But the forensic lab will still have the offender's DNA profile in their records?'

'On record but going nowhere.'

'OK, do me a favour.' Henry saw Rik cringe as from his inside jacket pocket he pulled out a clear plastic bag stuffed with human hair. 'From Ginny's waste bin, samples of her hair, some with roots still on . . . she was always combing her hair and dropping it into the bin. Get a comparison with the intruder's DNA will you? Off the record. Can you do that?'

Rik took the bag. 'I can, but why?'

'Just humour an old cop, will you? And in the meantime, two more things.'

Rik said, 'Bollocks,' despondently.

'This legend.' Henry waved the sheets of paper. 'If he's still using it, it could lead us to his whereabouts, or at least his locality. And secondly, give me the name of this spook who's playing you like a marionette.'

'Why?' Rik's voice was deeply suspicious and he didn't even notice Henry's veiled insult.

'Because I think it's time I spoke to him.'

NINETEEN

Henry Christie had never been a massive fan of London, but enjoyed the occasional visit and had sometimes worked there as a detective in the past, but not often.

However, that morning he was working in the capital as a grieving man with very much his own agenda, beholden to no one other than his murdered fiancée and her missing stepdaughter.

He was fighting for things that had so tragically been taken away from him and from a purely personal perspective he did not care if this turned out badly for him. At least he would go down fighting.

He had travelled down the evening before and stayed in the Premier Inn Hub on St Martin's Lane, just off the top end of Trafalgar Square. He hadn't had a greatly pleasant night's sleep – his mind was too busy, his pain still too intense both mentally and physically – but he'd managed a few hours and got up early to use the internet facilities in the hotel then took a stroll around the quiet streets, ending up by the Thames.

At eight thirty a.m. he was standing on Westminster Bridge with his rucksack over one shoulder.

There was an earpiece in his left ear connected to his mobile phone.

He was waiting patiently.

Now, he had all the patience in the world.

His mind rumbled back over the last forty-eight hours since his brow-beating conversation with Rik Dean.

It hadn't helped that Rik had never been formally introduced to the mysterious man from London in the chief constable's office. No name, no responsibility, no comeback. Just a description of a chubby, smug civil servant who expected the world to kowtow to his wishes.

Henry had encountered a few of them in his time.

He had told Rik to find out as much as he could about the man.

Rik whined, 'But, but, but . . .'

'You're a detective aren't you? How the hell did he get into the chief's office? As best as I can remember, unless you're summoned, an appointment has to be made.' Henry had leaned forward at that point. 'Check the chief's online diary, duh! And you said he came by military helicopter . . . where from? Flight plan? Duh!'

'Stop saying duh,' Rik complained.

'Duh – OK.'

Rik went into work and accessed the chief's online diary, which only officers above a certain rank were allowed to see. There was no entry for the time slot in which he had been to see the chief, it was blank. Rik thought the personal touch might possibly work, so he walked from his office over to headquarters and trotted up to the middle floor, the corridor of power as it was cynically known, and went into the Chief's outer office where the staff officer and secretaries worked.

Chief Inspector Riley was at his desk, tapping away at his computer.

'Morning, sir,' he said to Rik. His body language instantly informed Rik that he was being cautious.

'Hi.' Rik sat down on the chair positioned at the end of Riley's desk. 'Chief in?'

'No, with the crime commissioner.'

'I wonder if you could help me, then?'

'I'll try.' Meaning he wouldn't.

'The . . . er . . . two fellows who were in with the chief the other week, y'know, the government types . . . unfortunately I didn't catch the names or the departments they are in and I need to contact them as a matter of urgency. Can you give me their phone numbers and such?'

'No.' It was an instant response.

'Why not?'

'I've been told not to divulge anything to anyone.' He drew a pretend zip across his mouth, then tapped his nose with his forefinger. 'Secret squirrels.'

'I need the details,' Rik said, his face becoming dark.

'You'd have to ask the chief directly,' Riley said. 'I'm sorry, just doing what I'm told.'

'That it, then?'

The chief inspector nodded. Rik rose without a word and left the office making his way down to the canteen situated in the ground floor, bottom corner of the building but as he was about to enter, he had another idea and went to reception in the front foyer. The lady staffing the desk was one Rik had known over ten years and he recalled she had been on duty when he had been called across to see the chief.

'Morning, Rhona.'

'Mr Dean.'

'Need a favour.'

'Anything.'

'You were working the day that two guys landed in the military helicopter, the two men I came to see.'

'Yes, I remember.'

'Did they sign in?'

'All visitors have to sign in,' she said professionally.

Rik knew this. They had to sign in and be issued with a temporary pass for the duration of the visit. It applied to everyone, except police staff. Rik recalled both men had been wearing the passes on lanyards around their necks.

'Can I look at the log sheet?' Rik asked.

'Have I done something wrong?' Rhona asked.

'Far from it.'

'Let me find it.'

She showed him the book. Each visitor had to fill out their details, place of work, any vehicle registration number, and sign in.

Although the details required were not extensive, the men had written as little as possible in the space provided, but they had signed their names, which made Rik smile. It was often the little things that caught deceitful people out.

One gave the name Jenkins, the other Smith. Both gave their workplace as 'Home Office'.

'Which was which?' he asked Rhona.

Rhona looked and said, 'Jenkins was the tubby one in the suit, Smith the other guy, slim, in casuals. Looked like a soldier.'

'Brilliant, thanks,' Rik said and glanced up at the ceiling and noticed the security camera covering the entrance and front desk.

Henry walked along Bridge Street, then right into Parliament Street and started to head up Whitehall towards Trafalgar Square. There was some kind of early morning demonstration taking place directly across from Downing Street and as ever, even so early, gawkers had gathered at the security gates to rubber-neck Number 10 in the hope of seeing the Prime Minister.

Henry sidestepped the demo, carried on to Trafalgar Square.

It was a pleasant morning, busy with pedestrians and traffic, and the newly cleaned Nelson looked resplendent atop his column.

Henry paused on the corner of Northumberland Avenue, then cut across to stand on the junction of the Strand.

Rik managed to download a screenshot from the security camera of Jenkins and Smith signing in at the front desk. Through the whole process, Smith had kept his head lowered, very much aware of being caught on camera, whereas Jenkins was not as savvy. It looked as if he had been quite flirty and smarmy with Rhona, doing a lot of gurning at her, maybe trying to use his charm.

Rik had captured the moment, though, when both men raised their faces to the lens.

It was a good, clear, well-focused image.

He had shown it to Henry and given him the names from the booking in sheet.

Henry had stared at it for a long, long time after which he spent many hours trawling the internet, searching through government department websites including the Ministry of Defence, MI5 and SIS, and dug as deep as he could, not being the most skilled surfer.

He worked his way through lists of people awarded knighthoods, MBEs, CBEs and other such honours because he knew faceless people like Jenkins often received such recognition for services rendered and their lights were often hidden deep in the bushels.

A man called Alistair Arthur Jenkins did receive an OBE in 2007 for services to the Crown, whatever that meant. Henry found his photograph at a Buckingham Palace garden party the following year. It was definitely the man, ten years younger, thirty pounds lighter, with more hair, but still chubby and slimy looking.

There wasn't much else on him that Henry could find. And that told him something: security services.

Henry's next step was to send what he knew down to Karl Donaldson, who had returned to work in the American Embassy in London. Henry hoped that Donaldson might know where Jenkins worked.

It transpired he did not. He had seen Jenkins flitting about the press conference in Kendleton, but did not recognize him, nor did Rik Dean reveal anything about him other than to make a few cryptic comments which he did not elaborate on, so Donaldson had thought nothing about him.

However, he promised to ask around for Henry.

Good to his word, he came back to him within twenty-four hours.

Donaldson's boss knew Jenkins.

'One of the shady ones, definitely a spook,' Donaldson had explained to Henry over the phone.

'I think I knew that part.'

Henry was on the cordless phone in the Tawny Owl. As he spoke on it he wandered out from the private accommodation into the bar, which had reopened for business following a quick decision by Henry, who knew Alison would have wanted to keep it going. It had been her dream, he had become part of it and he was going to make it work and the staff were up for it. That was today's plan, anyway.

And the locals were mightily relieved.

It was early evening and the pub had a few regulars propping up the bar who Henry acknowledged as he walked through and outside.

'What does he actually do?'

'Top-secret stuff.'

'Get away,' Henry scoffed.

'No, I mean it. He runs a small unit that doesn't officially exist but straddles MI5, MI6 and SIS, and the MoD. It carries out off-the-book secret ops. The budget comes from all those departments, but they don't know that. Creative accounting, they call it.'

'And the name of this department is?'

'Er, The Unit.'

'Very original.'

'Word is they've been spectacularly successful in many fields of conflict and the removal, shall I say, of some very unsavoury characters. It doesn't take the Brain of Britain to piece the bits together, Henry.'

'He runs a hit squad.'

'In one – amongst other things. He has a very sordid remit, but all for the sake of national security.' Donaldson's voice became mock-cagey. 'If GCHQ hear this conversation, we're in the shit, you know.'

'Like I give a toss,' Henry said. 'And whose assets were already in Lancashire when Alison was murdered.' This was something Henry had learned from Rik, who had sheepishly, and reluctantly, told him about the meeting in the chief's office with Jenkins and Smith. 'Assets who were killing Lord Chalmers and his missus and who then tried to kill me because I was a witness.'

'RedFour,' Donaldson said.

'What does that mean?'

'The code name of the team he uses, usually made up of ex-SAS officers and other people who may have certain skill-sets.'

'OK, RedFour, better than the Unit, I suppose.'

'Just happened to be up there when your so-called David Jones struck.'

'So what had Lord Chalmers been up to that required a visit from them?'

'I don't know, Henry. Maybe we'll never know.'

'Not sure if I want to know . . . That's not what this is about, this is about Alison and Ginny and a man who knows more than he's willing to tell.'

'Yeah, yeah . . . Anyway, he works somewhere in the bowels of Whitehall but exactly where I don't know.'

'So I'll have to go and stand there until he walks past me?'

'You could do that – or you could have breakfast with him.'

When that phone call ended, Henry spent a few minutes in the bar with the regulars and speaking to the staff, then went through to the back where he logged on to the internet, booked a train to London Euston from Preston later that evening and booked the room at the Hub in St Martins Lane for that night. Then he sped down to Preston and waited for a Virgin Pendolino with just a rucksack over his shoulder.

He received a call on his mobile whilst he was standing on platform 4 which, although it did not surprise him, still stunned him.

He was now standing close to the entrance to the National Portrait Gallery, looking over to St Martin's Church and the glass entrance to the crypt below. Sandwich boards outside advertised the full English breakfasts served below.

Henry felt empty as if his guts had been scraped out, but he was not hungry.

Instead he was furious, confused and upset, fighting the urge to sink down to his knees and curl up into a foetal ball.

Suddenly there he was.

A. A. Jenkins. OBE. Spook. Chubby guy. State executioner. Bureaucrat. Civil servant. Butler to the Prime Minister. A man who slept soundly in his bed after sending other men to do the dirty work.

Henry added the 'C' word to that list.

Jenkins appeared from the direction of Whitehall, no doubt having slithered out from his lair, and turned into the crypt and disappeared down the steps with a battered briefcase in his hand.

Henry watched him go out of sight, then waited.

A few moments later and a black van with smoked-out windows drew up across the road and two people alighted from the side sliding door. One was a tall, lean man, the other a smartly dressed woman. They had hardly touched the pavement when the van edged back into the traffic again

The pair also went down into the crypt.

Henry heard a voice in his earpiece. 'Here we are, Henry.'

All of a sudden, Henry was ravenously hungry.

Henry was impressed by the vaulted ceilings and the whole set-up below ground. He ordered a breakfast and took himself off to a corner from which he could clearly see Jenkins at another table with the man and the woman who had arrived shortly after him without making it too obvious he was glaring at them.

His eyes were on Jenkins in the flesh, amazed there were such people in the world.

The trio were having an amiable breakfast meeting, maybe a catch-up, maybe real business.

Henry didn't care.

He was going to have his moment with this worm who knew the real identity of Alison's killer.

Henry was determined to wring the truth out of him one way or the other and maybe a crypt was the best place to achieve this, on the villain's home turf.

Henry dawdled over his meal, as did Jenkins and the other two, joking and laughing.

No other customers had yet arrived in the cafe, which was a good thing for what might follow.

Henry smiled grimly.

He knew one of the two people who had joined Jenkins for breakfast. His name was Karl Donaldson, his close friend.

As he sat there he recalled the conclusion of the phone call he'd had with Donaldson the previous evening when Donaldson had mentioned having breakfast with Jenkins, something that Henry did not quite get until Donaldson explained.

The American had run Jenkins' photograph and details past his supervisor, who immediately recognized him and sneered. When Donaldson had revealed why he was asking, the lady melted a little when he said that Henry Christie was desperate to confront the man over Alison's murder, giving her the full background. She asked how she could help without compromising her own position.

Donaldson said, 'You mentioned you've met him a few times?'

'Yes.'

'I won't ask why.'

'Don't,' she said.

'Would you like to meet him again?'

'He's a creep . . . On what pretext?'

'Could we offer him something . . . a snippet, maybe? And can I come with you?'

'We could,' she said thoughtfully. 'He'd be there like a shot anyway, snippet or not.'

'How come?'

'Desperate to get his hands into my panties, and maybe having this guy by the balls could be very useful.'

And so the meeting was arranged. Donaldson had listened to his boss's side of the conversation as she purred down the line to Jenkins. He had to admit he would have responded with the same alacrity because she was a very fine lady who ruled the FBI office in London with a rod of steel covered with silk.

'Nine a.m., St Martin's crypt,' she announced as she hung up. 'His usual breakfast haunt, apparently . . . off the beaten track. Shall we have some sport with the weasel?'

Henry had to admit that Donaldson's boss – he had only ever heard her referred to as 'K' (whether that was 'K' as in James Bond's 'M' or Kaye was her name, Henry didn't know) – was a stunning-looking lady, but like his appreciation of the crypt, it was something he put on the back burner.

He could see Jenkins fawning from where he sat, his body language spelled out in big fat letters.

Eventually their breakfasts were over.

'K' stood up and excused herself – a rest-room visit, as planned – leaving Donaldson and Jenkins at the table.

They chatted and waited for her return which, Henry knew, would not happen.

Henry pushed his plate away and stood up.

'She's taking her time . . . women, eh?' Jenkins twitched his thick eyebrows at Donaldson. 'Worth one, eh?'

Donaldson smiled thinly, wanting to be the one who planted a very big, thick, heavy fist into the man's face.

Jenkins frowned at him. 'We haven't met before, have we? No, didn't think so, but you look familiar . . . can't just place . . .'

Donaldson understood this man's role more than he had admitted to Henry as he himself had been unleashed by men like this. But there was something wrong about Jenkins and the whole set up of The Unit that he did not like.

Firstly the question of Lord Chalmers worried him. It seemed that Jenkins had used The Unit to murder a member of the aristocracy, but for what reason? Secondly, keeping the identity of a rogue killer under wraps just to save face was simply outrageous. Surely it would have been the best approach to admit it openly so this assassin could be brought quickly to justice? It was this side of things that had swayed K – as she was known – to help out this morning. The FBI could easily afford not be linked to a man like Jenkins. It would actually be in their interests to be on the side that brought the killer to book.

Donaldson rubbed the back of his right hand, then showed it to Jenkins.

'My, my, that looks painful,' Jenkins commented.

'It is, it burns like hell.' Donaldson looked into Jenkins' bloodshot eyes.

The civil servant shrugged, uninterested, but reluctantly asked, 'How did it happen?'

'Came across a bad guy.'

Jenkins' eyes narrowed, perhaps now placing Donaldson. He glanced around to see where K was, but all he saw was a man approaching across the crypt floor, like a monster from a Frankenstein movie, his eyes shrunken in their sockets, his head shaved, one ear a ragged mess.

'A very bad guy,' Donaldson added for effect.

Jenkins' sloppy mouth drooped open as something clicked with him. His head jerked around and he looked properly at Henry. He tried to stand up.

'I've been fucking set up here—'

Donaldson rose and stepped quickly behind him. He placed his big hands on Jenkins' shoulders, squeezed tight and slammed him back down on to the chair.

Henry moved in slowly, sat opposite and slid his rucksack on to the floor.

'What? What the damned hell?' Jenkins demanded. 'You let go, you big oaf.'

Jenkins waited to be set free but Donaldson simply held him in place and leaned to bring his lips close to Jenkins' right ear. 'You keep your voice level,' he whispered. 'You keep calm and maybe you'll walk out of here. Do something silly and I'll break your neck and leave you sitting here dead. Understood?'

With sweat instantly pouring out of his head, Jenkins nodded, but said, 'This is outrageous. You shall be receiving a formal comp—'

Donaldson smashed an open palm across Jenkins' ear, just hard enough to send shockwaves through his ear canal, but not burst his eardrum.

'Sit, listen, respond,' Donaldson said.

Clutching his ear, his face distorted in pain, Jenkins demanded, 'What do you want?'

Donaldson nodded at Henry.

'I think you know me, don't you?' Henry said.

'No, should I?'

'I have things you need to see.'

Henry unzipped the rucksack, reached in and extracted a blue A4 folder which he placed in front of him lengthways. He opened the flap and took out a photograph, twizzled it around and slid it towards Jenkins, who purposely did not look at it, knowing that once a thing is seen, it cannot be unseen.

'Look at it,' Henry said.

'Why?'

SMACK! Donaldson crashed the palm of his hand across Jenkins' ear again, sending another jolt of excruciating pain from one side of his skull to the other. Donaldson then gripped the back of the man's head, his fingers splayed as though he was holding a basketball and forced Jenkins to look down.

Henry laid his finger on the photograph. It was one he had taken from a frame on the sideboard in the living room of himself and Alison proudly standing outside the front of the Tawny Owl.

'Me . . . my fiancée, Alison Marsh,' Henry said, laying a fingertip on each person.

'Very nice.'

Henry took out another photo and slid it over the first one, covering it.

'My fiancée,' he said, 'Alison Marsh.'

This time it was a lurid crime-scene photograph, Alison dead and mutilated in the hospital toilet cubicle, a gruesome, terrible, blood-soaked scene.

There was just the merest hint of a reaction from Jenkins' eyes. His mouth did a little 'popping' noise.

Henry took out another photograph and placed it over the first two.

'My fiancée's daughter, Virginia – Ginny.'

Jenkins was breathing heavily, his fat nostrils dilating with the stress of the encounter. His face was becoming redder and a shade of purple at the same time. Donaldson was still holding his head in position.

Henry dipped his hand into the rucksack again and came out with a mini iPad which he placed on top of the photographs. It was already switched on. He turned it around and pressed play on screen and the short video, taken from the CCTV camera in the hospital car park, showed Ginny being kidnapped.

'Ginny being kidnapped,' Henry said simply, 'by your man after he had murdered her mother, my fiancée, Alison Marsh by cutting her throat and almost severing her head from her body.'

Jenkins watched unblinking.

Henry was relentless.

He took out another photograph. This was of Tod Rawstron's dead body, naked on a mortuary slab just after he had been moved there from the scene of his death and not cleaned up in any way.

'Tod Rawstron, nineteen years old, killed by your man.'

Henry went on, placed another dreadful photograph on top of the pile. This was of the crime-scene investigator, Ray Bower, who had caught the full blast of the grenade in the VW camper van.

'A wife and two kids, no dad any more.'

'Let me go,' Jenkins said.

Donaldson released his grip.

'He cannot be linked to us,' Jenkins babbled to Henry. 'I've already told your chief constable that.'

'He's not my chief constable,' Henry corrected him.

'Whatever . . . He went rogue after suffering a mental break-down, PTSD or whatever the hell it's called. He had been sectioned to a secure unit at a military hospital in Essex. He killed two nurses and escaped one night. We never expected to see him again. And don't you understand? If he is caught it can never be revealed who he really is because if it ever came out that the government has a unit that sanctions murder, it would be disastrous.'

'For who?' Henry asked.

'The government, you idiot. We are a civilized nation, we don't do things like that, bring ourselves down to the level of the people who are against us . . . except we do and I am the man who oversees it.'

'Let me tell you something, Mr A. A. Jenkins, I don't give a rat's arse about this government. I care about bringing this man to justice.'

'That will never happen.'

'Just watch me.'

'You're not even a cop any more,' Jenkins said.

'So you do know who I am!'

Jenkins blinked at his mistake.

Henry suddenly changed tack. 'Why was Lord Chalmers murdered?'

'I'm not going there,' Jenkins protested.

Donaldson slammed Jenkins' face into his plate and smeared his face in the remnants of the fat and egg yolk. The crockery clattered, Jenkins raised his egg-covered face.

'What was in the briefcase in Lady Chalmers' plane?'

'What briefcase?' Jenkins wiped his cheek with a napkin. His nose had started to bleed, just a dribble.

'The one she took on the plane with her, given to her by a man who was subsequently murdered by your RedFour team? Yeah, I know the jargon.'

'There is no briefcase, I can assure you of that.'

Henry shrugged. 'You are a liar, Mr Jenkins, OBE.'

'I have a job to do and I do it fucking well. I protect the government, particularly the Prime Minister's office . . .'

'So you are his private little army?'

'Possibly . . . What I do is not nice, but it's a necessary evil.'

'Ordering assassinations?'

'If the cap fits.'

'So . . . tell me about the man who murdered my fiancée and kidnapped her daughter. Tell me about him.'

'What's there to tell? Brilliant sniper. Trained up, sent out, did his job, was well remunerated for it, became a real hunter, then he lost it, had a breakdown, we tried to cure him, he escaped . . .'

'And somehow ended up in Lancashire? Now how the fuck did that happen? How did he end up in a one-horse town in rural Lancashire? Answer me that, you sack of shit.'

'Just happened, I suppose. No rhyme or reason for these things.'

'And you continue to lie . . . I'll tell you what "just" happened. What "just" happened was that he turned up in Lancashire at the same time as your RedFour team were sent to murder Lord Chalmers and then tried to murder me. That's what "just" happened, that was the coincidence and there is no connection between these events. But it was no accident that that your mentally scarred assassin escaped from a secure unit and decided to kidnap a girl in Lancashire, was it?'

'Don't know what you mean,' Jenkins said, wiping tomato sauce from his eyebrow and dabbing his bleeding nose with a napkin.

'Tell me his real name,' Henry insisted.

'No.'

He reached into his rucksack – Jenkins groaned – and pulled out two sheets of A4 paper with what looked like a complex of graphs and bar charts printed on them. He laid one on top of the other. He had printed these off earlier this morning at his hotel.

'Any idea what this is?' He tapped the paper with his fingertip.

Jenkins shook his head. 'Should I?'

'It's a DNA profile. This' – he continued to tap the sheet – 'is the DNA profile of your man.'

'How did you get that?' Jenkins asked with a hint of menace.

'A DNA sample was lifted from some of the items he left at the scene of the kidnapping at the Tawny Owl, the syringe, the gaffer tape. It was then analysed.'

'It was blocked,' he said desperately. His eyes zigzagged sideways and back as if he was weighing up an escape route.

'Blocked only when it was submitted to the DNA database
. . . just like the fingerprints were when they were checked. It
doesn't prevent an expert from making a comparison to another
DNA profile he or she might have access to.'

'You're talking riddles.'

'Yeah, I'm a real joker.' Henry slid the second sheet out from
underneath the first and laid it alongside.

Jenkins shrugged. 'And?'

Henry laid a finger on the second sheet. 'As you can see,
another DNA profile.'

Jenkins waited.

'This is the DNA profile of Ginny Marsh, my fiancée's stepdaughter. They are not blood related, therefore, but these two
people are.' Henry now looked Jenkins straight in the eye, firm,
unwavering, his bubbling rage evident in the look. Jenkins tried
to shrink away. 'A scientist compared these two profiles,' he
went on, 'and they conclusively show that the man who killed
my fiancée and abducted and may have killed Ginny Marsh is
her father.'

Henry reached into the rucksack once more.

His hands dithered as he placed an A4 photograph on top of
all the other documents. He had removed it from a picture frame
on Ginny's dressing table. It was a lovely family photo of Ginny,
aged around five, together with Alison and her father, Jack Marsh.

'They thought he'd died in Afghanistan,' Henry said, 'but he
didn't, did he?'

TWENTY

'Y ou don't have to be afraid of me. You're my darling
daughter, the innocent one in all this,' Jack Marsh cooed,
his eyes full of love. 'We can work through this, make
a good life for ourselves. Us – me and you, together.'

Ginny Marsh quivered in fear, her face pulsed, her breathing
laboured and dithery as she looked up at the man standing in
front of her.

'I'm your dad. I came back for you,' he tried to convince her.
Ginny's whole body trembled.

'Listen, my darling.' He squatted down in front of her, bringing himself to her eye level. He stroked her greasy matted hair. 'Do you want to talk now? Shall we talk? You know, dad and daughter things? I'll take the tape off but you must promise not to shout or scream or back on it goes. I know it's early days yet, I know this is a big change for you and I understand your trepidation . . . so?' He smiled encouragingly. 'You'll keep your voice down?'

She nodded.

'Obviously I can't untie you yet,' he said and slid his hand off her hair, across her cheek and with a swift jerk he ripped the gaffer tape from her mouth.

She gasped, sucked in air.

'Where's Mum? Where is she? What've you done to her?' Ginny demanded in a croaky voice.

'Here, here, calm down now.' Jack Marsh picked up a small bottle of water. 'Drink some of this. You need to rehydrate, then we talk, eh? A saline drip isn't like real drinking water, is it?'

He flipped the sports cap back and held the bottle towards her mouth.

Ginny was sitting on a creaky old metal-frame camp bed with her hands fastened behind her by plasticuffs, whilst her ankles were bound together by tape. It was only in the last hour that the drip had been removed, although a cannula was still in place on her inner right elbow, and she was only now beginning to think straight and realize that it had been much more than saline and water going into her system. She had been drugged, kept sedated, just on the verge of consciousness, a swirling, unfocused world that made no sense to her until the effect of the drugs began to wear off at last.

It had all been a terrible nightmare from the moment the syringe had been plunged into her neck on the hospital car park, right up until now. She had no conception of how long she had been held, it could have been hours or weeks, but as her mind cleared, she knew it had been a long time.

She did not know where she was.

In a room, possibly a cellar, with no natural light, reeking of damp and shit and piss.

As she inhaled these aromas and glanced down at her body, now dressed in jogging pants and a loose-fitting top, she felt nauseous at the thought that if he had been held for days, virtually unconscious, then she must have had 'toilet needs' and this man must have seen to them.

She took the water bottle between her teeth, tipped her head back and sucked. The water tasted cold and beautiful and she swallowed until she began to choke when the man removed the bottle.

'That's enough,' he said.

Ginny glared at him. 'Where's my mother?'

'You mean your utter bitch of a stepmother? We don't need her any longer. From now on,' his voice began gentle as he promised something as though she was desperate to hear it, 'it's just us.'

Donaldson changed the dressings on Henry's arm. The wounds were clean, uninfected and healing well, but they still hurt and Henry winced as Donaldson peeled the last strip away and tugged his hairs.

'Softie,' Donaldson said.

'That's me,' Henry agreed.

They had travelled out of London by train to Donaldson's house in the village of Hartley Wintney in Hampshire, where he had lived with his family for many years now.

His wife, Karen, appeared in the lounge bearing two mugs of tea. She had once been a cop in Lancashire and when they had first met – when she was a detective inspector and Henry merely a detective sergeant – they could easily have ripped each other's throats out. Now they were good friends. She had retired from the police after transferring to the Metropolitan, but still worked on short contracts delivering management training.

Henry took the mug, wincing again as he moved his arm. He wasn't a great tea drinker but was looking forward to it refreshing him rather than giving him a coffee-style kick.

'How are you?' she asked tenderly.

'I'd shrug, but it hurts,' he said. 'So-so.'

They looked at each other, neither able to find words.

'I need to catch up on paperwork,' she said to Donaldson and left the two men sitting in the conservatory.

Donaldson squeezed antiseptic cream onto the wound and carefully re-bandaged it as Henry sipped his brew.

'Think he'll keep his word?' Henry asked.

'I think you forced his hand, while I forced his head,' Donaldson said, 'but if he doesn't, then going to the media might not help because he'll just slap a D notice on it and kill it.'

'I could tweet it,' Henry said. 'Hashtag MI5 hit squad.'

'Yeah, OK,' Donaldson said dubiously. He finished the dressing and went into the kitchen to wash his hands as Henry eased his shirt back on. When he returned he sat opposite Henry on one of the cane-backed chairs with his mug of tea. 'I think he'll play – on his terms,' he said, 'and that's probably the best we can expect.'

Henry nodded, then said ferociously, 'How could they not have told Alison her husband was still alive?'

'Would sort have given the game away, wouldn't it? He – Jack – obviously made his own choice for whatever reason, probably money and kudos, then eventually went off the rails.'

'Fuck.' Henry shook his head.

'The bed's made up in the spare room,' Donaldson said. 'Get some sleep. You look like death warmed up, my old buddy.'

'It just bothers me that every second, every fucking second we waste puts us a second further away from finding Ginny.'

'Jack Marsh was one of the most natural marksmen I have ever come across,' Major Smith said.

Smith was not in uniform. He had arranged to meet Henry and Donaldson at a motorway service area on the M5 north of Tewkesbury to save the pair having to travel all the way across the country to Hereford, where he and the SAS were based. That said, it had still been a grim, almost four-hour journey in a sea of traffic first on the M4, then on the M5.

More time wasted, Henry had moaned.

But at least he had slept well in Donaldson's house. Hearing the sounds of a normal household, the TV, whinging teenagers, pots and pans clattering, even some bickering between husband and wife, had sent him off to bed feeling relaxed for once. There had only been one nightmare, when he woke clutching his head, sweating, trying to blank out the image of Alison's murdered body coming to life and walking towards him, pleading with him to save her.

Henry hadn't realized he had screamed, but Donaldson had quickly appeared at his bedroom door in his night shorts.

'You OK, pal?'

'Yeah, yeah, fine.' Henry flopped back on the bed, the fresh sheets now sweat-laden. He rested his head on the soft pillow, feeling a pulse of pain along the line where he imagined the fracture had been. He exhaled long and hard. 'You know summat?' he said, his Lancashire accent coming out.

'What?'

'Nah, nothing, I'm OK.'

Donaldson nodded and backed out of the room, closing the door.

What he had been about to say was that in all this mayhem and upset and grief, other than getting an occasional sympathetic pat on the shoulder, he had never had a long hug from anyone. He hadn't said this to Donaldson because it sounded pathetic.

He felt very alone.

He began to weep silently for himself and his loss.

Then he had slept well and after a quick breakfast he and Donaldson were on the road in the big Jeep after a confirmation phone call from Smith.

'He was a killer. Good with a knife – hence his codename Stiletto, but most people called him Blade . . .'

'His chums, you mean?' Henry interrupted sarcastically.

Smith ignored him. 'He was physically excellent too. Knew martial arts, kung fu, judo, could break a man's neck just like that!' Smith clicked his fingers loudly, the exact sound of a neck breaking.

'I've seen his handiwork,' Henry said.

Smith said, 'I know and I'm sorry.' He meant it, but went on, 'It's part of my remit to identify people like Jack to certain members of the intelligence services.'

'Yeah, right, I get that,' Henry said irritably. 'A hit squad. I can live with that, but how could he get chosen and his wife not find out?'

'Did she ever talk to you about him?' Smith asked.

'Not really. It was a very private matter and I didn't pry. Maybe when we got married more would have been revealed.'

'It was how it had to be,' Smith said. 'We were just at the point of approaching him for The Unit anyway, when it all kind of fell into our lap.'

'How so?' Donaldson asked.

Smith sighed uncomfortably. 'An army patrol in Afghanistan was cornered in a village full of Taliban hostiles. A firefight ensued and an SAS patrol came to assist. It got very bloody and a lot of good men lost their lives that day faced with over-whelming numbers and shit equipment. Two survived, Jack and one other and fuck knows how. Anyway, Jack went back the day after – alone – and laid up on a flat rooftop in the village for four days and subsequently took out two of the Taliban leaders responsible for the massacre. It was very messy but an opportunity was seen in it all for Jenkins to approach Jack and offer him something . . . his death and a life beyond. He made the offer, Jack accepted,' Smith concluded weakly.

'The offer being?' Donaldson asked.

'To be declared dead and then go undercover with another identity, or many other identities – and work for The Unit. Jack's dead body was put together from a few other mangled corpses who had been blown to bits and he was brought back to England and buried. His wife, she was a medic out there in Afghanistan, never knew. From what I remember their marriage was at breaking point anyway, wasn't working.'

'So she buried bits of other people thinking it was her husband?' Henry said in total incredulity. Smith nodded. 'You bastards,' Henry said. 'And he had – has – a daughter from his first marriage. Alison took her under her wing, brought her up, like a real mother and daughter.'

'I know.' Smith swallowed. 'It was his decision, he could have walked but he didn't. He played the game, was very well paid, lived in nice, but rented, apartments in Madrid, London, always close to an airport so he could drop everything at a moment's notice . . .'

'And go around the world killing people,' Henry finished, disgusted.

'Correct,' Smith said. 'And he was bloody good at it. He was regularly psychologically evaluated but about two years ago tiny cracks started to show. This is one of his assessments from about that time.'

He slid a sheet of paper across to Henry, who took it and read through a few paragraphs of what was clearly a redacted document. The psychologist's name had been blanked out, as had Jack's, so Henry only had Smith's word that it referred to Marsh at all. Certain words and phrases stood out, though.

'*I have evaluated this operative . . . he has become very morose and is prone to excessive bouts of bad temper and dark moods . . . he has begun talking about his wife and daughter again . . . he would like to see them again and lay down roots . . . go back to his former life, but realizes this is not an option. He says he dreams about them now and then, sees their faces . . . I believe he is becoming jaded and his future may have to be reconsidered. Some of his thinking is quite jumbled and incoherent and his decision-making in tests is flawed. I will re-evaluate in six months' time as per normal. For the time being I recommend he remains in active service as I believe his practical skills remain first class . . .*'

Henry passed it to Donaldson, who read through it.

'We knew he'd had enough when he executed some villagers in a failed West African state we were trying to assist in a civil war. He tied them up and blew their brains out. All were innocent people. That's when we brought him in,' Smith said then pushed another sheet across to Henry, similar to the first one, redacted with thick black lines and other crossings out.

'*The patient,*' it began – and Henry immediately noted the different phrasing, from operative to patient – '*shows all the signs and symptoms of bipolar depression and psychosis. He says he has been to see and watch his ex-wife from afar since our last meeting.*' There, Henry's insides curdled. '*He tells me she has betrayed him and he intends to "put that right". He has started calling her a "bitch" and "slag" and other such derogatory terms.*'

So Jack Marsh had been watching them even before this assessment took place. Watching him, Alison, Ginny.

'*His thought processes are now quite muddled but in a much more severe way than previously. He tells me he has seen too much violence and blood, too many dead and decaying people and now constantly dreams of exploding heads and has bouts of severe nausea when he recalls the reek of his kills . . . I recommend that consideration be given to removing the patient from active service.'*

'Consideration?' spat Henry. 'Typical mind-doctor, frightened to nail his colours to the mast. Jack Marsh was clearly raving mad at this stage. Pah!'

'I have to say,' Smith said, 'that his state of mind might be the only reason you are still alive. If it was him you surprised in the car park, and then in Ginny's room . . . yeah, yeah, I'm sure it was,' Smith defended himself off the look of horror on Henry's face. 'If he had been thinking straight, we would not be here having this conversation. He has the tools in his fingers on his left hand to kill you outright. He didn't.'

'Makes me feel a whole lot better to know I'm alive and Alison isn't. But that said, you lot had two bites at the cherry, didn't you? Even RedFour couldn't kill me,' Henry said sourly.

Donaldson cut into the tension between the two men. 'OK – do we need to know any more?'

'Only that he broke the necks of two nurses before breaking out of the secure unit.'

Henry sighed heavily and nodded. 'That it?'

'I was told to bring you up to speed with Jack Marsh's details, and I have done.'

'You could tell us where to find him, that might help.'

'I have no idea where he is . . .'

Henry sensed a 'but'.

'I haven't given you any of these,' Smith said. He reached into his attaché case and pulled a hefty pile of documents. 'Photocopies . . . Do whatever you want with them, but don't say I gave them to you. I want him captured as much as you. He was a good man and a good operative but sometimes a weakness up here' – he tapped the side of his head – 'can never be seen until it's too late. It happens. But he needs bringing in and that's down to you, I'm afraid. I hope you find him and I am truly sorry for your loss, Mr Christie . . . and one other thing: you underestimate and challenge Mr Jenkins at your peril.'

They stood up and shook hands.

'Could I possibly have a word with you alone, Mr Christie?' Smith said. 'Just before you hit the road.'

Donaldson cut back onto the motorway and up to Birmingham, where he dropped Henry at New Street Station. Henry caught a train back to Preston. He managed to get a single window seat with a small table and after buying coffee and a sandwich, he took out the file Smith had given him.

It contained Jack Marsh's military record from joining as a raw recruit at sixteen, following his career on to the SAS up to his untimely death at the hands of the Taliban. It included details of his two marriages and his only child, Virginia.

'The collusion of the establishment,' Henry grunted, drawing a stare from a man sitting across the aisle from him. After all, this was a quiet carriage.

Then Henry read something that made him sit up. He got out his mobile phone and called Rik Dean – which really annoyed the guy across the aisle – but after that he settled back. He watched the world whizz by at 125 mph and fell asleep, waking just as the train pulled into Preston.

After paying the extortionate parking fee, Henry picked up his car and drove the short distance to Preston nick, where a major incident room had been established by Rik, combining the murders and incidents that had happened at Kendleton together with the terrible events at RPH. There was a purpose-built MIR at the station, always ready and fully equipped with the technical resources necessary to get an investigation up and running. Just add staff.

Rik came to meet Henry at the front desk and signed him in, then took him to the MIR where Henry handed over the file Smith had given him.

'It might help,' Henry said. He looked beyond tired, the London trip having taken its toll. His head hurt, his arm throbbed and his heart ached. 'It's got all his army records in there plus details of all his undercover legends and details of all the debit and credit cards issued to him under his various aliases, and guess what? They are all still up and running and he has access to the funds therein.'

'You are joking me.'

'No I'm not. You need to access these accounts and get the banks watching them all for activity. He could still be using them.'

'They haven't cancelled them?'

Henry shook his head. 'Which might be a good thing now. Plus there is something else I didn't know but which could be good news for us . . . Look at his date and place of birth.'

Rik looked. 'Jesus! He was born and bred in Preston.'

'Yep, he's a local lad, which I had no clue about, but people always come home, don't they?'

'That's great,' Rik said. 'But when we do catch him, and we will, Henry, I promise, how will we explain this lot to the defence lawyers when it comes to disclosure?' Rik was referring to the duty of the prosecution to declare everything in their possession to the defence under the rules of disclosure. 'That we just found it?'

Henry chuckled mirthlessly and shook his head. 'What defence lawyers?'

'What do you mean?' Rik was confused.

'You know, you have the skills and abilities to become one of the best detectives this force has ever had, I shit you not. But at the moment, you're awfully naive.'

'What do you mean?' Rik asked, hurt.

'Are you for real?'

'Henry, what are you getting at?'

'This will never, ever, in a zillion years go to trial. I even doubt that Jack Marsh, or whoever we decide to call him, will make it as far as a police car. His brains'll be splattered all over the copper unlucky enough to be cuffed to him. He's too dangerous in too many ways and RedFour or The Unit will just take him out – and then you'll be in a whole new ballgame.'

'Oh yeah,' Rik said. 'You could be right.'

'I am right . . . So, how's it going?'

It wasn't going spectacularly well. At that moment Jack Marsh, aka David Jones, had covered his tracks too well and the police were stone-walled. Henry hoped the debit and credit card details would lead somewhere. They were an easy source of money and Jack definitely needed cash to keep operating. Henry guessed he would try and bleed them dry before his old bosses realized he was still drawing on them. Even if he had emptied them already, the locations of his withdrawals and spending could be followed up to at least give an idea of the area he might be in.

There was also a lot of legwork and telephone work to be done. There was a possibility he might have rented a property somewhere in Lancashire either before or after he struck and detectives were contacting estate and letting agencies to follow up any recent lets, as well as scouring newspaper columns for private lets. It was all slow, tedious work.

Rik had gone national with photographs of Ginny, appealing for anyone who might have seen her to come forward. That was getting little response.

It seemed Jack Marsh had gone to ground.

Henry left Rik's office feeling depressed on top of everything else, and slid into his Mondeo Estate.

He drove out of Preston onto the M6 and let the Rolling Stones blast out his brain for the whole of the journey back to Kendleton, killing all his bleak thoughts for half an hour or so with a concert from 1975. He drew up outside the Tawny Owl to see the pub open and, with Anna Niven at the helm, business was thriving. He would have found it preferable to slink in unobserved and put his feet up in the living room but was spotted as soon as he walked in and greeted with a cheer by a group of locals by the main bar.

He fixed a smile and dragged himself to them and if he was honest, they did cheer him up with their good, compassionate humour and support, plus a couple of pints of Stella, the taste of which, having flowed through pipes he himself had meticulously cleaned, was excellent.

After an hour he made his excuses and retired to the living room after having a chat with Anna, promising to speak to her about future plans tomorrow.

She gave him a hug and he let himself into the owner's section.

It was deathly quiet as the heavy door closed behind him. He stood looking along the corridor off which were all the rooms.

He swallowed and pushed himself off the door and walked slowly along and into the bedroom he had shared with Alison, sat on the edge for a moment then slowly lay back and felt the tears roll out of his eyes, down his temples and on to the covers.

TWENTY-ONE

The long shower refreshed him and he stepped out feeling almost human, towelling himself down. There was a full-length mirror in the bedroom, which Alison used regularly, but which Henry usually avoided.

But he caught sight of himself, stopped and stared at his naked reflection. He had lost so much weight, so quickly, which in some respects was good but in others, not. Skin now hung loosely around his man-boobs and the backs of his upper arms. 'Batwings' Alison used to call them. His neck was scrawny, eyes deep-set, lines etched at the corners of his mouth, his skin pale and drawn, the colour of old parchment.

That was all underneath what remained of his facial injuries.

He twisted to look at his wounded arm, having just bathed it, and was surprised to see a bruise spreading like lichen across his shoulder.

He touched his skull, letting his fingertips run slowly across his close-cropped hair.

Felt OK. He wondered if he had been lucky or whether there would be repercussions from the fracture.

At the moment he thought his brain was probably OK, although he still could not remember anything beyond seeing Lord Chalmers shot to death. He still had no idea why he'd crashed the Navara other than from what Jake Niven had explained. Nor did he have a clue as to how he had got out of the car and gone behind a rock. That whole part was blank.

He suddenly didn't care. It would all get swept under the carpet anyway and sitting there alone on that bed, he didn't have the will to fight that one or make a stink about it, even though he had ended up injured because of it. It would be a losing battle.

What he would fight for, though, was Alison's death, Ginny's death (if that was how it was to be), Tod Rawstron's death, the CSI's death and even Tod's dog's death, all at the hands of Jack Marsh.

Henry would never give up, even if Marsh ended up dead before a trial. He would embarrass Whitehall, he would parade and protest outside number 10 Downing Street with a placard. Might even get himself arrested,

'Fuck The Unit and fuck RedFour,' he said. 'Shit, what a mess.'

A loud knocking came from the connecting door into the pub. He wrapped a large towel around his midriff and slid his feet into his slippers and went to answer it.

Anna Niven stood on the other side. 'Henry, sorry to bother you, someone to see you . . . I said you wouldn't mind.'

He glanced over Anna's shoulder to see Debbie Rawstron standing there.

There followed one of the longest hours in Henry Christie's life, holding himself together whilst having to deal with the tsunami of despair pouring out of Tod's mother. By the time she left, he was mentally scarred and bruised and with a stone-like face he went into the bar, picked up a clean whisky glass and pushed it up twice under the optic containing Bell's whisky. It wasn't his favourite, but he wanted its sharpness.

He took it back into the living room where he settled on the settee, lifted his ankles onto the coffee table and held the glass under his nose to inhale the aroma and prepare his tastebuds for the assault they were about to experience.

Debbie Rawstron was in a place beyond grief and desperate to share it with someone who was feeling it as much as she was. Through her body-jarring sobs, she told Henry how her husband had withdrawn into himself, become cold and aloof and put up a barrier she was too weak to cross or understand.

Henry had dealt with all forms of grief over the years.

He had learned stuff about it. That everyone was different. That no one should be judged negatively just because they didn't cry or cried too much, too loudly, or threw crockery across the kitchen or rearranged the kitchen cupboards to make them tidier.

What he hadn't learned, though, was what bereavement was like when it hit home.

When it hit you in the gut.

How should you feel? How should you deal with it when it's affecting you, not someone else?

He had lost his wife, Kate, to cancer, now he'd lost Alison and maybe Ginny.

And he wasn't managing it greatly.

He told Debbie that her husband was dealing with his son's death in his own way and if she loved him ('Yes, yes I do, he's my world') then she should give him time and he would do the same for her.

Slowly she calmed down and began to talk more rationally about Tod, what a little rogue he had been, how he loved the outdoors and the job he'd just been given and how he had turned himself around from being a petty criminal to a life full of possibilities.

She finished the tea Henry had made for her, then stood up.

'Thank you, thanks for listening. I know Tod liked and respected you and Alison and I'm so sorry for your loss.' She wiped away her tears and took a deep, jerky sigh.

'I'm sorry for you, too. He was a good lad, and don't be too hard on your husband.'

'I won't.'

Henry got to his feet and showed her to the door where she turned.

'Would you hold me?' she asked. 'No one's held me yet, not John, not me mum . . .' Her voice trailed off weakly.

'Nor me,' said Henry, aware his bottom lip was beginning to quiver.

He held her tightly, she held him back, then they pulled apart.

'Will they ever find the man who did this?' she whispered.

'Yeah, they will,' he said confidently.

'Thank you.' She pecked him on the cheek. He opened the door for her and she stepped out into the pub.

A man sitting on one of the comfy chairs by the door rose quickly, awkwardly, to his feet on seeing her, then he stood with his hands at his sides looking helpless and very, very lost.

Debbie rushed across to him and embraced her husband.

Henry played all this through in his mind with the whisky held tantalizingly under his nose.

The phone rang. He almost ignored it.

Henry drove onto the car park of the multiplex cinema complex on Portway on the eastern edge of Preston Docks. The place was virtually empty and he had some qualms about leaving his Mondeo Estate there at this late time of day – almost eleven thirty p.m. – but he had little choice. He got out, leaned on it, folded his arms and waited.

Headlights appeared and a car sped towards him, stopping with a sudden lurch. One of the rear doors was flung open and Henry ducked in and slammed the door. The car shot off, rocking him against the seat.

The man in the front passenger seat turned.

'We might have him,' Rik Dean said.

There was a bank of three ATMs on the external wall of Morrison's supermarket on the retail park next to the old Albert Edward Dock.

Henry knew them well.

When he was an SIO based at headquarters but living in Blackpool, driving past Morrison's was a twice-daily occurrence, on the way to work and on the way home. He often used the ATMs to grab some cash. In fact he knew this whole area well, the Riversway Docklands as they were known. The big dock itself with the big retail units on the north side and all the former warehouses, now converted into apartments, lining the southern edge. The dock itself fed out into the River Ribble, which flowed to its estuary at Lytham.

He had been to many incidents here in his time.

And raided quite a few of the apartments for drugs and guns.

Rik's driver pulled onto the car park outside the McDonald's restaurant further on than Morrison's.

'What have we got?' Henry asked. He had been patient so far, but now it had worn thin.

Rik turned again.

'I've had analysts looking at the usage of the debit and credit cards Jack Marsh had access to, and the banks've been great too. He's been using all of them since he walked out of the nut house, almost all around here. The last one was used two days ago on Blackpool Road. He seems to have been rotating them and taking out money every two days, just before midnight and just after to get the maximum for each day. He's withdrawn thousands. There are four he uses around here – the NatWest ATM at Morrison's just here, one up on Blackpool Road, one at the Spar Shop on Water Lane and another near the university on Fylde Road. All within easy walking distance of each other, if that's what he's doing. We've got people on them all right now and we've got the banks looking at this in real time, we're set up in the MIR and comms to relay information immediately . . . but this one here, at Morrison's, should be the next to be used if he sticks to the pattern.' Rik was speaking quickly, easily.

'Which could mean he might be renting around here?'

'Yeah,' Rik said. Even in the darkness Henry could see the glint of excitement in his eyes. 'And on that note, a basement flat under a house in Tulketh Brow was rented two weeks ago by a mystery guy, paid cash up front, no name, no pack drill, description fits our man.' He paused, almost breathless. 'We cover the ATMs and if nothing comes of that, we go knock-knockin' mob-handed through the flat door. Teams are ready as we speak.'

'You moved quick.'

'Got lucky quick.'

'Nah, you make your own luck in this game.'

'As soon as a debit card goes in, we're on it,' Rik said.

'Fingers crossed.' Henry sat back in the knowledge that in most cases nothing ever comes of stakeouts like these other than boredom or frustration – although he did recall one years ago when he ended up getting shot in the chest in Marks & Spencer in Lancaster. Saved on that occasion by a bullet-proof vest, he still had the mark on his sternum where the bullet had struck.

'You can't get involved,' Rik warned him. 'You're just observing.'

'I'm too poorly anyway.'

'Yeah, right,' Rik said through the corner of his mouth.

Rik contact-called all patrols via the dedicated radio channel for this operation. There seemed to be an awful lot of people, all sat waiting, hoping something would happen. Henry didn't even bother to try and imagine where or how they had been secreted, but he half-imagined an ARV unit abseiling down from Morrison's roof like the SAS.

Then he heard, 'Alpha Golf 4.' It was whispered.

Rik held up a finger for quiet.

'Golf 4 – lone male, hood up, just appeared on Morrison's car park. Not certain where from but crossing east to west . . . possibly came through the hedge by Homebase. He is crossing towards the front of the superstore.'

'Roger,' Rik said.

Other patrols acknowledged.

Henry waited tensely.

'He's at the machine,' a patrol called up.

'Need to wait,' Rik told everyone. He looked at Henry. 'I think we'll check out this monkey even if he doesn't trigger an alarm.'

'Good plan,' Henry agreed.

Then control room cut in. 'Patrols on Morrison's – it's confirmed. Money being withdrawn from the highlighted account.'

'Hit him!' Rik said almost before the transmission ended.

With a flurry of voices and acknowledgements, all patrols shouted up and rushed from their positions to surround the person at the ATM.

Rik held back for just a moment. 'We'll let them nail him.'

It was quick and efficient. Less than a minute later a patrol shouted up, 'Suspect detained Morrison's car park.'

'Here we go,' Rik said.

As much as Henry wanted to believe this was true, he didn't, even though his heart was slamming quickly as the car raced to the arrest scene.

The suspect was laid out, splayed on his front, face down into the cold ground. His hands had been cuffed behind his back and two cops were standing with a foot each on his ankles. Two AFOs pointed guns at his head.

As Rik's car lurched to a halt, he jumped out and shouldered his way through the ring of cops and squatted down by the man's head and pointed a torch beam into his face.

Henry watched the quick interview take place on an audio/video loop feeding from the cells complex to an office in the MIR.

Rik was carrying out the interview.

The prisoner was a young man called Allan Roache.

Not Jack Marsh. Nothing like Jack Marsh.

'I tell you man,' Roache was whining, 'I don't know the dude. He was just very fucking scary but he said I could have fifteen quid for every two hundred I drew out for him, so I weren't gonna argue wi' that, were I? I'd a bin on thirty fat boys tonight for doing nothin'.'

'And you didn't wonder why it was such easy money?' Rik asked.

Roache shrugged. 'Dosh is dosh.'

Henry didn't even listen to any more of it. Roache was simply a local toe rag, a druggie, living off the state but eager to take any other money coming his way. He would not care one iota what was behind it all. Draw money, take your cut and no more (Henry knew the consequences would have been spelled out to him) and leave the balance in a plastic bag in the equivalent of a dead-letter drop, behind some bricks in a designated wall or in a litter bin. The location of the drop would be texted some-time in the early hours, so he didn't exactly know where it would be until then. He told police a different phone was used every time for this, and he was instructed to delete all traces on his phone.

Roache had also been shown a photograph of Marsh, but had just shrugged a 'Dunno,' at it.

Henry stood up and paced the MIR, believing that finding Ginny was getting further and further from his grasp.

He slumped on a chair in the SIO's office just as Rik came back from the cells looking stressed out.

'We should've just followed the fucker,' he said despondently.

'Maybe you still could, maybe he'll still text.'

'I'll bet you anything Marsh watched all this happen and he's laughing like fuck at us. He's not going to just let someone like Roache draw money for him unsupervised. He'll have been watching us and we've blown it. Now he'll just change location, hit other ATMs until his accounts are stopped.'

'Hey, you had to arrest him, you did right, save the post-mortem. Sometimes you have to show your hand. It's all a gamble . . . unfortunately it's a gamble with an innocent girl's life.'

They looked miserably at each other.

'Boss?'

Rik turned. The custody sergeant was at the door, a man Henry also knew of old.

He had a mobile phone in his hand, covered up by the palm of his right. He mouthed, 'Roache's phone . . . it's for Mr Christie . . . Jack Marsh.'

Henry took the phone from the sergeant, his eyes on Rik Dean. Henry now mouthed, 'Can we trace it?' Then he put the phone to his ear and said politely, 'This is Henry Christie, who is this, please?'

'You should be dead, Henry,' a male voice informed him.

'I'm sorry, who exactly is this?'

'I think you know who it is.'

Henry geed up Rik to move. He shot out of the office.

'No, I'm sorry, I don't.'

'Oh, and if you're thinking of trying to trace this, don't bother . . . I'm on my encrypted, non-traceable military phone.'

'I'm sorry, I still don't know who I'm talking to,' Henry said.

'I'm guessing you do, really,' the voice said smoothly. 'I'm also guessing that my bosses gave you details of my bank accounts, otherwise why did eight cops flatten that poor fucker tonight?'

'I don't know what you mean.'

Suddenly he was clammy and feeling very weak again. He tried to remain calm.

'Yeah you do, so let's just stop farting around, eh?'

'All right, Jack, let's stop farting,' Henry agreed. Keep calm, keep cool, his mind intoned. 'Where is Ginny?'

'Ginny? You mean my daughter, Virginia Marsh?'

'Yeah, yeah I do. Where is she, Jack? Because let me tell you something . . .'

'No,' Marsh shouted. 'Let me tell you something. You have stolen my family and all I did was take it back.'

'OK and, er, why not do that the way any normal, sane person would do – by discussion and negotiation, Jack?'

'It . . . it went beyond that,' he said. 'It went to betrayal, to lies, to fucking, to doing one over on me.'

'And then to murder, eh?' Henry said with contempt. He had been feeling weak, now he was feeling stronger with rage. He stood up, the phone clasped to his ear. 'You killed innocent people, Jack, people with no connection to you whatsoever.'

'People who stood in my way.' His voice was trembling.

Henry's jaw tightened. 'You slaughtered Alison and if you touch or harm Ginny in any way, I'll hunt you down for the rest of my life, if that's what it takes. If she's alive, you let her go now. You've had her too long, now you need to let her walk away and make her own decisions, not be forced into something she doesn't want.'

'She wants to be with me. Her *Dad*!'

'Let me speak to her, then. Let me see her.'

'Nah, she doesn't want to speak to you.'

'OK, fine . . . but how do I know she's all right.'

'Because I'm her dad. I've come back to claim my inheritance.'

'You're the one who chose to leave in the first place, Jack. Your decision, not theirs.'

'Is that what Jenkins and Smith told you? Two-faced, manipulating bastards.'

'Jack, let her go,' Henry said. 'You know it's the right thing to do.'

Rik Dean swung back into the office making 'Keep going' gestures by rolling his hands around each other.

'You know she doesn't deserve this,' Henry said. 'We can work this out now,' he cooed. 'The ball's in your park, I'm sure you can be reasonable.'

Jack laughed harshly. 'One minute ago you called me mad, not sane, now you say I can be reasonable. Make up your mind, Henry Christie, which is it, mad or sane?'

Henry hesitated.

'Thought so,' Jack said.

'Yeah, you are mad.'

'And you should be dead, matey. Do you know why you're not?'

'Go on, surprise me.'

'Because a great big red-deer stag got in my way, that's why!'

He ended the call leaving Henry with a dead phone in his ear. He peeled it away with a slurp as it was drenched with sweat from his earlobe. He gave it to Rik.

Rik was on the internal phone a minute later asking for an update re the phone conversation and a possible triangulation to get Jack's position.

He looked at Henry sadly as he hung up. 'Didn't get it, the signal's dead, untraceable.' He paused. 'We're going for the basement.'

Henry was not allowed to take part in the raid, but sat in Rik's car parked a couple of hundred metres away from the target premises. The fact Rik hooked him into the comms network with a PR so he could listen to the progress of the raid (on the proviso he did not butt in at any stage) did not make him much happier, but he understood. He was a civvie now and there was no way he could be involved for so many reasons and even letting him listen to the radio channel was pushing it.

In the past Henry would have been at the forefront of such operations. He had a reputation for leading from the front whilst other bosses usually took a back seat. There was nothing Henry liked more than knocking on a villain's door and, if need be, kicking it down, then looking into their eyes as he nicked them.

Now he was out of it.

His job had devolved to Rik Dean, who was just as enthusiastic as Henry had once been.

So Henry sat and listened.

The team got into place. Eyeball was established with the target premises.

There was a lot of breathlessness as heavily kitted up officers began to move and transmitted their progress up to the point where (and Henry had to visualize this) officers armed with rams positioned themselves either side of the basement flat door, fire-arms officers lined up behind them, weapons drawn, then all in position, then the 'GO' instruction.

They were inside within seconds, pouring through the door of a tiny flat Henry could only imagine.

'Entry gained,' came the first transmission.

'Living room, clear.'

'Toilet, clear.'

'Kitchen, clear.'

'He's in the bedroom.'

Henry's chest constricted, his teeth were grinding, sending echoes around his skull. His breath was held inside his lungs, his heart whomping.

Waiting for that next stage.

'Bedroom door in!'

Feet pounded, breathing was laboured.

'Down, down, down on your knees. Show me your hands.'

Then the agonizing pause.

'One male arrested.'

Henry exhaled and in spite of the warnings to keep off the radio, the tension of the next few seconds almost tore him to shreds and he couldn't stop himself from picking up the PR on his knees and pressing the transmit button. 'Is she there, is she OK?'

'Henry!' Rik's voice came sternly over the radio. 'Stop your transmission. We'll keep you up to date.'

Henry growled, 'You better fucking had.'

He waited. It seemed an hour but was perhaps five minutes before Rik came back on.

'Henry?'

'Go on.'

A pause, then, 'I'm sorry, Henry, Ginny's not here . . . and the man arrested is not our intended target, repeat not our intended target.'

TWENTY-TWO

'By default it was a bloody good arrest,' Rik Dean told Henry.

'That makes me feel a whole lot better,' he replied almost on the verge of crying.

By any stretch of the imagination it was an excellent arrest, actually. The man, who had rented the flat without providing personal details but with cash up front, was wanted by the police in Wolverhampton for a serious stabbing in the town centre that ended in death. He had been on the run for four months, skipping around the country, keeping one step ahead of his pursuers and had even featured on *Crime Watch*. His freedom had come to an end by accident.

'She's still out there. He's still out there,' Henry said bitterly.

They were back in the SIO's office at Preston police station. The local chief superintendent, James Lee, a man Henry had known for almost twenty years, had come on duty specifically for the raid, poked his friendly face around the door and commiserated with Henry.

'Thanks, James.'

'We will get him, you know,' James promised.

'I know, I know,' Henry said glumly.

James gave him a short wave, then left.

Henry shook his head wearily. 'Need to get to my bed.'

Rik slapped his shoulder gently. 'Sorry, pal, but now we know he's in the area we'll soon have him.'

'It's Ginny I'm bothered about. He's had her too long now.'

'Go home, go to bed,' Rik urged him.

Henry dragged himself out of the office and made his way to the car park out front where he'd brought his car up from the cinema and left it.

The night was still warm, a little stuffy. He took off his jacket as he walked to the car, pressing the remote control to unlock it. It made the little beeping noise that indicated the car was already open. It didn't really register with him as his mind was on other things more important than that.

How to hunt down Jack Marsh.

He opened the driver's door and slung his jacket across the front passenger seat, dropped in heavily behind the wheel and started the engine. He did not even register that the interior light did not come on as usual.

He sat there for a long time with his hands on the wheel, staring into dead space ahead of him, his thoughts tumbling and rolling, then he drove out of the car park onto the A6, going to take the same journey home as before, going up the M6 north, then off at Lancaster.

The first couple of sets of traffic lights were on green and Henry sailed through, his mind not really on driving. He was on automatic pilot up to the point where he was driving alongside Moor Park, with Preston North End's football stadium way across to his right.

That was the moment he realized exactly what was happening.

Why his car was unlocked.

Why the interior light had not come on.

Henry pulled in to the side of the road just as he felt the cold muzzle of an automatic pistol pushed into the back of his neck and hot breath down his left cheek and saw the flash of evil eyes in his rear-view mirror.

'Jack Marsh,' he said simply.

'Hello, Henry, we meet again.'

'So it seems.'

'Let's go and see Virginia, my daughter.'

With the gun at his head and Jack Marsh whispering directions and other things into his ear, Henry drove.

'I'm going to give you this opportunity because deep down I'm a good man . . . left here, keep going . . . I get it that you're fond of Virginia, but you know what? I get shivers of revulsion when I see you or even imagine you with her . . . next right, then straight on . . . the thought of you anywhere near my daughter disgusts me . . . not that I think you'd touch her or anything like that – you saved that for my wife, didn't you? No, because I'm her father . . . I'm the one who should be laughing with her, giving her a hug, not you . . .'

'You gave up that right a long time ago.'

'Is that what Smith and Jenkins told you? They brainwashed me.'

'You always had the right to pull out. You know what you did?' Henry turned his face and Jack jammed the gun into his cheek.

'Keep looking forwards . . . No, go on, what did I do?'

'You let Alison and your tiny daughter grieve over body parts that weren't even yours. Now that's what I call a cunt, not a father.'

Jack slammed the barrel of the gun sideways into Henry's face. He swerved the car with the stinging blow, corrected it and felt blood trickling from just under his left ear down his neck.

Jack moved his lips to Henry's ear. 'I am her father,' he whispered.

'Yeah you are, and where were you? Taking the Queen's shilling. A good life. Killing people.'

'Necessary.'

'Maybe, but don't bleat about your choices.'

'The marriage was as good as dead anyway. She was a bitch to me.'

'So that makes it all right . . . Just let me tell you one thing: being a father is never over. You can't pull in and out of it just 'cos you want to.'

Jack crashed the gun into Henry's face again. Henry's jaw slipped out of line, then back again.

'You really know how to wind me up, don't you?'

Yes I do, Henry thought, suddenly putting others first. He knew he had to keep himself calm and then keep Jack calm if there was any chance of survival here.

'Where are we going?' Henry asked, touching the cut inside his cheek with his tongue, tasting blood which he then swallowed.

'Next right.'

Henry complied with the directions.

'Keep going . . . pull in here.'

They were outside a terraced house in the Plungington area of Preston, that was all Henry knew. He stopped, said nothing.

'Here we are,' Jack said, sounding jolly. Then he became serious. 'I killed people for a living, Henry. I found it easy, then I found it hard, then I couldn't even think how I found it, and it all became a blur and I knew I wanted my family back and then I found you had stolen it.'

'So why not kill me outside the pub, or me and Alison in Ginny's bedroom,' Henry asked. 'You had the chance.'

'I really don't know. My mind . . . y'know, all over the place. But at least now I'm thinking straight and clear.'

'No you're not. You're warped and unstable. You're a threat to too many people, Jack. Just stop this shit here and now and you might come out of this alive.

'I'll survive,' he said. 'Me and Virginia. A team. On the road. There for each other.'

'I seriously doubt it.'

*   *   *

Henry walked ahead of Jack into the house. He pushed Henry along the narrow hallway into the kitchen at the rear, Henry stumbling, feeling dizzy and terrified. His ear was bleeding badly, the one that had been previously half-blown off by a shotgun blast. He despaired it would ever recover. He constantly swallowed blood.

Henry steadied himself on the sink.

'Stop here,' Jack said. The gun in his hand was a silenced Browning 9mm. He kept it steady on Henry as he said, 'Look in here.' He felt for the handle of the under-stairs cupboard and the door swung open.

Henry almost screamed as the crumpled, blood-caked and naked body of a female rolled out and unfolded on the floor. Henry saw terrible head wounds, huge holes exposing brain matter.

For a moment he thought it was Ginny.

But it was an older woman.

'First wife,' Jack said gazing down dispassionately at her. 'She was a bitch. When we split up – because she was shagging around – she didn't want Virginia, so I took her, I had to have her, I had to bring her up . . .'

'And then abandon when you became an assassin.'

'No – when I was brainwashed to become the best fucking hunter in the world. Don't you listen? Anyway,' he glanced at the dead woman, 'I paid her a visit, told her my plans and she went nuts, so I had to kill her. She got what she deserved.'

'Beginning to think no one deserves you, Jack,' Henry said. He wiped blood from his face. His shirt was saturated with it around his collar.

Jack stepped over the body and opened the cellar door. 'After you.' He gestured for Henry to go down the tight, narrow, very steep stairs ahead of him. At the foot, Henry turned left into the dimly lit room and saw Ginny.

Jack shoved him towards her.

She was prostrate on the camp bed, tape over her mouth. She shot upright as Henry staggered towards her, instantly recognizing him.

Henry swooped to his knees and carefully removed the tape and said, 'Ginny, Ginny,' softly. It was then he saw the thin chains securing her to the bed frame which itself was screwed firmly into the concrete floor.

'Henry, you came, you came,' she said groggily.

'Course I did,' he breathed, looking into her tired, sunken eyes. 'Always, always,' he said.

'So you see she's alive and well,' Jack said. 'I presume that's what you wanted to know before meeting your maker.'

Henry looked back at Jack with eyes glinting like the devil's. 'May you rot in hell, you sick bastard.'

Jack threw his head back and roared with laughter which stopped abruptly. 'I'll meet you there one day, Henry.'

'I very much doubt it.'

'OK, get away from her, over there, kneel with your head against the wall.' Jack hauled Henry across the cellar with his free hand and threw him against the wall. Henry slithered down and faced it. 'Forehead on the wall,' Jack ordered.

Henry shuffled on his knees, and placed his forehead against the cold, painted brick.

'Dad, don't,' Ginny pleaded plaintively.

'Virginia, sweetheart,' Jack said softly, 'I've explained all this to you. There are things that have to be done, and this is one of them.'

'Dad, Dad,' she sobbed.

Henry's eyes could not focus on the wall.

He waited. He knew Jack Marsh would kill him quickly. He closed his eyes.

He thought about Kate and Alison.

The muzzle of the Browning twisted into the back of his head.

And Jack Marsh was dead before he hit the concrete and the back of Henry's head and neck were covered with the splatter of hot blood from the massive wounds to Jack's head.

'This is the only justice you were ever going to get, so don't argue,' Major Smith said as he placed a shell-shocked Henry in his Mondeo. Ginny was already sitting in the passenger seat. 'Take her home, make her better, say nothing.'

'How the hell do I explain . . . this?'

'Which bit?' Smith said. 'I'll have a cleaning team here within the hour. There'll be nothing left, not your problem, OK? As for her, wing it, make something up, tell 'em you found her wandering the streets or something, whatever. Like I said, take her home, make her better.'

Henry nodded. He knew this was the best he would ever get. 'Thank you,' he said to Smith.

'I knew he'd come for you sooner rather than later. That was how he worked and, by the way . . .' Smith held out his hand.

'Oh, yeah,' Henry said. He reached into his jeans pocket and took out the tracker, which he handed back to Smith, the device Smith had slipped him at the motorway services when he'd taken Henry to one side. 'Good idea.'

'Go, leave this to us now, try and get some sort of life back.'

Henry started his car and set off.

Ginny was silent until they reached the motorway when she turned to Henry and said, 'Henry, will *you* be my dad, please?'

'Yeah, yeah, course I will,' he said. 'Forever.'

'Thank you.' She turned away and closed her eyes.

Henry gripped the steering wheel tightly and concentrated on getting them both home.

TWENTY-THREE

Six months later.

Henry was sitting in what he thought was probably his most favourite place in the world, with his most favourite view. The front of the Tawny Owl with its vista over the village green, the stream and up to the woods beyond. In fact he realized he had spent so much time there either in the morning with his breakfast brew or in the evening with a whisky, he had decided to have a section turned over to decking and make it a proper area in which his customers could also sit.

It was now almost perfect.

He was sitting on one of the new garden chairs with his legs crossed, looking at the accounts for the pub. He was no great mathematician, but they were looking pretty good to his untrained eye.

It was seven thirty a.m. and he was sipping a coffee he had

just brewed himself. It tasted wonderful in the cool spring morning.

He heard footsteps behind, looked and saw Ginny coming towards him with bacon on brown toast. He grinned. She was looking good, had recovered from her ordeal amazingly well and got on with her life. His only regret was that she had missed Alison's funeral, but the two of them had made up for that by scattering her ashes on the village green and sponsoring a bench which bore her name, and always remembering her.

'Here we are.' She swooped the sandwich with a flourish on the table next to Henry and gave him a kiss on the cheek.

'Thanks, sweetie,' he said. 'What's it like in there?'

'Four up already for brekkie. Two on the way.'

'OK. I'll be in shortly.'

She touched his cheek, then went back inside.

As he bit into the bacon butty Jake Niven pulled up in his Land Rover. Jake got out, as did Anna, who bade Henry good morning and went into the Owl to start work. Jake sat beside Henry and placed a briefcase on the table. It looked battered and weather-worn.

'Thought you might like to see this,' Jake said. 'But only if I get a free brew first.'

Henry thumbed him to go in and get one. He came back a minute or two later and sat down.

'Looking good around here now . . . nice decking,' he said appreciatively.

'Thank you. Now, what's that?'

'It's a briefcase.'

Henry waited.

'It was found by a gamekeeper on the moors, maybe a mile from where a certain light plane crashed, killing the occupant.'

Henry did not allow his expression to change.

'He handed it in last night. Found it jammed in a split between some rocks, really well hidden. Only saw it because he was standing on the outcrop for a view of a sparrow hawk or something. Otherwise, he'd never have seen it. He says he hasn't opened it, and I believe him. Looks like it hasn't been opened for, what, six months, I'd say but it does look like it's been protected from most of the bad weather, though.'

'Jake, open the fucker,' he said, desperate to look inside.

The PC produced a flat-bladed screwdriver from his pocket and began to prise it open, saying, 'I've already had a go at the combinations, but they're all rusted up to buggery, so it's down to a bit of elbow grease.'

He got the screwdriver under one of the locks and slowly broke it off, did the same to the other, then looked at Henry.

'I'll let you open it,' he said, and spun the briefcase towards Henry, who grabbed it, then slowly thumbed it open, recalling Jenkins' denial about the briefcase. Maybe he had been telling the truth. Maybe they didn't have it, maybe it wasn't in the plane, maybe this was it.

Henry opened it and suddenly his arsehole slammed tight shut. He looked slowly at Jake and said, 'OMG, Jake my boy, OMFG, looks like our Prime Minister's in a whole lot of doo-doo.'